THE PALM BEACH MURDERS

THRILLERS

JAMES PATTERSON

with JAMES O. BORN, TIM ARNOLD, and DUANE SWIERCZYNSKI

GRAND CENTRAL
PUBLISHING

NEW YORK   BOSTON

Copyright © 2021 by James Patterson

Hachette Book Group supports the right to free expression and the value of copyright. The purpose of copyright is to encourage writers and artists to produce the creative works that enrich our culture.

The scanning, uploading, and distribution of this book without permission is a theft of the author's intellectual property. If you would like permission to use material from the book (other than for review purposes), please contact permissions@hbgusa.com. Thank you for your support of the author's rights.

Grand Central Publishing
Hachette Book Group
1290 Avenue of the Americas, New York, NY 10104
grandcentralpublishing.com
twitter.com/grandcentralpub

First Edition: March 2021

The Palm Beach Murders was first published as *Let's Play Make-Believe* by Little, Brown in August 2016
Stingrays was first published as an ebook by Little, Brown in June 2017.
Nooners was first published as an ebook by Little, Brown in July 2017.

Grand Central Publishing is a division of Hachette Book Group, Inc. The Grand Central Publishing name and logo are trademarks of Hachette Book Group, Inc.

The publisher is not responsible for websites (or their content) that are not owned by the publisher.

The Hachette Speakers Bureau provides a wide range of authors for speaking events. To find out more, go to hachettespeakersbureau.com or call (866) 376-6591.

ISBN 978-1-538-74998-2 (paperback) / 978-1-538-70445-5 (large-print paperback) / 978-1-538-75407-8 (hardcover library) / 978-1-538-75004-9 (ebook)

Cataloging-in-publication information is available at the Library of Congress.

Printed in the United States of America

LSC-C

Printing 1, 2021

CONTENTS

THE PALM BEACH MURDERS

JAMES PATTERSON

with **JAMES O. BORN**

PROLOGUE

THE YOUNG REPORTER TRIED to keep her eyes on the camera as it tracked past her to the mansion facing South Ocean Boulevard and the Atlantic on the island of Palm Beach. She thought back to all her journalism and broadcast classes and tried to keep calm. Even with that effort, her voice cracked when the studio anchors cut to her live.

She said, "I am here in the town of Palm Beach as the police try to sort out what has occurred at this South Ocean residence. We know that at least one person has been shot to death, and the killer is believed to be still inside, possibly with a hostage." The young reporter threw in a few improvised lines, then hit the points the producers wanted her to make. "Police have closed this section of South Ocean, and early-morning traffic is backing up as far as the Southern Boulevard Bridge, as we wait to hear exactly what has led to the tense standoff with police on the island of Palm Beach."

Someone off-camera was directing her to step to the side so that the early-morning sun didn't reflect off the lens. As the camera panned to follow the young reporter, there was a growing crowd of neighbors gawking at the scene. Nothing like this had ever happened east of the intracoastal. Police activity of this nature was much more common in West Palm Beach or Riviera Beach. Most of the locals thought Palm Beach was immune to serious crime.

The reporter motioned for the camera to focus back on her and said, "We've heard reports that the town police chief has asked for assistance from the Palm Beach County Sheriff's Office in case they have to make a forced entry into the house."

In the background, near the front of the house, a police officer started to speak into a megaphone. The reporter stopped talking so the camera operators could pick up the audio and show the police officer crouched behind a cruiser.

"Martin Hawking, come out of the front door with your hands up and empty. No one will hurt you if you do it now." There was about a twenty-second break. Then the police officer said, "Come out right now, Mr. Hawking."

CHAPTER 1

I SOMEHOW MANAGED TO slide onto a stool at one of the prime high-top tables near the front door of the Palm Beach Grill. From here you could see the bar, get waited on easily, and keep an eye out for anyone of note who wandered through the main entrance. Landing this high-top was close to a miracle on a Friday evening at seven o'clock, when the place was clogged with Palm Beachers. Julie, the sweet and personable maître d', stopped by, and I gave her a hug.

I needed a night out and a few laughs with my friend Lisa Martz. Like me, Lisa was going through a rough divorce, but she'd hit the ground running and never looked back. The whole thing had struck me a little harder, mainly because it had come out of left field. Lisa was happy to be out of her prison, whereas I'd never thought I was in one.

Lisa signaled to the waitress that we needed another round of margaritas.

I laughed and said, "That'll be my third drink tonight! I'll have to run twenty miles to burn it off tomorrow."

Lisa put her hand on my forearm and said in her sweet

Alabama accent, "Don't even talk to me about losing weight. You look fabulous. When Brennan asked for a divorce, it was the best thing that ever happened to you. Everything about you has changed. You look like a cover model with those cheekbones and that smile. If you tell me you're a natural blonde, I might have to stab you with a fork right now."

I had no desire to be stabbed, so I kept my mouth shut. I appreciated my friend's attempt to build my confidence. The fact is, I had been going across the bridge and working out at CrossFit in West Palm Beach, as well as jogging on the beach a couple more days a week. My husband, who was six years older than me, had turned forty a few months ago and decided I was too old for him. He may have phrased it differently, but I'm no idiot. It stunned me then and it still stings now. But I was making every effort not to let that loser dictate the rest of my life. As my dad used to say, "Life is tough enough, don't be a dumbass."

Suddenly, Lisa was waving frantically at a guy across the room, who smiled and worked his way toward us. He was about my age and got better-looking with each step. In good shape, a little over six feet tall, he was dressed casually in a simple button-down and a pair of jeans. A nice change from the usual show-offs on Palm Beach.

Lisa said, "Christy, this is my friend Martin Hawking. Marty, this is Christy Moore. Isn't she gorgeous?"

I admit I liked the goofy, shy smile and the slight flush on Marty's face as he took my extended hand. He had a natural warmth that was intriguing. His short, sandy hair was designed for an active man: it required minimum styling. Before I knew it, we were sitting alone as Lisa got on the scent of a recently divorced gynecologist who was having a few drinks at the other end of the bar.

I said, "I'm sorry if Lisa messed up your evening by dumping you here with me while she went off on the hunt."

Marty let out a quick, easy laugh and said, "I have to be completely honest. When I saw the two of you walk in and she stepped up to the bar beside me, I asked if she would introduce us. I know her from working on the addition to her house over on the island."

"Are you a contractor?"

"No, I'm legit."

He made me laugh, even at such an old joke.

"Actually, I'm an architect. That's just a general contractor who doesn't have enough ambition to make any money. What about you? What do you do?"

I wanted to say, *Make poor choices in men;* instead I said, "I'll tell you when I grow up."

"What would you like to do until then?"

I thought about things I did as a kid growing up in New Jersey. My friends and I kept playing the same games but adapted them as we grew older. I said, "I like games." His hand casually fell across mine on the table and he looked me directly in the eye.

"What kind of games?"

I wasn't used to flirting. I felt like I was crushing it after being so out of practice. Instead of telling him about some lame game I liked as a kid, I said, "Maybe you'll get to find out."

I liked being mysterious for once, and this guy seemed nice and was enjoying it. I couldn't ask for much more right about now.

CHAPTER 2

AFTER OUR MARGARITAS AT the Palm Beach Grill, we ended up at the HMF inside the Breakers Hotel. By then we were on our own, and Lisa was firmly attached to the divorced gynecologist. Marty and I just chatted over drinks. We talked about everything. It was easy, light, and fun. I even found myself opening up about my separation and the pending divorce. He told me a little about his own divorce and how his wife had moved to Vero Beach just so they wouldn't run into each other. It was a good plan.

We threw down some specialty drink at HMS that, as near as I could tell, had vodka, some sort of pink fruit juice, and a lot more vodka. Marty thought we were drinking at the same pace, but I was being much more careful.

I thought hard but just couldn't find the right words to tell Marty how much I'd like him to come back to my place. In my whole life, I'd never picked up a man for a one-night stand. It was new and a little bit scary to me, but I'd be lying if I said there wasn't an element of excitement to it as well.

He gazed at me and said, "You have the most beautiful eyes."

"That's just the alcohol talking."

"No, I mean it. All four of them are beautiful." He weaved his head back and forth like someone pretending to be wildly drunk, and it made me laugh out loud.

That was all I needed to screw up the courage to say, "How would you feel about coming back to my place for a nightcap?"

"How far is it?"

I gave him a look. "It's in Belle Glade, about an hour away."

"What?"

"No, Mr. Clueless, it's here in Palm Beach. No one's ever more than ten minutes from their house when they're on this island."

We grabbed a cab back to my temporary residence at the Brazilian Court Hotel. Although Brennan was beating me out on almost everything in the divorce based on some prenuptial agreement I signed when I really believed he loved me, he didn't want the locals to view him as a complete jerk, and he had put me up in a nice apartment inside the hotel. The cost meant nothing to him, and at least I had a base of operations on the island.

No one asked questions at the Brazilian Court, and Allie, a girl from my CrossFit class, was the evening clerk there. She gave me a heads-up whenever she saw Brennan stomping through the lobby to confront me about one thing or another and generally looked after me like women our age usually did.

Once we were in the room, I realized I was still a little tipsy. I had never used that word in my life until I moved to Palm Beach. Everyone was always getting "a little tipsy," no matter how much they'd had to drink, but in this case, I really was just a little tipsy.

The tiny apartment consisted of a living room and a comfortable bedroom, with a bathroom in between. The balcony in the back looked into the thick tropical foliage that rimmed the property, which was about three blocks from the ocean. This was a trendy place to stay, and the bar could get interesting some nights.

Marty took a look around the place and turned to face me. "We could use some music," he said with a slight slur to his words.

The next thing I knew, we were blasting an older Gloria Estefan song through the oversize external speakers for my iPhone. We also managed to make it to the bamboo-framed couch, and started to make out like teenagers. It was fun and I was getting swept up in it. I lost track of time until I heard a rap on the front door. It might've been going on for a while because it just sort of crept into my consciousness past the music and Marty's kisses.

Someone was now pounding on the door.

CHAPTER 3

MARTY REACHED BACK AND shut off the music as I stood and straightened my cocktail dress. He gave me an odd look and scooted to the bedroom. I realized he was doing it for my benefit so no one would ask any embarrassing questions.

A smile crept across my face as I slowly stepped toward the door, giving Marty time to disappear into the rear of the apartment.

I carefully opened the door a crack, to see my friend Allie's face. I could tell something was wrong.

"What's up, Allie?" I said, without slurring any words. The pride had to be written across my face.

She kept her voice low but said, "My God, Christy, you may want to keep it down a little bit with your new friend. We had complaints from downstairs, as well as people on either side of your room. It sounds like a South Beach nightclub in here." Her slight Serbian accent made it a bit hard to understand her.

"What are they gonna do? Call the cops?"

Her smile told me not much was going to happen.

The old me would've been unbelievably embarrassed; instead, there was something liberating about showing off how much fun I was having. After Allie left, but before I could slip back to tell Marty, there was another knock at the door. I thought Allie had come back.

This time I flung the door open to scare my friend, but then I saw that it was two uniformed Palm Beach cops. I recognized one of them from around town. A typical buff, tan, friendly Palm Beach cop.

He said, "Allie told us she spoke to you, but we have to follow up because someone called us directly and made a complaint."

I used a serious tone even though I wanted to laugh. All I said was "I understand."

"Do you?"

"No more loud music."

The tall cop sighed and said, "We've got enough to do."

"Do you? Do you really?" I couldn't help myself.

The cop smiled and shrugged. "Maybe not, but keep it down anyway."

He could've been a jerk, but luckily, Palm Beach cops are known for being polite to residents, and at least for now I was still considered a Palm Beacher.

I headed back to the bedroom and found Marty looking sober and ready to flee.

"What's up? You're not leaving, are you?"

"I heard the cops. I wasn't sure what was going to happen."

"It was nothing. Just a complaint about the noise. You don't have a problem with cops, do you?"

"Cops and I have a great understanding; I don't bother them

and they don't bother me. It works out for us all. Especially in a place like this, where they wouldn't like my West Palm Beach address."

I wasn't sure what he was talking about. "Paranoid much?"

When he didn't seem to get it, I gave him a smile and said, "It's fine. I don't need loud music to prove I'm having a good time."

"You're enjoying yourself?"

"Of course I am, aren't you?" I asked. It was the natural concern of the recently separated.

He sat down on the bed and patted the spread next to him.

I stepped back, then jumped high in the air to land next to him on the king-size bed.

"Let the people downstairs bitch about that," I said as the bed made a tremendous thump on the hard wooden floor. We laughed in bed together until we started kissing again and I lost all track of time. I couldn't remember the last time falling asleep had been so entertaining.

The next thing I remember was a bright light in my face. I was thinking, *Who the hell is shining a light at this time of the night?* When I opened my eyes and everything came into focus, I realized it was the next day and that the bright light was shining in everyone's eyes.

Marty's arms were wrapped around me, and he nuzzled my neck. I could tell by his scratchy voice he didn't feel great when he said, "What time is it?"

I looked at the clock on my nightstand. "Jesus, it's two in the afternoon."

This wasn't a game; I'd had one of the best nights of my life. And I was pretty sure Marty had too. It felt like the smile on my face wouldn't come off all day.

CHAPTER 4

THE NEXT TWO WEEKS were a whirlwind, and I saw Marty Hawking all but two nights. We'd made the focus of our relationship amusing ourselves and keeping things exciting. I felt like a teenager with her first boyfriend. Life can be harsh and people can be rude, but when you're in a fresh romance, everything is easier. That was what the last two weeks had been: fun, thrilling, and unexpected in every way. We went to the Palm Beach Improv in CityPlace and rode the Diva Duck through the streets of West Palm Beach right into the intracoastal. It may have been a touristy thing to do, but having Marty with me made it special.

I adored the way Marty was full of life, just like a big kid. He got so much joy from everything and loved to see me smile. Almost as if he lived for my approval. It was such a nice change from my life with Brennan. He was so reserved. Even though I had been swept off my feet the first time I saw him playing polo, I'd never felt this comfortable around him. It even made me wonder if his obvious wealth had played some role in my feelings toward him. Growing up the daughter of a schoolteacher and a UPS deliveryman had left me wondering what it was like to live without any concerns about money. One thing I'd learned was, even with money you have a lot to worry about.

I was discovering that Marty was an educated, funny guy. He seemed to have made enough money but wasn't consumed by it. His parents lived in Delray Beach, or as he said it, *Everyone's parents live in Delray Beach.* And it sounded like Marty regretted not having any kids. I could relate, but that was the last thing on my mind now. I was too enthralled with this carefree relationship that seemed to revolve around enjoying life.

So when he picked me up early one evening in his slightly dinged twelve-year-old BMW, I was open to his idea to take a leisurely ride all the way down to South Beach, which was more than seventy-five miles away.

We were lucky and found a spot in front of Marjory Stoneman Douglas Park, so we walked down the boardwalk, holding hands the whole time. Unlike Palm Beach, this beach was busy with runners, sightseers, and bicyclists crowding the boardwalk. It was an entirely different vibe from home. Everyone here looked happy.

We ended up at a place called Prime 112 on Ocean Drive and munched on appetizers and sipped incredible wine. It was magical. We moved on to our meal and a wonderful bottle of wine paired to our fillets. If Dwyane Wade or Khloé Kardashian had walked through the tony restaurant, I wouldn't have been surprised.

It was nice to see Marty enjoying himself and acting so relaxed, until our waiter, Diego, brought the bill. In my time with Brennan, I'd rarely had to worry about the cost of things.

It was so different from how I'd grown up. When I saw the look on Marty's face, I had to ask, "What's wrong, babe?"

He showed me the bill, and I saw that it was something over a thousand bucks. For some reason the whole idea started to make me giggle. That in itself struck me as funny and I started to laugh out loud.

That got Marty laughing too. I don't know what it is about a man who laughs easily, but there is almost nothing as attractive to me.

I reached for my purse, and he said, "No. No way. I was the one who dragged you down here and insisted on the most expensive wine." Then he gave me that crazy smile and said, "You ready to play another game?"

"Anything you want."

He pulled two hundred dollars out of his wallet, and when Diego walked by he held it up and said, "I want to make sure you get your tip in cash. No one likes to declare what they earned in tips." Diego smiled and thanked us both, kissing my hand like the South American gentleman he was.

Then Marty said to me, "We're going to make believe we left a card to cover our outrageously expensive meal. Is that okay with you?"

Maybe if he hadn't tipped Diego, I would've been more hesitant. Instead, a tremor of excitement ran through me. "You don't think we'll get caught?"

"Diego got his tip, and he's happy. We'll be blocks away before he even realizes it." Marty reached into his pocket, pulled out his keys, and slipped off his car key, leaving three keys on a ring on top of the bill. "That'll make it look like we're coming back."

"Don't you need your keys?"

"I've got extra keys, and it won't cost me a grand to replace them."

I got the idea that Marty had done stuff like this before.

We stood up from the table, and my heart was pounding. I wasn't sure what the criminal charge would be, but I knew it had to be a felony. This was one thousand dollars we were walking away from. Marty looked casual and unconcerned as he gave me a wink and then reached out to take my hand. Slowly, we turned and looked along our path toward the front door. *Shit.* The manager stood there, chatting with a couple of the waiters, including Diego. Marty took one step that way while I held firm.

"That's crazy. A suicide move," I said in a low voice.

"It's bold and dramatic." He gave me a smile that somehow set me at ease.

I had a better idea. I pulled him back toward the table and around the partition that concealed the way toward the bathrooms. There was another door at the end of the hallway. It led to the little outdoor dining area, where one waitress, who appeared to be thirteen years old, was wandering around. Taking the right angle, with the right pace, we could step through the patio area and over the velvet rope and be only a few feet from freedom. The question was, would the manager and Diego figure out what was going on if they saw us?

We had to do something. I tugged on Marty's hand and pulled him along the corridor. I turned to him and said, "Last chance to pay or use the bathroom. Do you want to do either?"

"Hell, no, I'm an outlaw. I'm with you all the way."

I pushed open the door and was relieved to see there were only two couples on the patio. We wouldn't have to awkwardly step past anyone. The waitress looked up and smiled, eager to have someone else in her section. I just shrugged like we'd walked through the wrong door and then turned quickly to my left, stepping over the rope that sealed off the area as Marty followed me. We took a few steps down the sidewalk and then heard a man's voice shout.

"Wait!"

The manager had seen us.

My impulse was to freeze in place and come up with an excuse, like we were going out to get money from the car. But Marty took off at a sprint and I followed. The CrossFit classes came in handy as we shot north toward Second Street. Just as we turned the corner, I looked over my shoulder and saw the manager and Diego on the sidewalk coming after us.

I said, "We should probably get to the car. We can outrun them easily, but I doubt they'll be happy about us walking out on the bill. They'll have the cops down here looking for us in a few minutes."

Before I knew it, I'd lost any fear and was laughing as we trotted along the sidewalk toward the park, where the car was waiting for us.

I couldn't believe how this guy had brought me out of my shell. I loved that he was so unpredictable and had an edge to him. I never would've thought a respected architect would act like a teenager and do something like dine and dash. This was the most excitement I'd experienced in a long time. Definitely since I'd been locked in this nasty divorce. I'd had no idea life could be this much fun again.

CHAPTER 5

WE DECIDED TO TAKE the long way back to Palm Beach and drove north on the oceanfront US Highway A1A, having to make several detours around inlets, but once we were back in Palm Beach County, it was a steady, comfortable ride with a cool ocean breeze in our faces. The night was beautiful, and Marty seemed to be opening up more and more.

For the first time since we'd met, he started to talk in detail about his divorce. I hadn't wanted to pry, but I was curious. Every divorce has its own story, and it's told by two different people, but in this case, I believed everything Marty said.

Marty changed his voice in an effort to imitate his ex-wife. It wasn't like a comedian who just raises his pitch; Marty actually sounded like an annoyed woman. In his odd falsetto, he said, "Marty, I'm going to need an extra twelve hundred dollars for the trainer this month so I can learn how to properly work my arms. Marty, I'm going to New York this weekend to go shopping with my girlfriends, have you paid off the credit card from last month yet? Marty, why haven't you designed any skyscrapers like John Nelson, a boy I grew up with whose second major building is going up in Seattle?"

All I could say to him was "I'm sorry, babe. It sounds like you're better off without her. What happened to finally end it?"

He kept his eyes on the road as he spoke. "There's really not much to tell. She fell for an AC contractor. You know how women love air-conditioning." He let out a laugh. "Some tall, goofy guy from Boca Raton. I think he was originally from New Hampshire, and whatever he had, she wanted. The hell of it is, I like him. He's a funny guy. And as much as I try to stay away from both of them, I hear different rumors. Most of them come from the contractors who use me as an architect. I heard he's taking jobs up in Vero just so he can see her and keep his own wife in the dark."

"He's married?"

"Someone's got to be doing the cheating. I read some stat that claimed fifty percent of married men cheat. That means they've got to be finding an equal number of women to cheat with."

"Does that make it harder for you?"

"That she cheated on me? Yeah, it hurt. The fact that we had no kids made the divorce work its way through the system quickly. No-fault. That's all I kept hearing. It's a great idea until you realize your ex-wife gets nearly half of your earnings for the next eight years. It's brutal. Now I live in a rented condo in downtown West Palm and work my ass off just to stay afloat."

"I hope you realize you don't have to spend money just to impress me."

"I'm having a hard time spending enough money just to keep eating. I figured you were impressed with my sexual skills." That sly smile of his made anything he said adorable.

I leaned across the seat and gave him a kiss on the cheek. Then I couldn't help but bite his earlobe.

Somehow I couldn't resist asking, "What's your ex-wife's name?"

"Teal. I swear to God my ex-wife is named Teal."

That made us both laugh.

Marty said, "She told me she'd always supported me emotionally when I was working. She said I only wanted her happy, in shape, and at home. Then, at the last court proceeding, she said, 'Now I *am* happy, in shape, and at home, and you gotta pay for it awhile longer.'"

Marty took a moment to gather himself. "You know what else she told me?"

"No, what?"

"She told me I should meet someone, I'd feel better." He took his eyes off the road to look at me. "You know what?"

"What?"

"She was right." He had to pull the car to the narrow shoulder of the road in Highland Beach just to kiss me the way he wanted to.

CHAPTER 6

ONCE WE WERE PAST the Lake Worth beach and still heading north on A1A, I told Marty to slow down just a little. I pointed out all the local landmarks I knew so well: the tennis courts at Phipps Park; the condos on Sloan's Curve; and the big houses that sat just off the road, whose residents I named for Marty.

When we were north of the Bath and Tennis Club and clear of Donald Trump's Mar-a-Lago, I had Marty park in one of the spots next to a tiny beach bungalow, more like a cabana, on the beach side of South Ocean. I knew there was no one inside. It was only used occasionally, and even then, just as a way to shower off after swimming in the ocean. I pointed across the street to a mansion that looked like it was surrounded by a golf course.

"See that castle over there? Twenty thousand, two hundred twenty-seven square feet. I've measured it. To the inch. That used to be *my* house. That's where I lived and planned to stay the rest of my life. I loved that place. And my dick of a husband took it away."

"I've heard about your husband. Everyone on the island knows Brennan Moore."

"Don't get me started on that guy." Then, without meaning to, I launched into my own imitation. I tried to put on that irritating, fake accent, as if he had gone to Yale. "This just isn't working out, Christy, dear. I think it's best we go our separate ways." Then I returned to my own voice, trying to keep the bitterness out of it without much success. "That was it. No emotion, no anger. Just his assessment of what was going on and how he intended to correct it. Of course he was bold, because he knew he had a prenup and could lock me out of most of his assets. Not to mention, he had the best attorneys, who I'm sure were ready for this for some time before he said anything to me."

"How's it make you feel now to look up at that house?"

"Angry. Really, really fucking angry." I thought it was best if I didn't go on. I wasn't proud of this side of me. But the fact was, I didn't deserve to be in this position. I was a good wife who'd never even thought about straying and always put Brennan's interests first. I thought that was what couples did. That each wanted the other to be happier than them. Now I was in the real world and I knew that kind of thinking was some part of a fantasy life.

I barely responded when Marty slipped his arm around me to give me a supportive hug. All I could think of was the Italian marble I'd picked out and the true craftsman I'd hired to lay it, and the bamboo wallpaper that set off the study from the rest of the house. That place was mine, and it had been stolen from me.

CHAPTER 7

IT WAS A SHORT ride back to the Brazilian Court, and Marty was in an odd mood that I couldn't decipher. He was quiet and perhaps sullen but clearly deep in thought. I hadn't meant to upset him by showing him the house I used to live in. Maybe he was bothered by the fact that he couldn't pay the dinner bill. All I really wanted to do was make him feel better. I wanted to see that smile. He had one of those smiles that was so sincere it was infectious. It was like a drug, and I needed a fix.

We had a glass of wine from a bottle I had been saving. Then he pulled out a little multicolored pill and said, "Should we try something really wild?"

"What is that? Is it dangerous?" My experience with drugs consisted of trying pot a couple of times in college and hearing stories about some of my friends using cocaine.

Marty said, "It's a new version of Ecstasy that's supposed to completely break down your inhibitions. It's almost like it relieves you of responsibility for your actions. But it keeps you focused and sane. It might be just what we need to take a step further away from our divorces."

I thought about it for a minute, considering what could go wrong. Then, without saying anything, I snatched the pill out of Marty's hand and broke it in half. I didn't wait or think about it again as I popped my half of the pill into my mouth and took a big gulp of wine.

A smile spread across his face as he did the same thing. He reached into his pocket and pulled out another pill as he said, "I have a few of them."

Before long we were back on our favorite couch, making out. The music coming from my speaker system seemed to form colors in the room. It felt wild and natural at the same time.

The pill didn't seem to affect my judgment, just my perception of sight, sound, and touch. The feeling of Marty's hands across my neck and bare shoulders made me shudder with excitement. I could tell I was having the same effect on him when I slipped off his shirt and undid his belt.

That's when there was a knock at the door. A tap at first, then a little louder, until it turned into a good, solid pounding that indicated it was an official visit and not just someone coming by to say hello.

Marty slipped his shirt back on as I stepped to the door and opened it a crack. Once again Allie was standing a few feet from the door with her hands on her hips like she was a schoolmarm about to deliver a lecture. Her long, dark hair was in a loose ponytail, and her pretty, tan face couldn't hide her smile, despite her annoyance. This time I invited her in and introduced her to Marty.

Before she could say anything, I had a glass of wine in her hand. She sat down on one of the bamboo chairs that matched the couch and said, "I'm trying to head off trouble, Christy. I just got off duty and thought it was best if I came up to tell you we had another complaint about noise. Management is thinking about telling you to find another place to live. I'd hate to see that happen."

Even as she spoke, I realized I was just focusing on the way her mouth moved. She was gorgeous. Even the dowdy hotel uniform couldn't hide her curvy body. The combination of wine and Ecstasy had really done a number on me. I wish I could say I didn't like it, but it was so new and exciting.

After a few minutes, Allie picked up on it and said, "What's with you two? Are you high?"

Marty showed her the pill, and my giggle pretty much explained what was going on. Allie simply reached across and plucked the pill from Marty's hand and popped it into her mouth. I was shocked and pleased at the same time. Now, this was a party.

Before any of us could change our minds, we were all scampering to the bedroom and losing our clothes along the way. The bed felt like it was swallowing us whole as Marty and Allie planted themselves on either side of me. Maybe I had been a good girl for too long. This was the kind of night I had fantasized about but had never told anyone.

It really was fun being a bad girl once in a while.

CHAPTER 8

THE NEXT MORNING I was surprised to find myself alone in bed. Somewhere in my foggy brain I realized Allie had left in the middle of the night, but that didn't explain Marty's absence. For just a moment, it flashed in my head that he had left with her. But that wasn't how I recalled it. The night was a wild, sweaty, and exhilarating blur. I wasn't sure I could give any details if I was asked to. But I didn't regret it. Not for a moment. I just hoped it wouldn't be awkward with Allie. Then again, thinking about some of the things she'd done in bed made me realize she wasn't much for feeling awkward. And that last night hadn't been her first time in a threesome. Live and learn.

I sat up in bed, and it took a moment for my vision to catch up with me. I slipped into a sundress and looked through the apartment, trying to figure out if Marty had left a note or any clue about where he had gone. Then I noticed his wallet and keys on the desk in the living room. He had made coffee for me as well. I gladly took a cup and sipped it as I sat back on the couch and tried to piece together everything that had happened the night before. I had gone from feeling angry about the divorce and losing my house to the wild delight of a new experience that I would never get to brag about. Not bad for a Wednesday.

A few minutes later, Marty came through the door wearing his short swim trunks and an old T-shirt with the logo completely faded. He looked great. He was trim and tan and had just enough muscles to prove he wasn't a slacker. Every inch of him was covered in sweat.

I was surprised how relieved I was to see him. I couldn't explain the doubts I'd had when he wasn't in bed with me when I woke up. And I'm typically not that insecure.

"You were quite a ninja leaving this morning. I had no idea where you went."

He grabbed his left foot and held it behind his back to stretch his quadriceps as he said, "You looked so peaceful when I woke up that I slipped out and used the workout clothes you let me keep here. I went for a run along the public beach and kept heading south, all the way to your former house. In the daylight, it's even more spectacular. I could see that even the bungalow on the beach was beautiful. Something about running on the deserted beach and seeing that big house really pissed me off. As badly as I was treated by my ex, I feel like you were treated worse."

Obviously I agreed with him, but I didn't want to sound vindictive or petty. I just gave him a quick kiss on the cheek to show my appreciation. But the look in his eyes told me there was more to what he was saying. Seeing that house had sparked something in Marty. He wasn't exactly who I'd thought he was when I first met him. And I wasn't sure if that was good or bad.

CHAPTER 9

THERE WAS NO WAY I could risk the scandal of a dine-and-dash at a local restaurant, so when the bill came at Charley's Crab, I snatched it right out of Marty's hand. We'd had lunch and only had a few cocktails. I hadn't been a midday drinker since I was in college, but it was kind of fun and there was something about doing it with Marty that made it seem okay.

Before I could get to the bottom figure on the bill, Marty had grabbed it back and handed his American Express card to the waitress.

I didn't want money to become a problem between us, so I said, "We don't have to keep eating at fancy restaurants every day. I'm a simple girl from Jersey. A sub or a hot dog can keep me filled up for a long time." I hadn't meant it as a double entendre, but the smile on his face told me that was how he took it. A typical guy. But in his case, he was so good-natured that anything I said to make him smile made me happy.

Marty said, "It's fine, I have jobs lined up back to back that will carry me through next summer. I may not be designing the next New York library or be considered the Addison

Mizner of my generation, but at least I have a good reputation. And it's nice to have the money coming in." He paused for a moment, then added, "Teal is happy about it too."

I caught the bitterness in his voice. Recently, I'd been trying to judge if he was getting over his ex-wife and the circumstances of his divorce, or if he was focusing on them more. It was hard to tell. In a way it made him more human, like a regular guy. He wasn't flawless, even though I found him engaging and caring.

As we were standing by the covered front entrance to Charley's Crab, I looked up and was shocked to see Brennan driving by us on Ocean Boulevard in his Jaguar convertible. It was the blue one that I'd picked out for him. I couldn't keep a "son of a bitch" from coming out of my mouth.

Marty looked up quickly and said, "What's wrong?"

I nodded toward the Jag and said, "There's Brennan looking like he owns the world." And he did. It looked like he should be wearing a commodore's cap. Then he did the worst thing I could imagine him doing. It cut me like a knife and left me shaking.

He waved to me.

Not a nasty wave. Not a condescending wave. Just a casual raising of his right hand like we were old acquaintances passing on the street. Like I meant nothing to him. Not only was he over me, it was like I had never existed.

I couldn't let Marty see how this was affecting me, so I pretended to sneeze and put my hands over my face.

Marty was too smart for that. He slid an arm around my shoulder and said, "Let's find a place to sit back and talk for a while."

CHAPTER 10

WE WALKED ACROSS THE street to the public beach and found a park bench on the south end. It was a breezy day and the sun was behind us as we looked out over the choppy Atlantic. A lot of people say the Palm Beach public beach is the least-enticing beach in Florida. Parking is expensive and the locals clearly don't want people visiting from off the island, but our comfortable bench, just off the road, provided a vista most people can only see in magazines.

Marty put his arm around me and didn't say a word. He didn't try to solve my problems or analyze me or give me advice. We just sat quietly, and I found my head rolling onto his shoulder. It was exactly what I needed. Before I knew it, I started to talk. I talked about Brennan and our marriage for maybe the first time.

When people hear you're going through a divorce, it's almost like you have some communicable disease. They stay at arm's length and let you know they're still your friends, but that this is probably something you should get through on your own.

Not Marty. He just listened.

I said, "Brennan was so dashing the first time I ever saw him. He was playing polo in Wellington and I was there with a girlfriend. He looked like a knight sweeping through the pack and swinging his mallet, or club, or whatever they call that thing that hits the ball. It was almost like a dream, it was so perfect. And he was charming. I mean actually charming, not faking it. He had an accent like a yacht club member on Martha's Vineyard, but he was also funny and extraordinarily polite. A sense of humor and good manners go a long way with most women.

"Until about our third date, I hadn't even known he'd been married before. They had been college sweethearts, and it sounded like she hurt him pretty badly. At least that's how I interpreted it. I never heard many specific details, except when he'd tell me she never made him feel like I did. What a load of shit."

Marty didn't seem fazed at all by my rambling as we both watched the few families on the beach build sandcastles or run through the shallow water along the shore.

"Brennan proposed to me after six months. Two days before the wedding, he said his father insisted on him signing a prenup with me. He assured me it was no big deal, but the family wanted to protect the assets that provided the income for him. I didn't care about money. I really still don't. At least not that much. Anyway, I never even bothered to consult an attorney. All I wanted was to be his wife, maybe have a few kids, and live with this dream husband. I signed the prenup. Ugh. What a rookie mistake."

Marty said, "You didn't talk to any of your friends about it?"

"None of them had any experience with prenups. They were all married to teachers, insurance agents, or firemen." I wiped a tear from my eye and regained my composure. I hated that Brennan still got to me like this. Then I said, "He never really kept any promises. We were going to travel, have a kid, be a family. He never even took me to Disney World like I wanted. He said there was no time. It was Disney World, for God's sake. Was that too much to ask? My parents couldn't afford a trip from Jersey when I was little, and my husband didn't have time for fun. I've still never been to the Magic Kingdom." I looked out at the ocean in an effort to hide my emotions. Marty had done nothing to deserve this kind of baggage.

After a long silence Marty said, "What happened in the end? I mean, why'd you guys break up?"

"Maybe he wanted a younger woman, but I think the real reason is that he just got bored with me. Then he threw me out on the street. I was so stunned, I barely made a squeak."

Marty kissed me. "That's where he's wrong. You are anything but boring. You've revived me."

That was exactly what I needed to hear him say.

CHAPTER 11

OVER THE NEXT FEW days, Marty and I got in the habit of walking the beach and talking. We always started from the north end of the public beach and strolled south, right past my former house. I liked being seen with such a good-looking man. I wanted people to know that my life wasn't over just because someone like Brennan was trying to divorce me. It was simply a lot of fun to be with a guy like Marty, who listened and made me feel wanted. What a change from Brennan.

Some days, I agreed to jog on the beach because I knew Marty preferred the faster pace. I wanted to prove I could keep up with him. It was the competitive streak of a girl raised by a man who had wanted a son. Some days I ran hard on the sand, making my heart race. Marty appreciated the effort. Brennan never would've even noticed.

I wondered why I was trying so hard to please Marty; then I realized just how serious my feelings were for him. He'd rescued me and changed the trajectory of my life, and I was actually happy. It was incredible.

The one thing that seemed to interrupt my joy was when I flashed back to my life with Brennan.

It's hard to explain, but every time I saw the house from the beach, I got a little angrier. I know there are people in the world with much more serious problems. I had my health, a new boyfriend, and a lot more life to live, but it sure would have been nice if that house had been part of my life. I could picture Marty sitting by the pool or working on house plans in the den.

Just when I thought I couldn't get more annoyed, one day we noticed Brennan getting ready to pull out of the driveway. He wasn't in the Jag. The bastard was driving a brand-new Bentley. A black Bentley Mulsanne that seemed to shimmer in the sunlight. He'd bought a more formal car to go with his convertible.

Marty and I were running out on dinner tabs and this son of a bitch had a car for every occasion. Something just wasn't right about it.

Marty said, "What an asshole. Anyone under seventy who drives a Bentley is, by definition, an asshole."

I reached out and gripped his hand. Marty really was on my side. His face was red and he looked like he was ready to burst through the gate next to the bungalow and charge Brennan in his brand-new Bentley.

Marty said, "I could punch that guy in the face."

I stared at Marty, wondering how serious he was. He stepped toward the gate, and I reached out to hold his arm. We watched as Brennan, oblivious to the world as usual, pulled out and drove away in the Bentley.

Marty took a breath and shook his head. "I should welcome you to the club."

"What club?"

"The getting screwed in your divorce club."

His color had already come back, showing off his pleasant tan complexion, and there was a hint of a smile on his face. He looked like he had just been blowing off steam and Brennan was a convenient target.

Then Marty said, "Don't worry, it gets better."

"Really?"

"It did for me."

"How long does it take?"

"It got better as soon as I met you."

I had to kiss this sweet man.

But thinking about the house and Brennan's new car, I did wonder about what, exactly, that jerk deserved. Not just in the divorce, but in life as well.

CHAPTER 12

ON FRIDAY OF THAT week, I saw Brennan again. This time at Family Court in the Palm Beach County Courthouse. Even though Brennan didn't feel like family to me anymore. He gave me a smirk when I walked in with my attorney.

The judge had read both sides' briefs, and I felt confident he'd grant our motion to throw out the prenup.

I listened quietly while the attorneys answered questions about the progress of the divorce and who would be testifying today. All three of Brennan's high-priced attorneys against my cute little mama's boy from Boca Raton, whose mother was my hairdresser and had said he was good and cheap. And that he needed the work.

My attorney shuffled nervously through papers as I looked over at Brennan's crowded table. Brennan was impeccably dressed in one of his many dark Ralph Lauren suits, but hadn't been able to resist the typical Palm Beach touch of a turquoise flowered tie. Not a power tie. He didn't need one.

My chance to testify had finally come. It wasn't in the witness box like I had imagined. The judge instructed me to stand right next to where I was sitting and answer his questions.

The older, dignified man kept looking down at some notes, until finally he said, "Mrs. Moore, has your attorney explained the three main reasons that are grounds for dismissing a prenuptial agreement?"

"Yes, Your Honor."

"And you understand that *duress* means the agreement was presented too close to the date of the marriage, or some similar issue?"

"Yes, Your Honor."

"And *coercion* would be like offering ultimatums, and *fraudulent financial disclosure* explains itself."

"Yes, Your Honor."

The judge nodded. "Very well, let's get started." Now he gave me his full attention and said, "Mrs. Moore, what did you do for a living before your marriage?"

"I was in marketing."

"And do you have a college degree?"

"From Rutgers, yes, sir."

The judge said, "Ah, a Scarlet Knight, very good. I'm from Trenton. We're the only state without a university named after it."

"Yes, sir." I didn't know what else to say. At least he was trying to put me at ease.

"And would you say your income was low, high, or average?"

I kept focusing on breathing and keeping cool. "Average, Your Honor." I paused and added, "To low average."

The judge nodded and wrote down a few notes, and then, in a very calm and quiet manner, said, "How long before the wedding date was the prenuptial agreement presented to you by Mr. Moore?"

"Two days before the date we had set."

The judge said, "Did Mr. Moore offer any ultimatums? Did he ever say anything like 'If you don't sign this, we're not getting married'?"

This was another important question. I gathered my thoughts and said, "Brennan said his dad needed the agreement signed, and if not, we'd start off our life together broke. I told him I was used to not having any money. He said he wasn't and then just stood silently until I signed the agreement. I later learned that he was really concerned about his own assets."

I stood, trying to hide my smile at having been so concise in showing duress, coercion, and false financial disclosure in my brief exchange with the judge. I had hit this one out of the park.

But then it was Brennan's turn.

CHAPTER 13

THE JUDGE HAD SOME of the same questions about background and how we met. Brennan pointed out that he'd graduated from Georgetown and worked in finance. I guess if you manage your family's hedge fund you are, sort of, working in finance.

Then the judge asked him about the intent behind the prenup.

At that moment, I wished Marty was sitting next to me so I could hold his hand. Also, I wanted him to see firsthand how pompous Brennan was.

Brennan finally got to the meat of his answer. "The intent of the prenuptial agreement was to protect not only my assets, but assets that had come to me through my family. The prenuptial agreement was something I had discussed with my parents and lawyers long before I'd ever met Christy."

"Did you feel you waited too long to present the agreement?"

"No, Your Honor. Not at all. We'd talked about it for months before I presented it to her."

That was a lie, but my lawyer's death grip on my arm told me we'd get a chance to straighten out the record.

The judge said, "Would you still have married Mrs. Moore if she had not signed the agreement?"

This was what I was waiting to hear. This was a question I had been asking myself since Brennan had tossed me out.

Brennan said, "It never came to that, Your Honor. Christy signed immediately. I never had to consider any alternatives. I loved her, Your Honor, but I do have certain responsibilities. I'm glad I didn't have to make that choice."

The judge said, "Do you feel the absence of a prenuptial agreement would have affected the marriage in any way?"

I had never even *thought* about the agreement until Brennan dumped me. So clearly the damn thing had not affected our marriage one bit. At least from my perspective.

Brennan said, "Looking back, Your Honor, I feel Christy might have been more interested in my *lifestyle* than me. And the fact that we're having this hearing confirms that theory." Then he added, "I can't say she ever showed any genuine emotion toward me."

There was no reason for Brennan's last remark. He knew it wasn't true. I'd loved him and thought he loved me.

He just stood there as if he expected applause.

I felt a tear well up in one eye. Why was I crying now? Maybe because not only was it over, but I was realizing that nothing had ever actually existed between us. I was just some kind of trophy for him.

The judge said, "Thank you, Mr. Moore. You may sit down now."

My husband, because he was still my husband, in fact and

in the eyes of the law, turned in his chair and looked right at me. When he had my full attention, he winked and gave me a smug smile.

The judge considered everything he'd heard and told the attorneys to hold their questions. Then he looked up and cleared his throat. This was it. He had recognized that I'd signed the agreement under duress, I'd been coerced, and Brennan had presented me with false financial data. I looked at my attorney, who was also smiling. He was optimistic too.

The judge said, "Gentlemen, I have carefully considered your motions on behalf of your clients, and after hearing from both Mr. and Mrs. Moore, I've concluded that Mrs. Moore is a very intelligent, educated woman who signed the agreement willingly, without undue pressure or while under duress; therefore..."

I didn't hear the rest, but then again, I didn't really need to. All I heard was the judge's final comment. "Mrs. Moore's motion to dismiss the prenuptial agreement is denied." He looked up at both tables and said, "Let's start to move this along now, shall we." Then it was over. My best shot at recovering part of my old life had been a failure.

Brennan stood with a broad smile on his face and shook all of his lawyers' hands like he was O. J. Simpson and had just avoided a double murder rap.

I spent the next few moments consoling my attorney, who felt like he had let me down. I wrapped my arm around his shoulder and hugged him. He sniffled and nodded.

As Brennan passed me on his way out of the courtroom, he

stopped and leaned down. "You look great, babe. Sorry about your little motion."

"Why are you doing this? Why humiliate me on top of everything else?"

Brennan just grinned and said, "Because I can, and there isn't a damn thing you can do about it."

CHAPTER 14

OUTSIDE THE COURTHOUSE, MY lawyer said it was all his fault. As I looked at him and his off-the-rack suit and Supercuts haircut, my thick file tucked under his right arm, I realized he had no idea the hearing had been fixed. He'd followed the rules and assumed everyone else would as well. I'd done the same, and look where that had gotten me.

My lawyer said, "I'll keep looking for something we can exploit. But at some point you have to get on with your life. Christy, you're a beautiful woman, and you shouldn't let this experience sour your outlook on love."

That was an easy thing for a father of three who had been married twenty years to say. I gave him a hug and sent him on his way.

That evening Marty had to work, so I sat in my quiet room at the Brazilian Court Hotel and did nothing but search the Internet for legal precedents and articles about situations like mine. I wanted to explore every possible option I had.

That night I barely slept, tossing and turning, my stomach tightening every time I thought about the hearing.

The next day, Marty came by around lunchtime, when I was only barely starting my day. He talked me into taking one of our usual walks along the beach. I was quiet for a while; then, after we had gone a way in the soft sand, he said, "Sorry I didn't sleep over, but I had a ton to do. But because I worked during the night, now I have a few hours to spend with you on a beautiful day like this."

I said, "It's all right. I was on my iPad all night doing legal research anyway." That seemed to catch his attention.

"I thought your attorney was supposed to do that kind of thing for you. Did you at least find anything interesting?"

"A few things." I wasn't sure if I was playing coy or worried about trusting Marty completely. It was easier to make him work for the answers so I could decide what I might say.

Marty said, "A few interesting legal leads? Can you give me a for-instance."

I decided to jump in with both feet. "Did you have a will when you were going through your divorce?"

Marty said, "I had nothing to leave anyone. Teal was getting it all anyway."

"Did you know that if you die without a will, it's called dying *intestate* and generally the spouse is in line to get everything?"

That made Marty stop in his tracks. He even glanced around to make sure no one was near us on the beach, but by now we were blocks from the public beach and there wasn't a soul in sight. He looked right at me and said, "That can't be right. Even in a divorce."

I told him what I had read. "As long as the divorce isn't

final, and there is no will, all of the precedents say the spouse is entitled to the estate."

"Aren't wills filed in court?"

"No. They can be held by the attorney, but usually they're just kept right at the home of the deceased. It's convenient and doesn't cost anything. And most people really don't think they're gonna die anytime soon. It's just one of those details that floats by in life."

Marty started walking again and just said, "Really? Good to know. Next time I'm wealthy, I'll make sure to give a will to my attorney just in case. One less thing to worry about." He gave me that adorable smile that made all my troubles melt away. That was a rare quality in a man and something that couldn't be faked. I started to realize just how lucky I'd been to find Marty at this time in my life.

CHAPTER 15

IT TOOK ALMOST A week for me to get back to normal, but Friday afternoon Marty surprised me by showing up at the Brazilian Court, looking like a true Palm Beacher in his linen shirt with a cashmere sweater draped over his shoulders, khakis, and loafers with no socks. His fake Rolex would pass all but the closest of inspections.

As I assessed him spinning in my doorway and looking a little like a model, all he said to me was "Got any plans?"

I let the smile spread across my face as I said, "None at all."

I almost thought he'd take me for another walk along the beach, but he told me to dress up and not expect to be back at the hotel for quite a while. I had no idea what that meant.

We hopped into his BMW and drove across the bridge into the center of downtown West Palm. Traffic was much heavier than it was on the island, and I was curious where we were headed.

He turned onto some side roads, obviously to throw me off and have some fun. The man took his games seriously, and I loved that. Then we found ourselves westbound on Okeechobee once again and crossing over I-95.

Finally I had to ask, "Where are we going?"

His goofy smile was infectious as he said, "You'll see. We're just going to play a game. Are you up for that?"

I could've said *That depends,* but I really was in the mood for something different. I needed to get my head out of my troubles, at least for a little while.

So I grabbed his free hand, which was resting on the gearshift. "Yes."

When Marty pulled in to the Bentley dealer off Okeechobee, I became even more curious. This was a fun game, and I had no idea where it was headed. I knew there had to be some connection to seeing Brennan in his own Bentley the other day, but I was happy to watch the whole thing unfold.

I was in a dress that was more appropriate for an evening event but could pass for business attire at some of the higher-end jewelry stores or any of the shops on Worth Avenue. The Christian Louboutin pumps on my feet weren't the easiest things to walk in, but they made my calves pop, so I had thrown a pair of comfortable shoes into the bag Marty had told me to pack.

I resisted the urge to ask questions and spoil the spontaneity as we walked, hand in hand, through the front door of the dealership and stood next to a dark red Mulsanne. Marty looked through the window of the car and down the hood like he was checking for imperfections. That drew a salesman like chum draws sharks.

We endured the introductions and a few minutes of small talk until the tall salesman, about forty-five, who could've been selling Mazdas as well as Bentleys, said, "So what, exactly, brings you out here today?"

Marty was very casual as he said, "My wife and I are in the market for a new car, and I thought it was time to seriously consider a Bentley. Brennan Moore recommended you guys."

That line shocked me, but it had the desired effect on the salesman.

"I sold Brennan his Mulsanne, just like the one sitting right here." He patted the hood of the car like it was a racehorse. "Brennan is a great guy, and I'm so happy he recommended us."

The salesman looked at me for some kind of response, but all I could do was mumble, "Yeah, yeah, he's the best."

Marty said, "We see him over on the island quite a bit, and I like the look of his new car. But we usually don't go for long drives."

The whole time, I marveled at Marty's inventive deviousness. I still had no idea what this game was.

Marty said to the salesman, "Although we've considered a Flying Spur, we're seriously looking at a Mercedes across the street at Mercedes-Benz of Palm Beach. I just wanted to show her a couple of Bentleys." Then he turned toward the door and took a few steps.

It was genius. I had never seen anything like it. Immediately the salesman lunged for us, saying, "Wait, wait, you don't want a German car on the island. Bentley is the only way to go."

Marty was masterful. The salesman essentially begged us to take a Flying Spur for a test drive.

Marty remained aloof and said, "I'm not sure driving a few

blocks in the car is gonna give me the confidence I need to buy it."

The salesman said, "No problem. All I need is a little information, just your cell phone and maybe your driver's license, and you can take it home overnight and really get a feel for it. We'll even come by and pick it up if you don't like it, or we can complete the paperwork right at your house."

Even though the salesman was a little aggressive, I felt sorry for him. He was standing in front of us like a puppy waiting for a treat.

Marty hesitated and then gave him his cell number.

When the salesman said, "We just need a little bit more information," Marty countered with "I don't have time for paperwork."

Then he looked at me and said, "Let's go." He turned like an impatient Palm Beacher would, and the salesman jumped up with the keys, telling us to just give them a call if we needed anything.

A few minutes later, after we had retrieved a few things from Marty's BMW, we pulled out of the parking lot, but instead of turning east toward Palm Beach, Marty turned west on Okeechobee.

I said, "Where are we going now?"

A satisfied smile popped onto his face as he said, "You'll find out."

I loved this game. We held hands and chatted as he pulled onto the turnpike headed north. I didn't ask any questions. I just enjoyed the ride as we took the turnpike farther north until Marty pulled off onto Osceola Parkway and then off again at an exit just south of Orlando. I had to fight the urge to ask questions, but when he pulled into the Four Seasons right outside Disney World, I couldn't help but show my surprise. Who doesn't want to visit Disney World? I had just told him how Brennan had promised but had never taken me. I threw my arms around Marty's neck and planted a big kiss on his lips.

As we got out of the car I had to tell him, "This game of make-believe is fantastic."

CHAPTER 16

DISNEY WORLD WAS ALL I had dreamed it would be. At least the attractions were, anyway. Somehow, when I was a kid, I'd never calculated how many people were crammed into the park every day. Especially on a beautiful Saturday like this. We managed to make it onto most of the rides, though the longest waits were at Space Mountain and Pirates of the Caribbean. I might have enjoyed a trip to the Magic Kingdom more when I was eleven, but being here today with Marty was really special too. Maybe the most important thing was that I realized how carefully Marty had listened to me and how badly he wanted to see me happy. This guy would do anything for me, and no one had ever made me feel like that before.

Walking hand in hand with Marty made me feel like no matter what choices I had made, I had the right man in my life now. He was just what I needed.

But after lunch my mood started to change. It began with the salesman from the Bentley dealer calling Marty and asking how he liked the car. Marty handled it perfectly, telling the salesman we were still undecided but we'd bring the car back later this afternoon.

As Marty stuffed the phone back into his front pocket, he smiled at me and said, "I just won't answer the phone again until we're about to drop the car off."

The call had brought me back to reality, and my problems were no longer a world away. I started thinking about the court hearing and that pompous ass Brennan. While we were floating in our boat through It's a Small World, I noticed our conversation had turned darker as well.

Out of nowhere Marty said, "Disney makes a fortune separating people from the real world and the ugliness around them."

"Whoa, what brought that on?" The little girl in front of us had been peeking behind the seat since the ride had started. She might not have understood what he was saying, but she picked up on Marty's attitude and quickly twisted around to sit low in her seat, out of sight.

Our conversation drifted back to normal, Magic Kingdom–related topics as we shuffled our way through the Haunted Mansion and Frontierland. Once we landed in comfortable seats and under air-conditioning at the PhilharMagic 3-D, with no one sitting close to us, I acted on the urge to kiss him.

Marty said, "I'm glad you're having a good time. I'm sorry you missed out on Disney for so long, but I'm glad your ex-husband didn't hurt your sense of joy."

"First of all, he's not my ex-husband yet. And he didn't hurt my sense of joy, but he did come close to ruining it. He was never the man I thought he was. It turns out *you* are the man I thought *he* was."

We kissed again, deeply and passionately. I felt Marty's hand around the back of my neck, and I wanted to hold him tight. As the show began and objects came flying at us in 3-D, we continued making out, grabbing at the visual effects before us. I'd never thought I'd enjoy the PhilharMagic 3-D so much.

Somehow I knew Marty was a guy I could depend on. He would protect me, and since he had taken me to Disney World, I knew he just wanted to make me happy. Who could ask for anything more?

CHAPTER 17

I THOUGHT THE SALESMAN was going to kiss Marty when we dropped off the Bentley. He darted out of the showroom and met us in the parking lot.

The salesman blurted out, "I thought you'd—"

Marty was back in character as the annoyed rich guy and said in a sharp tone, "What? You thought we'd what?"

The salesman stammered and said, "F-forgotten us. You just surprised me by keeping the car a little extra. You must have really loved it." He was standing in front of us, almost hopping in place with excitement, like a kid about to open a Christmas present. "What do you think? Will you pull the trigger on it? I can have everything ready for you to sign in just a few minutes."

He was following along in the parking lot as Marty walked toward the back where his car was parked. The salesman didn't even seem to realize he was being led away from his office.

Marty waited until we were right next to his car so we could enjoy the look on the salesman's face when he opened the door of his beat-up BMW. The salesman's expression said it all.

As Marty and I slipped into the car, Marty said, "Think I'll stay with my Beemer for now."

We giggled about it all the way back to Palm Beach.

The night ahead of us ended up being one of the best endings to one of the best weekends of my life. I tried another one of Marty's crazy little pills, and this time we didn't wait for Allie to show up. I called her. And she brought a friend. A tall, very young, and really hot Czech bartender from Café Boulud, the restaurant right in the hotel. He had blond hair and blue eyes, and he eagerly accepted one of Marty's homemade Ecstasy tabs. I couldn't even pronounce his name, which didn't sound like it had any vowels in it, and his accent was thicker than Allie's. But he wasn't here to talk.

Before I knew it, we had our own disco going, with my speakers blaring out dance songs from the eighties on Pandora. We left the music on as each couple started to get more intimate and clothes started to fly onto the floor.

The young bartender looked like he belonged in a Tommy Hilfiger ad, with his flat stomach and ripple of muscles that popped perfectly against his tightie-whities.

Suddenly, I heard a knock on the door. It wasn't like when Allie would tap and then rap a little harder. This was an immediate pounding.

Allie scooted from the couch and said, "I'll get fired if I'm caught in here."

"Me too," added the bartender.

I shut off the music and called out, "Who is it?" Trying to keep my best homemaker's voice.

From outside the door I heard, "Palm Beach Police, Mrs. Moore."

That had an effect on Marty, who sprang up and started toward the bedroom. I said, "You need to stay out here with me this time. These two have to go into the bedroom. They can't be caught in here or they'll lose their jobs."

Marty said, "Leave it to me. They won't get their names." He scrambled to get dressed as I slipped my blouse back on and pulled up a pair of shorts. I opened the door a crack, like I was worried about who was there. It was the same two cops who had crashed our first party. That must have been how they'd known my name.

I opened the door and waved them inside.

Only one of the cops spoke, just like last time. He was tall and handsome, with blond hair and great arms. They strained the sleeves of his polyester uniform.

He glanced around the room and noticed the other clothes, and even I could see the shadows of Allie and the bartender under the door of the bedroom. They weren't particularly discreet.

The cop said, "Looks like you're having quite a party."

Marty smiled and said, "Wanna join in?"

Neither of the cops thought that was very funny, and they got it across with a long, surly look at Marty. That made Marty clear his throat and say, "Just kidding, you guys."

The cop pulled a pad from his back pocket and said, "I'm sorry, Mrs. Moore, but we had another complaint about the noise. I just need to write a quick report about it. If you promise to keep it down, we'll let this one slide too."

"I promise." I was in no mood to deal with the police.

The cop looked at Marty and said, "And your name, sir?"

Marty hesitated. "Why do you need my name?"

"Why don't you want to give me your name?"

"Why *should* I give you my name?"

"Because we were called here on a complaint of noise and you appear to have been contributing to that noise. I think we've been very polite and pleasant during this encounter, but that is going to end if you don't give me your name. Now."

I immediately understood that Marty was distracting the cops from Allie and the bartender, but I also saw how serious the cop was, so I was surprised that Marty stood his ground. He really didn't want to give the cop his name. The whole encounter was kind of thrilling, at least through my drug-enhanced view of it. I just hoped Marty's ploy worked and the cops didn't go to the bedroom and get Allie's and the bartender's names as well.

Finally Marty said, "My name is Martin Hawking." He didn't give the cop any more trouble as he provided his date of birth and address.

On the way out, the cop said, "You guys need to keep it down. Palm Beach goes to bed early and it doesn't like scandals."

Allie peeked out of the bedroom as soon as she heard the door shut, and Marty excused himself to go to the bathroom.

Allie said, "I could hear everything through the door. Your boyfriend just saved our jobs. He's fantastic."

I looked at her and said, "Yes, yes, he is."

CHAPTER 18

THE NEXT MORNING I woke up with Marty's arm draped across me. For a few seconds I panicked, wondering if Allie and the bartender were still in the apartment. I had never experienced that kind of fear in the morning and vowed right then never to take another one of Marty's crazy pills. I'm not saying I regretted it. Everyone needs to get wild once in a while, but things had gone a little too far last night. I wasn't completely clear on what had happened after the cops left.

We knew to keep it quiet, but there was still more drinking, and the bartender had some really potent pot. The night got wilder, and now I vaguely recalled Allie and the bartender slipping out sometime in the early-morning hours.

Marty stirred and I turned in bed, giving him a kiss to wake him up. That put the smile that I wanted to see on his face.

Without prompting, he said, "Maybe we don't need any pharmaceutical help to have fun anymore. I'm not sure I'll ever say the sentence 'It's not really a party until the cops show up' again."

That made me laugh as I rolled onto my back and looked up at the ceiling. It wasn't just the small square footage of the apartment that was such a change from my previous residence; it was the overall feel of everything, from the low ceilings to the tiny bathroom. It immediately got me thinking about my house on South Ocean and the jackass who'd thrown me out of it.

Marty said, "What would you like to do today?"

An idea popped into my head and I just said it out loud: "I have a key to my old house, and I'd like to pay a visit if Brennan isn't there."

"You want to burglarize your old house?"

"Technically, I think we would just be trespassing."

"No, I'm pretty sure you're talking felony."

"Anyway…" I turned to look Marty in the eye and said, "Are you game?"

He shrugged his bare shoulders and said, "Why not? The Palm Beach cops already love me."

That was all there was to it. After a little breakfast, our usual walk on the beach ended up at the beach bungalow across the street from the house. It didn't take long for us, sitting on the beach together, to see Brennan pull out in the Jaguar. He headed south, which meant he was crossing the Southern Boulevard Bridge, and I knew he'd be gone for at least an hour. It isn't worth leaving the island unless you're going to be gone for more than an hour. That was plenty of time.

We had to jump the gate at the beach and cross the street quickly, but then we just walked up the driveway, and I led Marty past the front door and through an unlocked gate into the backyard. The key I had was to the pool house, and as we walked through it, I realized that it was almost twice the size of my current apartment.

We paused for a minute before we stepped through the door that led to one of the rear patio rooms. I listened and didn't hear anyone. Generally, Brennan kept a very small staff, just a housekeeper and a guy who supervised the lawn and pool care. He wasn't here every day.

I also knew that Brennan activated the alarm system only when the house was going to be empty for a few days or more, when he was traveling. It was his typical arrogant attitude that nothing could ever happen to him. That was the attitude I was counting on.

CHAPTER 19

I OPENED THE DOOR and we stepped into the cool patio room that looked out on the pool. Part of the roof was made of glass panels that let the sun in. It was a transition from the main house to the outside and had been a sanctuary for me. Slowly, I led Marty into the main part of the house.

Marty, of course, was drawn to the architecture of the interior. His face was turned up like he was a tourist in New York City. He said, "This is an unbelievable house. Some of the crown work and the fireplace have to be a hundred years old. Done by true craftsmen, too."

I said, "I picked out most of the furniture and the art." As I was standing next to a landscape painted by an up-and-coming Miami artist, I decided to make myself comfortable and slipped over to the wet bar in the corner of the room. I made us a couple of Grey Goose vodkas on the rocks with a splash of cranberry, and we took them back into the patio room, which had loungers and a great view of the pool and yard.

I wanted to prove I wasn't scared, so I stretched out on a

lounger and sipped my drink. Marty followed my lead. The house was so well made, it was difficult to hear anything outside, and I realized that if I was wrong about my calculations, Brennan could show up unannounced at any moment. I wondered what the confrontation would be like. Would it hurt him to see me here with a guy like Marty? Would Marty really try to punch him in the face? These were valid questions, but I was determined not to show any fear.

Brennan had a temper, and I knew there were a few guns in the house. He had bought us a matched set of Walther PPKs one Christmas. He'd made it sound like they were for me, but he really wanted one and pretended I'd appreciate an identical gun for myself. The thought of the guns made me worry about a violent confrontation. Suddenly I started listening for every creak of the house or other sound. We had to be alone.

To fight my fear, I stood up and let Marty look at me for a moment. Before he could ask what I was doing, I slipped out of my shorts and T-shirt and kicked off my flip-flops. Standing there naked, I was waiting for him to tell me I was crazy, but he did the same thing with his bathing suit and tank top.

So there we were, naked, casually sipping drinks inside my former home like we didn't have a care in the world. I tried to imagine what a life like that would be like. A life with Marty instead of the one I'd had with Brennan. It was a nice fantasy.

My doing something like this was all inspired by Marty and his love of dangerous games. This was so outside my comfort zone that Brennan might believe he was seeing things if he walked in right now. I almost wanted to show off the body I'd worked so hard on since he'd given me my walking papers.

I wondered what I might say to the cops if they showed up unexpectedly. Someone might've seen us slipping in from the driveway, or maybe there was a new silent alarm I wasn't aware of. Suddenly, I started thinking of the downside of this adventure that had initially been so exciting. I resisted the urge to jump up and flee. My heart was starting to race, but I kept a pleasant smile on my face as I looked over at Marty, who was examining the room in detail from his comfortable lounger.

Then I heard the mechanical click of a key drift through the house.

Someone was opening the front door.

CHAPTER 20

I FROZE EVERY MUSCLE, naked on the lounger, for just a moment, making sure I hadn't imagined the sound of the key in the dead bolt of the front door. Then I heard the door and I saw the look of panic on Marty's face. What had I done? His games were fun and involved Disney World, and my games were creepy and could lead to jail time.

We both sprang off the loungers and tried to slip into our clothes as quietly as possible. I could hear someone inside the house, and I didn't see how this could turn out short of a disaster.

Marty was dressed faster than me and stood, pulling his shirt tight like he was about to have his photograph taken.

I could hear the footsteps on the marble floor. A steady *click-clack* that could be from hard-soled loafers, the stupid cowboy boots that Brennan occasionally wore, or maybe a policeman's shoes.

We were screwed.

I heard the footsteps more clearly.

Click-clack.

Just as I was about to make a last-ditch effort to lead Marty through the pool house and out into the backyard, where we could be seen through just about every window on the first floor, the French doors to the patio room opened.

We were caught. There was nothing to do but act casual, so I just stood there with the vodka and cranberry in my right hand. I willed myself to turn slowly and then saw the figure in the doorway.

It was not Brennan. The wide waist and short body with flowing dark hair immediately told me it was Alena, Brennan's housekeeper for the past ten years. She'd been here before me and would be here long after me. Most important, she had no beef with me. I'd always treated her well and, frankly, considered having her as a housekeeper as opposed to a younger, shapelier woman a major plus. It was one less thing to tempt Brennan.

Alena gasped when she saw us; then she recognized me. She wore a simple white polyester uniform that stretched tight around her hips and bosom. She held her hands to her cheeks, then rushed toward me with her arms out to envelop me in a massive hug.

"Miss Christy, I have missed you so much. Are you well?" She stepped back and a tear ran down her cheek. "Look at you. You look wonderful. Maybe you could eat a little more, but you are still so beautiful."

That made me shed a tear as I stepped forward and gave Alena my own hug. I'd forgotten how sweet this woman from Guatemala could be. I also knew that not having her phenomenal pastries around was probably one of the reasons I had lost weight quickly after I moved out.

THE PALM BEACH MURDERS

I said, "How are you, Alena?"

She shrugged, and I knew what she meant. She worked for a jerk, but what are you going to do?

I introduced Marty quickly, brushing over our exact relationship.

Alena gave me a sly smile and said, "Very handsome, Miss Christy."

"He's an architect, so I wanted to show him the place. Do you know when Brennan will be back?"

"Not for a long time. He had to go with his father to Miami on business. I was just using the day to run errands."

Now it could get tricky. I hesitated, then finally said, "Alena, do you think you could keep my little visit a secret?"

"I would do anything you asked after the way Mr. Brennan treated you. Besides, now that you're not around, he doesn't even pretend to treat me with any respect. If I didn't need the job so badly, I would walk away and never come back."

I gave Alena another hug before she headed out on her next errand. Now Marty and I had some time to look around.

CHAPTER 21

I DECIDED TO GIVE Marty a grand tour of my former castle. It was a lot like the tours I had given friends and neighbors after we'd had work done around the house. As I was showing him some of the guest bedrooms upstairs and recognizing all the improvements I had made in my years as the mistress of the house, I started to realize that maybe I had been covering up flaws in our marriage by throwing myself so completely into home renovations. It wasn't an uncommon practice among the bored housewives of Palm Beach, but I'd had no idea I was doing it at the time.

I had purposely saved the master bedroom suite for last. It sat on the east side of the second story, and the main windows looked out over the ocean. The view was remarkable. There was a separate walk-in closet on each side of a hallway that led to a bathroom, which included a small steam room, a Roman tub with Jacuzzi jets, Italian marble counters and sinks, and even a massage table that pulled out from one of the marble counters. That saved Brennan's personal masseuse the trouble of carrying a table with her when she stopped by to give him one of his three weekly massages.

I enjoyed the look on Marty's face as he inspected every inch of the house. He said, "This is just unbelievable. Even a spread in *Architectural Digest* wouldn't do this place justice. And most of these renovations were your idea?"

I nodded while trying to hide my superior smile. "That's right, I made this place what it is today. When I got here, Brennan had literally thrown some rugs across the floors and hadn't updated the house in any other way since the 1960s. When I found mold—and I'm talking some serious mold, like up the walls and everything—in two of the guest bedrooms, Brennan's response was 'No one stays there long enough to get sick, so why worry about it?'"

"Peach of a guy. I'm glad I've never had to meet him face-to-face."

"You're in another class. There's no reason for you to ever have to deal with that jackass. He'll be out of our life soon enough."

Marty smiled and said, "Now, that's an attitude I can get behind. As long as you don't need all this again, I can't see why I won't make you happy."

Instead of answering him, I turned and wrapped my arms around his neck, then planted a long, lingering kiss on his lips. It felt nice to have this kind of passion in this particular bedroom. The room certainly hadn't seen this kind of action from me in a long time. I had no idea what Brennan was up to on the dating front, and I didn't care. If I really had to admit it, this house had always meant a lot more to me than Brennan had. At least that was what I kept telling myself.

I pulled Marty by his hand and said, "I have one more thing I have to show off, and this one will blow your mind." I ignored his questions and pulled him into the walk-in closet, which was really just another room, to the left of the hallway leading to the bathroom. This was Brennan's formal closet, with one entire wall covered by over a hundred suits, organized by cut and color. I knew it would shock Marty.

He was silent for a moment, then whistled as he walked along a row of suits, dragging his finger across the sleeve of each one. He looked up at the dozens of shirts, in colors ranging from white all the way to black, arranged in perfect order. It looked like a paint chart from one end of the closet to the other.

Marty said, "And he wore a different suit every day?"

"Sometimes two; one to work and one to go out at night. The man loves his clothes." I watched Marty poke around the closet; then I said, "Go ahead, take a couple of sports jackets. He'll never notice. Take anything you want. Brennan might be a little taller than you, but you're about the same size. I'm telling you, that asshole will never miss them."

Then I noticed Marty pulling a box from a shelf at the end of the closet and holding it up to show me. It was the box that our matched set of Walther PPK pistols had come in. Brennan's blue steel pistol was still in the box, surrounded by foam padding; an empty space in the shape of a pistol showed where mine used to reside. Now it was safe in the nightstand in my hotel room.

I didn't say anything when Marty pulled the gun from the box and checked to make sure there were cartridges in the magazine. He looked at me for any sign of disapproval, and when I gave none, he slipped the gun into the pocket of his shorts. You couldn't even notice it.

He put the box back right where he'd found it. I knew it would take Brennan months to find out it was empty. Even if he decided to go shooting, he had other guns and might assume he'd stuck the PPK somewhere else. Things like that didn't bother Brennan.

As we slipped out of the house and locked the patio door behind us, I realized I was about to walk down the beach with a man who had just stolen a gun and was carrying it illegally in public in one of the wealthiest cities in America.

This was an exciting game.

CHAPTER 22

MARTY HAD A MANIACAL grin when he turned to me, raised his eyebrows, and said, "This is the big one. You ready for it?" He looked perfect, framed by the rail and the overhang where we were sitting. The sun was just over his head with the Gulfstream Park racetrack behind him.

He held a handful of tickets for the third race and threw in a cartoon madman's laugh. Who wouldn't smile at an act like that? He looked cute, dressed casually in a polo shirt and jeans. This was just another one of his surprises, and I had never been to a horse-racing track before.

Marty knew I loved horses but had been avoiding the polo fields of Wellington because I didn't want to risk running into Brennan. I had casually mentioned it the evening before as we shared a bottle of wine on the beach. That was when he'd come up with this perfect alternative. We'd left this morning for the track in Hallandale Beach. It was a nice ride, about an hour away, and on a weekday, the place wasn't too crowded. The hot dogs were good and the beer was cold. Marty had managed to sweep me off my feet once again.

When the starting gun sounded, the gates opened and the horses burst out like water from a broken dam. It didn't bother me that there weren't enough people around to make the cheers sound thrilling; I screamed for our horse anyway. We'd put no real thought into making a dozen bets on a horse named Sullivan's Dream. Marty had showed me how to bet on the horse by itself, as well as in combination with other horses, and now we were about to see the result of our leap of faith.

Everything looked good until the third turn, where our horse slowed considerably, and before the race had been decided officially, we realized we were out of the money. Marty said, "Had enough of horses for the day?" He scooped up the losing tickets and stuffed them into his pocket.

"What did you have in mind?" It was warm, and I didn't mind the idea of avoiding Broward County rush hour.

A few minutes later, I found myself on the shuttle heading toward the far reaches of the sprawling parking lot and my white Volvo S-60.

Marty said, "I'll drive, if you don't mind."

I smiled as I thought about what a gentleman he was. Then we slipped onto I-95 and started cruising north.

I said, "This is great. Just what I needed. A few hours away from Palm Beach." I realized that was the opposite of the opinion most people held.

Marty kept his eyes on the road as he said, "Glad you liked it."

"What would you like to do now?"

He thought about it for a few seconds and then said tentatively, "I have a game in mind."

"Anything you want. You've definitely earned it."

Marty just gave me one of his smiles and didn't say anything else. I was content with that. We let Adele's music fill our silence as we zipped along the interstate northbound. I didn't say a word when we passed our exit. Marty had already proved that his surprise trips were always worth the effort.

When we were more than an hour past Palm Beach, I finally said, "Is this all part of your game or are you lost?"

He kept a smile as he said, "All part of the game."

"Want to fill me in?"

He just smiled, and I liked it. He looked a little nervous, with his fingers thumping on the steering wheel and his constant shifting in the seat. I didn't really know what it meant, but I was willing to go along with the game.

We pulled off the interstate and took the long road east until we were on the edges of the city of Vero Beach.

I said, "Okay, I can guess that this game has something to do with your ex-wife. She lives here, right?"

Marty nodded. "She does. You still in?"

"Sure, I said I'll play."

"Then do me a favor and reach back into my jacket on the rear seat."

I twisted and reached for the Windbreaker and immediately felt something heavy in the pocket. I pulled out the pistol and held it up.

"Is this what I think it is?"

Marty grinned and said, "If you think it's the pistol I took from Brennan's closet." He made it sound innocent, like it was a shoe he had taken.

"What's it for?" I kept my voice as even as possible.

"Our game."

"What's the game?"

"It's called *scare the shit out of my ex-wife, Teal.*" He kept driving, taking a few turns, and said, "Come on, it'll be good for a laugh."

I didn't say yes or no as we parked on a short cul-de-sac a few blocks from the ocean.

Marty pointed at one of the three houses on the right side of the road. A vacant lot took up the space on each side of it, separating it from the houses next door. "That's her house."

It was nice. Nothing like my old house, but it was clean and cute. A short walk to the beach. I was getting nervous as I considered all the crazy things that could happen. But I didn't want to let Marty down, and frankly I was curious as to how he'd scare her. He was a smart guy. I was certain he had put some thought into this.

A brown Audi whipped down the street, then pulled into the driveway.

Marty said, "And heeeeere's Teal." Then he looked at me and said, "Are you sure you want to play? I could really use the help."

I hesitated, then blocked out all the reasons I should say no. Instead I said, "Yeah, I'll play."

CHAPTER 23

MARTY EXPLAINED MY PART of his plan quickly, and I just nodded like a robot. It all sounded crazy to me. All I had to do was distract his ex-wife and he would do the rest. I still had no idea how badly he was going to scare her, but somehow, the idea was enticing. Maybe it was because I wanted to scare Brennan badly that I agreed to go along with everything. This was as close as I could get for now.

We both slipped out of the car, and Marty darted toward a row of bushes that would keep him out of sight. I just started to walk slowly down the street in the direction of Teal's house. I noticed that of the few houses, one of them was empty, with a For Sale sign in the yard, and another house on the corner had no cars in its gravel driveway. On the other side of the street, where we were parked, there were no houses, just the rear of a church soccer field.

Teal was unloading groceries and had to make a couple of trips from the front door to her open trunk.

When I was on the street in front of her house, I got my first good look at Marty's ex-wife. She was a beauty: tall, with a creamy complexion and long, wavy hair. I realized I had never seen a picture of her. I'd done a little snooping on Facebook, but she had no profile.

She noticed me, and I felt my stomach jump. My pulse was racing. I wasn't sure I liked this game.

Teal stared at me for a moment. That pushed me to say, "Hi, I, umm, I'm sorry to bother you, but I just had a stupid flat tire. I was hoping there might be someone who could give me a hand." Marty had said to distract her, but I really hadn't put much thought into it. I hoped this was doing the trick. I figured he'd just slip into the house or do something equally juvenile.

Teal said, "I don't think I'd be much help, but we can call someone. There's a service station less than a mile away."

She didn't sound anything like I'd thought she would. Her voice was warm, and she genuinely seemed interested in helping me. That was a stark contrast to the portrait Marty had painted for me of his ex-wife. She was wearing a simple yellow floral print sundress and looked like a suburban mom who'd brought her kids back home from soccer practice. Suddenly I didn't like the idea of helping Marty scare her.

Teal took a few steps past her open trunk toward me and was just about to say something else when Marty burst out of the bushes and stepped into the yard next to the driveway.

If this was his prank, it worked. Teal jumped and squealed, turning to face her ex-husband. Then she said, "Martin? What the hell are you doing here?"

Right at that point, I realized the game was already spiraling out of control.

CHAPTER 24

NOW THAT MARTY WAS out of the bushes and ready to confront his ex-wife, I didn't see where the real scare was. He didn't have the gun in his hand, and they immediately started to bicker. It was really more awkward than scary, and I have to say I was disappointed by the outcome.

Marty even looked a little confused as Teal started to make her points.

She said, "All you do is complain to me about not being able to pay alimony. How you're so busy you don't have a free minute in the day. But somehow you have time to drive all the way up here from West Palm Beach with your bimbo? That doesn't make any sense, Martin."

Marty just stared at her for a moment, and in all honesty, I felt embarrassed for him. Then he said, "Do you have any idea how you sound? How you are more like a shrieking bird than an actual woman? You've never even met Christy. How dare you call her a bimbo."

"Really, Martin? Really? You're at *my* house, where I moved to get away from your crazy jealousy and stalking, and now you're lecturing me on jumping to conclusions about a woman I've never met?"

Then Teal looked at me. She did not have the scared, confused expression I had been expecting. Instead she said, "Are you part of his plan? You seem bright enough. How did he trick you? Did you just get sucked in slowly to his crazy schemes? It's easy, I know. Everything seems normal until all of a sudden you realize he has no boundaries. His concept of reality is very different than it is for the rest of us. My advice to you would be to run. Just like I did. But apparently I didn't run far enough."

Teal turned back to Marty and said, "Congratulations, Martin, way to impress your new girlfriend. Now, I've got a lot to do, so if you'll excuse me, I need to finish bringing in these groceries."

That felt like a pretty definitive end to our little escapade. I knew Marty wanted the experience to last. He wanted to see fear on her face and maybe expected her to be jealous of me. I'd never really been clear on the goal, but now I could see that coming here had been a mistake. His plan to scare her just hadn't worked out.

Marty reached behind his back, and when his right hand came in front of him he was holding the pistol. I have no idea how badly it scared Teal, but at that moment, I was in absolute shock. I could feel the acid in my stomach back up into my throat. I had never seen a gun pointed at a person before except on TV. I could feel my knees starting to get shaky.

Marty wasn't wearing his normal good-natured smile. He shouted, "You know why I came all the way up here?"

Teal was mesmerized by the gun as she took a step away

from Marty. The pretty yellow sundress fluttered in the breeze, but I could see Teal's legs start to shake. Was this the moment Marty had been looking for? Was the terror he was causing his ex-wife enough for him? It was for me.

Teal held both hands out in front of her and said, "I don't know what you're doing, Martin, but this has gone far enough. Put the gun away and we'll forget about this whole stupid encounter."

That sounded good to me. Maybe we hadn't ruined every-thing. I was about to tell Marty that I wanted to leave when I heard two loud pops. They dissipated in the wide-open space and didn't sound the way I thought gunshots should sound, but the noise, coupled with the bright flashes from the barrel of the gun, told me Marty had snapped.

For a moment, I just held my breath. Time felt like it had stood still. The two of them stood facing each other and hadn't moved a muscle since he'd pulled the trigger. Then Teal slowly turned to face me and I could see two red stains on her pretty yellow floral print dress. One was just below her sternum and the other was along the top of the dress, closer to her right arm.

Teal's mouth moved like she was trying to say something, but no words came out. For a moment I just heard an unsettling bubbling sound; then she kept turning until she fluttered to the hard gravel of the driveway in a heap. Her long hair drifted behind her and settled around her face like a soft blanket.

Slowly I looked at Marty, who was still frozen in place with the gun out in front of him. He looked as if he was as surprised as anyone that the gun had gone off. But he still didn't move. He just stared at the lump of flesh that was his ex-wife, Teal.

Maybe I should've been in shock longer, but immediately the practical part of my brain kicked into gear. I'll admit I had let out a quick scream as soon as Marty fired, but my first real thought was to wonder if anyone had heard the gunshots.

I turned my head, quickly scanned the soccer field behind us, and saw that there was no one outside the church. There were those vacant lots on each side of Teal's house, and when I looked up the street I saw nothing but one car passing on US 1. I didn't think the sound of the shots would've carried very far. They'd happened so close together that it would be difficult for someone to pinpoint where they had come from.

Taking everything in and making a quick assessment led me to yell at Marty, "We need to go, right now!"

God forgive me, but it wasn't until we were in my car and Marty was driving south on US 1 that I even thought about whether we should have checked Teal to see if she was still alive.

CHAPTER 25

"HOLY SHIT, WHAT HAVE I done? Holy shit, what have I done?" Marty kept chanting that same phrase like it was some kind of mantra that would bring him back to reality. Or maybe it would *keep* him from reality. Because at this moment, as we tried to gain some perspective and figure out what we would do next, we knew that we were both involved in a murder.

My car swerved as Marty overreacted to a car pulling up to a side street.

I screamed, "What the hell are you doing? We need to draw *less* attention to ourselves, not more!" I immediately regretted being so sharp. I was on edge, and looking at Marty, who was perspiring uncontrollably and leaning into the steering wheel, I knew he was, too.

He took the turn onto Kings Highway, and I knew we'd be cutting through some odd little neighborhoods just north of Fort Pierce.

"Where are you going?" I asked with the stress still evident in my voice.

"The turnpike."

"Listen, Marty, we have to take a deep breath and think this through. You want to go to a road that will photograph us entering and ping off my SunPass as we pay the toll? We need to stay on the back roads, or at most, get on I-95."

I could see that my words were registering with him. He said, "Do you think anyone saw us? It just sort of happened. I didn't even know what I was doing."

I felt like I was about to throw up. I'd never been involved in anything at all like this. I had talked to the cops more in the last couple of weeks than I had in my whole life combined. If I'd been counting on Marty being my rock, I could see I'd made a mistake. Even if I went to the police right now, I'd have to explain why I'd driven all the way up to Vero Beach with Marty and why we'd both fled the scene. This wouldn't play out well in any courtroom. Now we had to jump in with both feet.

Marty turned onto one of the main roads and then took the entrance ramp to I-95. I didn't want to question his every move; he was already so far over the edge that I even wondered if he might pull the gun and use it on himself or maybe even on me. If we got stopped by a cop now, it would all be over. There was no way he'd be able to look calm with the way he was acting.

"Speed up and get into the center lane. You're drawing attention," I snapped when I looked at the speedometer and saw that he was only going forty-eight miles an hour. Cars whizzed past us like we were parked.

Marty mumbled something as he got into the flow of traffic. He was still staring straight ahead, and I tried to figure out how to get the gun from him. That would be a good first step. Eliminate the possibility of more murders or a suicide.

I leaned over and patted him on the shoulder and rubbed his neck for a minute. He didn't respond. The guy was a wreck. Then I let my hand drift down between the seat and his back until I felt the grip of the pistol tucked into his belt on the right side of his back.

I didn't say anything; I just pulled out the small semi-automatic pistol and slipped it into the console.

Marty saw where I put the gun but didn't say anything. I felt like I might have relieved some of the pressure he was feeling by taking the gun from him.

I said, "Marty, we're going to have to come up with a decent alibi to get through this."

"I know, I know. I still can't believe what just happened."

"The last place anyone can prove we visited was Gulf-stream Park. I think I have one of the betting slips in my purse."

"I have a whole bunch crammed in my pocket."

"Good, good. We just say we stayed at the park until later in the afternoon, then took I-95 back to Palm Beach. We'll make sure someone sees us as soon as we get into town. We can go to the Palm Beach Grill and have a drink. If we hurry, we can be there by five thirty and it will match up with leaving the racetrack about four." I waited for some kind of response from my semicomatose boyfriend. Then I said, "We're going to have a drink and gather ourselves. We won't mingle with anyone unless we have to, but we at least want the bartenders to see us."

He took his eyes off the road and stared at me for a moment but didn't say anything. I had to gasp and point at the slow Mazda in front of us to get him to look back at the highway and swerve into the right lane.

"Trust me, babe, this is the only thing we can do."

He took the exit at Jupiter before I could say anything. He said, "I don't know why, but I feel like it's a better idea to drive down to US 1 here and then south to Palm Beach. Maybe it's an instinct. Does that sound right to you?"

Suddenly he sounded coherent and in control. "Yeah, that sounds good, Marty. Just keep cool and it'll all work out. But there's one other thing we need to talk about."

"What's that?"

"No matter what happens, you know the police are going to talk to you, if for no other reason than the fact that you're Teal's ex-husband. You have to face them and be cool and composed during the whole meeting. They might come as soon as tonight. They'll try to trip you up on details. You have to be careful with what you say."

"Talk to me about what? We've been at the track all day, then stopped for a drink at the Palm Beach Grill. I can account for almost every minute of my day."

"And I'll back you up on every single thing you say. But we need to practice our story over and over. And not be on the phone to each other every few minutes."

He nodded. "Smart, very smart. I'm lucky I have you." He focused on the street in front of him, careful not to cause an accident or draw any attention. If someone spotted us up here at the north end of the county, it would blow all our plans instantly.

I leaned back in the seat and took a deep breath. I tried to clear my mind, but all I could see was that dark blood spreading across Teal's pretty flowered dress. I was an accomplice to murder.

CHAPTER 26

ABOUT MIDDAY, I TURNED on my phone and called Marty. We didn't want a lot of phone calls that could be verified by the police. We felt it would be more natural if we had just one call during the day like any normal couple. That was all part of the plan we'd formulated on our frantic drive down from Vero Beach when we decided to try to cover up our involvement in the murder of his ex-wife. Once we'd made a conscious decision to hide it, we were committed.

We met at TooJay's, a decent local deli chain that was in the same plaza as the Palm Beach Grill. It was later in the afternoon, so the place was nearly empty except for a few of the elderly residents who'd walked over from the Biltmore Condos and a couple of traders from the local financial companies grabbing a late, late lunch.

We picked at a platter because neither of us felt much like eating, and when we were sure no one was around, Marty said, "So the cops came by my apartment late last night. It was a Vero detective and an agent from the Florida Department of Law Enforcement. I guess they needed the FDLE for jurisdiction. They didn't call first. Just knocked on my door around eleven. I acted like they woke me up, but of course I couldn't sleep."

This was what I had been anxious to hear all night. I couldn't believe I'd managed to keep my cool. I'd wanted to race over to see him or call him the entire day. "What'd you tell them?"

Marty leaned in close and said, "Just like we practiced. We went to the racetrack, then drove almost straight home to the Palm Beach Grill. I dropped you off at the Brazilian Court about nine. I hadn't heard from or talked to Teal in a couple of months. I even left my betting slips in the front pocket of my jeans so I had them when the cops asked if I had any proof I'd been at the track. It worked out exactly like you said it would."

I said, "They came by to see me about noon. Maybe they were checking some other details about your story first."

"What'd you tell them?"

"Same thing. Just like we practiced. Not too much detail. The difference is *I* really was asleep when they knocked on the door."

We sat for a few minutes, nibbling corned beef and turkey off the platter. Then Marty said, "I'm still in shock over what happened. It was like I wasn't even there. I have no idea what came over me. I hope you can see that wasn't the real me yesterday. I want you to know I'm a good man."

I took the opening to a question I needed to ask. "Teal said you drove her to move. What did she mean?"

Marty shrugged. "Nothing. She said I couldn't let it go, but I could. She overreacted and got a restraining order during our divorce proceedings. The judge seemed like he was only listening to her and didn't care about my side of the story at all. But the restraining order was just to make her look like a victim. It was a horrible experience that got me really down on myself. But once I met you, it was a lot easier."

I said, "You saved all those betting slips and asked me to use my Volvo. I have to ask: Was shooting Teal part of a spur-of-the-moment game or did you plan it?"

He gave me a puppy-dog look and said, "I'd never put you in that position. It just happened. I was just as shocked as you were that it happened, but now I think it might all work out. I think if they had enough, the cops would've arrested me. We're in the clear, and I feel like this is all going to be okay."

I said, "I hope so, because..."

"What? Come on, you can tell me."

"Marty, I love you. Sometimes it takes stress or danger to reveal exactly how you feel about someone. I love you, and I would do anything for you."

He looked relieved. Finally he said, "I've been wanting to tell you how I feel for a long time, but I was afraid I might scare you off. I mean with your divorce and all, I didn't want to add anything to your plate. I love you, too." He reached across the table and lifted my hand so he could kiss it.

I couldn't keep from glancing around the nearly empty restaurant and wondering if any of the patrons could be cops.

CHAPTER 27

IT WAS DARK BY the time we left TooJay's, and we decided to just walk around to the other side of the plaza and stop into the Palm Beach Grill for a few drinks. God knew we could use some alcohol.

We sat at the same high-top as the night we met. The waitress, Suzie, a cute little thing I'd known since she started here, gave us an odd look. A minute later she was back with two Grey Goose vodkas with cranberry. Both doubles. Marty threw his down quickly and looked at Suzie and said, "May I have another, please." Then he stood up and said, "I have to go to the bathroom."

As soon as he was away from the table, Suzie looked at me and said, "The cops were here right when we opened. They asked about you and Marty. They asked if we saw you in here often and if you were here last night. Is everything okay?"

"Just a misunderstanding."

"But you're sure you're okay? I mean, there's nothing funny going on with Marty?"

I let out a laugh. "No, he's not holding me hostage or

anything. He is a little stressed out, so if you don't mind making his drinks a little stronger so he can relax, I'd appreciate it. We're going to have a serious talk."

Suzie was a good waitress and kept the drinks coming without either of us having to ask. After a while, Marty and I shared a hamburger and nibbled at the fries. Marty had walked over to say hello to one of his clients from the island who was putting in a separate pool for his children and wanted a new patio with two enclosed rooms built around it.

There was a TV on in the corner, and I saw a local news piece on Teal's murder. Vero Beach was on the very edge of the local news territory, and the story had gained some interest because shootings generally didn't occur in an upscale town like that.

I stared at the TV, relieved Marty wasn't at the table to see it. The pretty, young female reporter spoke in front of Teal's cute house, and the story was interspersed with footage and earlier interviews. One of them was with a police detective who said absolutely nothing about the facts of the case other than to give the information that they had a body and no witnesses. A photo of Teal flashed on the screen. She was dressed up like she was going to a fancy party or a ball. It suddenly struck me as sad.

The reporter said, "Anyone with any information about this horrendous crime can call Crime Stoppers or the Vero Beach Police Department." It made me think about what had happened and how Marty had snapped so unexpectedly.

The news story headed for its conclusion with the reporter saying, "Police are working around the clock to solve the murder of Teal Hawking. Evidence is still being analyzed, and interviews are being conducted." Then the story ended with the police detective declaring, "We won't stop until this case is solved."

Marty walked back to the table as I processed that last remark. We sat, silently watching all the rich and wannabe-rich people as they came and went through the restaurant's door. After Marty had downed a double vodka, I finally said, "You feel like another game?" His eyes were a little woozy, but he was still in control.

"Sure. What'd you have in mind?"

"A good game of make-believe."

CHAPTER 28

MARTY JUST STARED AT me. "A game of make-believe?"

"It's only fair. You owe me this one."

Marty leaned back and raised his hands. "I'm not arguing. Anything you want."

I said, "Anything?"

"Anything at all." That smile said he was sincere.

I let him consider his words and just gazed into his eyes. He really was a good-looking man and a lot of fun to hang out with. I said, "Let's go see Brennan. I need a little confrontation with him. I want to settle our differences, and he needs to see I've moved on. I want the satisfaction of him seeing us as a couple. Then I'm going to tell him you make me feel like he never could."

"What do I have to do?"

I smiled and patted his hand as I said, "Just look pretty."

"I can do that." He gave me a sly smile and said, "I can do a lot more if you want. I'd like to see that prick piss his pants."

I thought about it, imagining Brennan with urine staining

his expensive slacks, and it made me smile. Marty tended to make me smile.

"I just feel like there's something I have to get off my chest with that guy."

"Are you kidding? Brennan treated you terribly, and you have a right to get anything you want off your chest. He needs a dose of his own medicine."

"I couldn't agree more."

When Marty wandered off again, I grabbed four twenties from my purse and laid them on the table. I wanted to scoot out of there with minimum fuss.

My friend Lisa Martz, who had introduced Marty and me, came through the front door and saw me. She came right to the table and gave me a hug.

Lisa said, "Look at you, aren't you a vision. How's it going with Marty?"

Before I could answer, Marty was next to her, ready with a hug.

I didn't feel like chatting. I was focused. I wanted to have it out with Brennan. I felt my impatience grow as Lisa chatted about the most Palm Beach of things: houses, cars, and scandals.

When Lisa moved on to another table to spread the gossip of the island, Marty and I were alone. He said, "When do you want to play this little game of yours?"

"Why not tonight?"

CHAPTER 29

I HAD TO STOP at the Brazilian Court and left Marty in the car. I stopped and spoke with Allie at the front desk, then rushed to my room. One advantage of living in such a tiny space is that nothing ever takes long to find. I was back in the car in a few minutes and found Marty listening to the Moody Blues on the radio.

As I drove through Palm Beach with Marty in the passenger seat, he surprised me by showing some nerves. It wasn't about a confrontation, either.

Marty said, "Do I look all right to meet Brennan?"

I laughed and said, "You're not going to date him. You look fine."

"I mean, will I impress him the way you want me to?" He blew into his hand and smelled his breath. "God, I need a mint at least." He dug in the glove compartment, then turned to the console. That was where he found the pistol I'd stuck in there the day before.

He reached down, pulled out the gun, and examined it for

a second, then said, "We'll take this, too. I hate to admit it, but somehow it makes me feel more confident."

If Marty was hesitant to play this game, it didn't show as he slipped the gun into his pants and pulled his shirt out over it.

By the time we were in front of my old house, Marty was looking around to make sure no one was on the street. This was Palm Beach and it was after nine o'clock, so that wasn't even a worry.

Both the Bentley and the Jaguar were in the driveway, and I could see the downstairs den lights on. That meant Brennan was home. He was the only one who used the den; he'd sit in there when he was working late to keep up with the foreign stock exchanges. We sat in the car and watched the house for a few minutes. Then I saw Brennan's silhouette as he stood up from the desk and walked to one of the file cabinets that were built into the wall.

There was no traffic this time of night, but I kept twisting my head from side to side just to make sure. I was nervous, and there was no hiding it. Not only was my heart still pounding, but I felt a thin sheen of sweat across my forehead. Maybe this wasn't such a good idea.

I turned to Marty and said, "Okay, when we get out, don't slam the door, just close it quietly." He nodded obediently.

I said, "You sure you're still up for this, babe?"

"Anything for you."

"Brennan can be a lot to deal with. For all his bluster, he does have a mean streak, and he's not afraid to show it."

"I can handle myself." Marty sounded confident.

"I just want to say what I have to say and get out of here. Okay?"

"Okay, okay. I'll behave."

I looked up at my grand house and thought about how much my life had changed in the past six months. It made me angry.

Before I had time to dwell on my emotions, a splash of light fell across us. A car had just turned and was coming down the street slowly. We were parked awkwardly on the curb where there wasn't supposed to be any parking. We stuck out like a sore thumb. Then I realized that at this time of night, it was likely a police car on patrol. I didn't feel like answering questions in front of my estranged husband's house.

Then I thought of the real problem. What if they pulled us out of the car and found the gun on Marty? That would not go over well here in Palm Beach.

I looked at Marty and saw the same concerns on his face.

We both stared at the car as it came toward us at a steady pace like a shark moving methodically through the water. Neither of us could find the will to move.

Marty was about to say something when I held up my hand to keep him quiet. I needed to think.

Then, as the car was almost on top of us, I noticed it was a bright red. Not the blue and white of a Palm Beach police car. And it was a Cadillac. A big one. As the car passed us, I could see the tiny white head that barely reached over the dash, and I realized it was a local, someone who probably always drove slowly after dark.

The elderly woman never even looked in our direction.

I let out a long breath and grabbed my purse from the backseat, and we slipped out of the car.

CHAPTER 30

WE MADE IT UP the driveway to the front door without making a sound. For some reason, when we stood in front of the door I found myself out of breath. I pressed the doorbell and could hear the chimes inside the house. Chimes I'd picked out and had installed to replace the stupid *ding-dong* sound that was attached to the doorbell when we got married. I looked around, making sure no one was watching us. Marty tapped his foot as he stood next to me.

It was a typical humid Florida night, and the breeze off the Atlantic felt like heaven. The excitement of facing Brennan built inside me. I turned to Marty, and in a low voice I said, "I can't wait to see the look on Brennan's face."

Then the door opened, and Brennan didn't disappoint me. He was utterly shocked and couldn't hide it. Dressed in a polo shirt and golf slacks, he looked good. Almost like a model. His hair was perfect, and he had a few lines on his face, like a man who spent much of his time outdoors. For a change, he was speechless, and his blue eyes were wide with surprise. He looked from me to Marty slowly, then settled back on me. This was exactly what I wanted. He was shaken.

After a long silence, Brennan said, "Christy, what are you doing here at this hour? I thought we were speaking only through our attorneys."

I took a moment to gather myself, looking Brennan straight in the eyes as I said, "I need to say something. Not in court, where I can be censored."

"I'm listening," he said slowly, still looking back and forth between me and Marty.

Somehow with just those two words he managed to be condescending.

"Do you realize what a pretentious, pompous ass you are? Is it intentional?"

Brennan made no comment.

"You're rich, so what? You've never had any hardships, so basically you're spoiled, and I enabled you for four years. You didn't need a wife, you needed a caretaker. I didn't complain when you left me at home alone on Christmas two years in a row so you could windsurf with your buddies in Aruba. You basically ignored my parents and to this day don't know my mom's first name. And you had no reason to try in our marriage, so you just threw me out like the trash. I've got news for you, Brennan. I'm not who you thought I was." I took a breath, then said, "I gave you four years and you gave me nothing in return."

"Except a phenomenal lifestyle."

"And the privilege of being Mrs. Brennan Moore."

"Glad you finally get it."

That arrogant smile cut into my soul.

I kept going. "You spent more on a massage table built into the bathroom than on my engagement ring. That should've given me an idea of what to expect when I married you. You told the judge you didn't think I had ever shown any real emotion toward you. Well, be careful what you wish for. Now you'll see all my emotions at once. All my well-earned anger and frustration, followed by relief and joy. Now you get to know what it feels like to be powerless."

I think Marty could sense my anger, but he shocked me when, without any warning, he yanked the pistol from under his shirt, fumbled with it for a second, and then pointed it at Brennan's groin. He held it steady in his hand as he brought his face up to look at my reaction.

I was at a loss. He'd moved so quickly I hadn't expected it.

Marty was smiling.

Brennan staggered back half a step and said, "Jesus Christ, that's my gun."

CHAPTER 31

I FELT LIKE SINGING. Why not? I was back inside my house. For the moment I could forget the awkward fact that Marty was holding a gun on Brennan. We shuffled in through the foyer, then turned into Brennan's den, where it was clear he'd been working. His computer screen was still showing active trades on the foreign stock exchanges, and he had papers laid out across his giant oak desk. The one I had found for him in a furniture shop in North Carolina. It was magnificent, with hardwood inlays and drawers that felt like they moved on air.

Brennan had been remarkably quiet up to this point, but he still had that self-assured, superior look on his face, even with Marty standing a few feet away pointing the gun at him. It was clear Brennan didn't think we were going to hurt him. Obviously, we'd been drinking, and I'm sure Brennan just viewed it as another immature prank by a dull wife he thought he'd gotten rid of. But after a minute or so, he was tired of the game and anxious to get back to work.

He had his hands up slightly, like he was being robbed. It must have been human instinct. He kept his voice low as he said, "Could you point that somewhere else, please."

Marty just said, "Nope."

It was the best possible response to unnerve Brennan. It also shut him up. He stared at Marty but wisely remained silent.

Marty cut his eyes to me in an effort to get a clear idea of what we had planned. He was visibly more agitated than when we'd started this little prank and was hopping from one foot to the other like a nervous kid who needed to go to the bathroom. He was probably wondering if I expected him to gun down Brennan like he had Teal the day before. I stepped over to him, patted him on the back, gently wrapped my hand around the gun, and eased it from his tight grip, quietly saying, "It's going to be okay." He visibly relaxed as he relinquished the pistol and took a pace backward.

Now I held the gun. I took a breath to calm down. Marty was about to snap, and I was sure I'd taken the pistol just in time. As I stepped away from him, closer to Brennan, I told Marty, "Just wait right there, sweetheart, and keep calm."

Brennan picked up on the fact that I was trying to keep Marty from doing anything crazy, and he thought we were looking for a way out. He waited while I made sure the pistol was pointed down, away from anyone's vital organs.

Marty appeared a little hurt that I had taken the gun from him. If I had acted a little faster the day before, maybe poor Teal would still have been alive. The gun was heavy in my hand. Heavier than I remembered it from the range. I carefully slipped it into the pocket of my jeans. It fit snugly.

Brennan was visibly relieved and regained some of his

swagger. He raised his voice and said, "You found some moron you can order around and you think it's love? Christy, what in the hell are you guys doing here? This doesn't help anyone. You guys need to get out of my house and sober up."

That's when I straightened up and looked him right in the eye and said, "I'm not drunk. In fact, I've barely had a drink all night." I realized that surprised Marty, too, as he looked at me with a puzzled expression.

Then I reached into my purse, the one large purse I owned, and easily drew out another pistol. The second one of the matched set. It looked identical and rendered both men absolutely mute. I liked that.

I gave my full attention to Marty. "I'm afraid there's a lot you don't understand, sweetheart. And I don't think you'll ever realize how much this bothers me." He still had that look like a puppy as I stepped closer to Brennan, standing just behind him and facing Marty. "I mean it, Marty, I am really, really sorry." Then I aimed the pistol and squeezed the trigger. Just like I had been taught. By Brennan. The pistol bucked in my hand and the noise inside the house, with all the marble and tile, sounded like a nuclear blast.

But I still managed to hit my target and shot Marty once, almost dead center in his chest.

The flash from the muzzle blinded me temporarily. I didn't even see any bloodstain on his shirt before he dropped straight to the floor, and thankfully, he didn't make any sounds like Teal had. He rolled onto his back, and then everything stopped. He was absolutely still. My ears rang from the gunshot, and the air had the acrid odor of gunpowder. Marty was dead. It had been quick, and he was now flat on a hard wooden floor that would be easy to clean up.

I'd noticed how much Brennan had jumped when I pulled the trigger. I couldn't see his face, but I could imagine what he was thinking right now. His legs were already trembling.

Good God, this was what I had been waiting for.

CHAPTER 32

I WAS STILL STANDING behind Brennan, who dared not turn his head. He had a perfect view of Marty's crumpled body about fifteen feet in front of him. My ears still throbbed from the noise of the gunshot. Now I knew why we always wore earplugs when we went to the range. My guess was that right about now, Brennan was regretting our days shooting together and his detailed lessons. At the time, he'd just enjoyed being able to tell me things. It had been a power trip for him.

Brennan's voice cracked as he said, "Christy, Jesus Christ, what have you done?" He choked up on whatever he was going to say next as he tried not to vomit.

"How's it feel, Brennan? Knowing you're helpless. Is it a new sensation?" I let a brief silence fall over the room so I could enjoy seeing Brennan squirm. Now he was shaking as he tried to maintain his composure. The air was still filled with the odor of the gunshot. This old house had never seen anything like this, and Brennan had never experienced anything like it either. He deserved it. Not just for the way he'd treated me, but for the way he treated the rest of the world. It was time he learned he wasn't better than anyone else.

I said, "I doubt the sound of the shot even penetrated the walls. No one outside this room has any idea what just happened. No one is coming to help." I let that sink in, then said, "Stand there perfectly still, looking straight ahead. Got it?"

He nodded frantically. Sweat stains were now visible on the back of his shirt near his underarms. I don't think I'd ever seen Brennan sweat.

I said, "I'd like to savor your reaction to this, but I have a lot to do."

"What—what are you talking about? What do you have to do?" He started to whimper and added, "What's going on? I don't understand what you're doing."

"I think experts call it 'arranging the crime scene.'" I stayed behind him as I snapped on a pair of gloves. I'd figured out the right trajectories and what the residue tests would show. "You see, Brennan, it took a lot of research to learn that the cops might connect the gun to Teal's murder. I had to take all that into account and come up with the right story."

"Story? What story? You're going to try to make the police believe I shot your boyfriend?"

I chuckled. "I have no doubt I could sell any story to the cops at this point. It's all the other details that take concentration." There was a long silence as Brennan thought things over.

He finally said with a cry, "What are you doing? I don't understand."

"Well, Brennan, dear. This was my backup plan. I admit I had another one in the works for quite some time, almost from the day I met Marty, who I recognized as being very nice and extremely easy to manipulate. I knew if my legal challenges to your ridiculous prenuptial agreement failed, I'd need an alternative. This is it.

"I knew I wanted to go through with the plan the day you crushed me in court just because you could." I let him think about that and how he had abused me. "Yesterday, Marty shot his ex-wife. You might've seen it on the news. He got away with it, too. At least he thought he'd gotten away with it. I told him I had backed up his alibi"—I leaned in close to Brennan and whispered in his ear—"but I didn't."

Now I pulled the gun from my pocket and held it in my right hand. The other was loose in my left, hanging by my side. I slowly strolled around in front of Brennan until I was standing near Marty's body. "Marty was crazy for Teal and everyone knew it. She even got a restraining order on him. I told the cops we left the racetrack early and I didn't know where Marty was most of the afternoon until I met him at the Palm Beach Grill." Now I could enjoy Brennan's expression as I laid out my story.

"That's why I'll say I broke up with him earlier tonight at the Palm Beach Grill and why I told my friend Allie, at the Brazilian Court, that I had already broken up with him and I was a little scared. I also told her Marty went crazy when he heard you were interested in reconciling with me. It's also why I'm sure the police are at Marty's apartment waiting for him right now."

I held the gun steady in front of me. "The best part, the one thing that just fell into place, was when Marty found your pistol. I may have moved it so he'd notice it, but he thought it was all his idea." I saw that Brennan was confused. "That's right, he found it in your closet one day when we came to visit. I didn't say a word when he stole the pistol. Because I knew the cops could tie the gun that killed Teal to the gun used here tonight, I had to switch them on poor, simple Marty. Wild, huh? He used *my* gun to shoot Teal and I used *your* gun to shoot him. All I have to say is that Marty stole my gun from the nightstand in my hotel room. It will work out perfectly. Brilliant, right?"

Brennan was trying to keep from sobbing. "What are you talking about? Why are you doing this?"

I grinned. "Because I can. And there's not a damn thing you can do about it."

CHAPTER 33

I COULDN'T BELIEVE HOW thrilling it was to have this much power over another person. It almost made me understand why Brennan had done some of the things he had. Now it was time to explain exactly what was about to happen as I stood in front of him, holding the gun in a remarkably steady hand.

"It's really a simple story. The key is to always keep things simple. Marty asked to go for one final drive together. Then he pulled the gun, the Walther PPK you gave me as a present. He must've gotten it out of my nightstand at the hotel. Then he forced me to drive here so he could prove he loved me, because he was, you know, crazy.

"He came into the house and you shot each other. I was terrified and fled upstairs to call 911. Simple and believable."

Brennan just stared at me. "But why? This could ruin your whole life. What do you really have to gain?"

I let out a quick laugh. I'd never realized Brennan could be so funny. Then I looked at him with a deadpan stare and said, "You have no will. I checked the wall safe the other day when we were here. And I know you're far too cocky to leave it with an attorney."

Brennan had a real hitch in his voice now. "So what? We're divorced. What good does all this do you?"

"Actually, we're in the *process* of divorcing. We might even reconcile. If you die intestate—that means with no will—I get my house back. It's really all I wanted. I couldn't care less if you live or die. And frankly, I would've preferred a nice fella like Marty to live with. But shit happens."

"I can make this right, I swear. You can have the house. You can have a great settlement. You name it."

"It's a little late to negotiate, Brennan. You had your chance to do this the right way. Now I've just turned it into a big game. A game of make-believe. Let's make believe we're part of a fantastic murder mystery. Now you have to make believe you're going to die."

I let that realization dawn on him so I could see it in his face. It was amazing. One moment he thought I was ranting and raving, and the next he realized I was following through on a carefully laid-out plan.

I said, "Every game has a winner and a loser. I'm afraid in this one you're the loser, babe." I squeezed the trigger and the gun jumped in my hand. The bullet flew a little high, hitting Brennan in the upper chest. He toppled backward and fell with a thud on the hard floor, gurgling for a few seconds. This time the noise didn't shock me so much and the gunpowder smell wasn't as jolting. Everything is easier the second time around. Even shooting a man.

It took only a minute to wipe down the guns and stick one in the right hand of each of the dead men in the room. I pulled the trigger with the gun in the hand of each man and didn't really care where the bullet went. It was all part of the story I had planned.

I stepped back to make sure everything looked just the way I wanted it to. The bodies were well separated, and the police measurements would show that the bullets had traveled about the right distance. I went to the nearest bathroom and, using the back of my hand to avoid leaving fingerprints, double-flushed the gloves. Perfect.

I strolled through the house and started to climb the stairs, then dialed 911 on my cell phone, and as soon as the operator answered, I screamed, "They're shooting each other, they're shooting each other, what should I do?" Then I threw in a convincing cry.

The operator, keeping calm like they're trained to, said, "Ma'am, ma'am, where are you? What's the address?"

I continued to climb the stairs. Through a series of sobs I gave her the address. And told her, "He's crazy and he has a gun."

The operator said, "Where are you in the house? Are you safe?"

I gave her a good moan and said, "I'm hiding upstairs in a closet. Think I'm safe for now."

The operator said, "Stay there. Help is on the way."

When the cops found me in the closet, they would see that I'd been crying. What they wouldn't understand was that they were tears of joy. I had just gotten my house back by winning a game. This game was called *let's play make-believe that I can get away with the murder of my husband.*

NOONERS

JAMES PATTERSON

WITH **TIM ARNOLD**

CHAPTER 1

"SO, TIM, HOW would you describe yourself in a single sentence?"

Friday lunch, and I was sitting across the table from Linda Kaplan, the president of one of the most successful advertising agencies in New York, Kaplan-Thaler. She's in her mid-fifties, attractive, and exudes the confidence of well-deserved success.

I'm your typical New York adman, Madison Avenue through and through, but after a second stint at Paul Marterelli & Partners, I'd hit a wall. It was time to move on. Past time.

And at this lunch, it's taking all I've got to stay in the moment. A lot of bad, crazy shit has come crashing down around me, and I'm trying to figure out what it all means.

But I'm getting ahead of myself....

We're at Soho House, a members-only restaurant, hotel, and spa down on 9th Avenue in the Meatpacking District. Linda Kaplan launched her agency in 1997 with the Herbal Essence shampoo *"Yes! Yes! Yes!"* campaign—think Meg Ryan in *When Harry Met Sally*—and never looked back. Now the agency is part of the Publicis Group, a global organization with the financial means to pay their people well. My head-hunter hooked us up because Linda is looking for a co-partner and managing director to assume responsibility for all of the agency's clients.

I'm getting a good vibe. The light in her eyes suggests she has a good sense of humor and doesn't take life—real life—too damned seriously. Just her job.

This is a big deal. Our first interview. I want this job. *A lot.* Possibility of a 25 percent salary hike, plus bonus. I know I'm qualified, and so does she.

I'm wearing a necktie for the first time in years. I usually just wear jeans and a button-down to work, unless we have a client in or a new business pitch, but this meeting calls for a tie. Lots at stake here. And the damned thing feels like a noose tightening around my neck.

This was the day of the first murder. Somebody I knew. By the end of next week, my life will have changed forever.

CHAPTER 2

Yesterday...

ON BAD DAYS the advertising agency profession can get old fast. Especially with lousy clients. But this day is set to remind me why I got in this business in the first place.

We're presenting a new campaign to a client who's sat on the same advertising for five years: Chubb Insurance— Marterelli's biggest client—has become one of those "un-approachable" insurance companies lost in the morass of indistinguishable brands in a category that's competing on price, and little more. Worse, Chubb is premium priced. We've got a scary idea—the kind I love—to take Chubb to the next level. The plan is to confront consumers with the inevitability of some painful loss of assets during their lifetimes. Then we let them know that Chubb will be there to help, with a campaign built around humor to balance the grim forecast.

It's enough to distract me from the real-life bullshit swirling all around me.

The meeting's scheduled for eleven a.m. I'm in the office by eight; I stop by the break room, crank up the coffeepot, and head upstairs to go over some notes.

I'm wearing jeans, for sure—Ralph Laurens—pressed, and an oxford cloth open-collar long-sleeved shirt. Got my black-on-black brocade sports jacket slung over a chair, ready for the client. So I'm going formal. Cool New York formal.

"Hey, *buenos dias, amigo.*" It's Ramon, our tech guy, at my cubicle door. A tall, dark, and handsome guy, as they say, with a bright, persistent smile on his face. "What's up? And what am I doing here this early, you ask?"

"Looking for . . . ?"

"No one. Just here to set you guys up in the conference room. Big meeting, huh?"

"Yeah, totally. But we're ready to kick some client ass. Thanks, man, I'll see you later."

"Ciao." I will definitely see Ramon later.

Back upstairs with my coffee. Now it's Mary Claire Moriarty, my junior account leader—that's what I like to call all of us account types. Early twenties, straight out of the Missouri School of Journalism, and she's a terrific writer, too, so I've given her a small part in the pitch. It's all about teamwork, and providing experience in the trenches for these bright up-and-comers.

"Good morning, *sir,*" she says. Her bright eyes are beaming. She's a spark.

"MC, I keep telling you, no '*sirs*' in this business—or anywhere else for that matter—except the military. Anyway, how are you? Ready to rock?"

"Yeah. Just wanted to thank you for the opportunity. Hope I don't screw it up."

"Girl, you won't. I know you won't. Now *you* need to know it. Got it?"

"Yeah, yes...yeah, I've got it, thanks. See you downstairs."

My mind is wandering....

Will we be through with this meeting in time for a late lunch?

It's a sixty-minute meeting. Done. No wordy slides. No extraneous BS. We headline the pitch with an innovative brand strategy to convey that Chubb understands life's risks, and can relate to customers' needs. Two fabulous ideas, both on strategy: the one with the most potential upside scarier than the other.

Mary Claire describes the brand personality in the colorful language she authored herself.

Then our creative director reads the last scripted line from another satisfied Chubb customer appearing in the TV spot and turns to me for the capper, the tagline that will separate this client's business from the rest of the category....

I look the CMO in the eye and announce in my rehearsed voiceover *"Insurance Against Regret"*...and the room is as quiet as a funeral. For an instant. And then an uncommon reaction in the agency business: applause! Our clients are smiling from ear to ear, and *clapping!*

They buy it on the spot. Damn, I love this business.

"Tim," said the Chubb CMO, Kevin Magnus, shaking my hand, "you've just reminded me in dramatic fashion why I hired you guys in the first place. Send me the summary and a production estimate, and let's get it done!"

My team hears all this and responds with enthusiastic, polite applause of their own. The client's not out the front door before we're gathering into a group hug, backslaps all around.

"Guys, this is the result of some fabulous teamwork. Never forget that. Together, we make shit happen.

"Now, get your asses back to work!" I say with a broad smile, which is returned in kind by every one of them.

Perfect timing for a lunch break. And I think I've earned a long one.

CHAPTER 3

BY THE TIME I get back, it's four-ish, and the proverbial cocktail hour is within reach.

"Well done, MacGhee!" Paul Marterelli is at my door before I can get my jacket off. "Magnus just called me to say how excited he is about the possibilities! I've never heard him so enthusiastic. Must have been great. Obviously he bought the big one. . . ."

"Absolutely. Thanks, Paul, really appreciate it. It's days like today that remind me why I came back to work with you," I tell him. Hey, I'm an adman.

"Wanna grab a beverage?"

"Damn, man, would love to. Can't. Got plans."

"Ah, okay, see you tomorrow," Paul says, and heads downstairs.

I first met Paul Marterelli right out of the Marines. With my Columbia journalism degree there was only one gig for me: adman! Soon enough some good networking connected me with Paul, and we clicked instantly.

Paul was a creative guy, a writer, and a good one. Clean-cut, glasses, conservative dresser; would have assumed he was an account guy if you didn't know better. Met him the first time downtown at McSorley's. We hung out, had beers, told stories. Tells me he's got the CrawDaddy account, an up-and-coming tech company, with their kick-ass cowboy CEO— an ex-Marine!—and wants my own Marine self to take him on. Perfect—at least for an advertising moment. More on that later.

Paul founded Marterelli & Partners in 2003, positioning his team as a feisty "ad store," and soon established his agency as an early and proactive user of social media on behalf of their clients.

On my first day, he called the agency team together to introduce me. "Okay, guys, listen up," he said. "It is my great pleasure to introduce Tim MacGhee, a kindred spirit if there ever was one. An adman in the truest sense of the word. New to our business, but he's got a couple of years and some genuine leadership experience under his...ammo belt. A natural leader. A teammate. He's joining us to, well, call CrawDaddy's bluff and help us get their kick-ass brand on the Super Bowl!"

There was warm applause all around. A couple of whistles.

"Tim, as a small token of our sincere welcome, I want you to have this, a present from all of us." He handed me a gift-wrapped box.

"Wow, this is amazing!" I patted my heart a few times. "Thank you, Paul. Thank you all." They'd given me a really nice canvas attaché. I recognize the maker—J.W. Hulme. Damn!

"And by no means does this suggest that you are a bag-carrier."

"Beautiful. And it sure beats the hell out of my Marine assault backpack!"

A genuinely wonderful reception. Turns out it was the perfect gift. I offered a few positive words of appreciation, and Paul showed me to my desk. That was day one, about three lifetimes ago.

Now I'm on my way back up to my corner cubicle on the fifth floor, and I'm getting universal smiles and nods in the hallways, colleagues glowing in the shared success of our Chubb meeting. Feels good. Word travels fast.

I've got time to kill, and here's Ramon to help. As you can tell by now, I'm not one of those stuffed suits that wears his title on his tailored sleeve, looking down his nose. I love the troops. I'm a team guy. And over the years I've discovered I have a lot more in common with some of these guys than I do with my so-called peers.

"Everything work?" he asks.

"Like a charm. Thanks, as always. Well done."

"I'm here to serve," he says with a grin.

"So, meet you up on the roof?" I say.

"Let's do it," Ramon says. What a good guy. And a good partner.

"Okay, man. I'll get it wrapped here—then I've got to run out for a quick stop. Back in a flash. Sun's already dropping. See you upstairs."

The agency occupies the top three stories of a five-story brownstone in downtown Manhattan, so we have exclusive access to the roof, a convenient escape that offers a view of historic surroundings and fresh air—as fresh as Manhattan air gets. A place to hang. On nights like tonight, it's an after-work gathering space for us kindred spirits.

Got to get to the bank first, down on Canal Street. I grab my attaché and catch a cab on Second Avenue. "Canal and Broadway," I tell the driver. "Wait for me, okay? I'll be in and out in a flash."

"Sure," she says, and off we go.

Thirty minutes down and back, and I'm on the roof in another fifteen. Ramon's already there with a handful of other agency types, each one with a beer in hand from various coolers downstairs.

It will take an hour or so for me and Ramon to be left up there, alone.

CHAPTER 4

TOUGH NIGHT. COULDN'T sleep. *Since when does this kind of stuff get to me?*

Now I'm in the kitchen at three a.m. when my wife, Jean, comes up close behind me and puts her arm around my waist.

"You okay?" She's asking because I'm never like this. I'm the calm at the center of the storm.

"Yeah, sorry. Had a crazy day. Crazy good, most of it. Worked late, you know? No big deal. Just need to unwind."

She heads back up to the bedroom and I look in on the kids, stop by the bathroom, pop a rare Xanax and shuffle back to bed, reminded again that I am part of a wonderful, loving family. A gift.

I crawl in under the covers and the love of my life slides over next to me.

"Honey?" She's not convinced I'm okay.

"Don't worry, baby. Got this important interview tomorrow at lunch, great opportunity, a job I really want." Little does she know how much I need this job.

"Anyway, I can hang in here a little later in the morning."
She's already asleep again.

The alarm erupts at seven a.m. and it feels like I've been struck by lightning. Shower, shave. Pull on some selvedge denims and a cashmere sport coat, both black, out of the closet along with an Essex multi-check lavender shirt and the hand-painted tie I bought down in the Village.

First impressions are important. Never thought of myself as a slave to fashion, but this is the advertising business and I'm headed for a critical interview.

The office doesn't expect me in until early afternoon, which means I have time for a rare breakfast with the kids before Jean takes them to school. A second cup of coffee with the *New York Times* and I'm off to the train station.

I'm about to experience the kind of day that most people could never imagine, not in their wildest dreams. Or nightmares. Neither could I.

CHAPTER 5

THE 8:57 HUDSON Line express from Croton-on-Hudson into the city gives me enough time to make a quick stop and grab one more cup of coffee downstairs at Grand Central Station, so I can get focused on my meeting with Kaplan.

But now, pitching myself for a job I absolutely must have, there's a thousand conflicting thoughts spinning around inside my head that have nothing to do with the agency business.

She's familiar with my résumé. This is about chemistry.

Me...in a single sentence...?

"That's a damned good question," I say to this agency superstar, snapping back to the here and now. "I've thought about how best to describe what I do, who I am. And here's my answer, if you'll pardon my French: I'm a guy who makes shit happen."

"That's certainly to the point." She chuckles. "Especially

in our business. And especially for an account guy. Great attitude."

The waiter sets our salads in front of us, escarole for me, farro and quinoa for her, and asks if we want any more iced tea. Tea? I want a martini.

"Read this column in *Adweek* right after I started at Marterelli. Headline was 'Making Stuff Happen,' but what the columnist wrote about was making *shit* happen. Especially for account leaders. That was all I needed. It spoke to me."

"You've got a great track record," she says, "a strong, unique résumé, that's for sure. Loaded with references."

"Thank you! Hey—I'm an ex-Marine. Heard the call, 9/11 changed my whole perspective on life. Signed on for two years right out of Columbia University, and ended up in Iraq, 3rd Battalion, 1st Marines, Platoon Leader...."

"Thank you for your service! Where?"

"Fallujah. Second Battle—the bloodiest conflict of the entire Iraqi war. We lost a lot of soldiers. They lost more. Tough stuff. I saw things I'll never be able to erase from my mind. But we ran the insurgents out and took the city back. And I helped make it happen."

"Your résumé isn't quite that...colorful."

"That was a lifetime ago. Honorable discharge, and I leverage my journalism degree and my leadership experience from the real world into a starting job with Marterelli. Fabulous, for a little while. Did the CrawDaddy thing. Then we lost the account—no fault of ours, hell, we made history with that spot, blew their business through the roof! Anyway, back then the agency was far from flush, had to pare down. So I jumped ship, painful for both Paul and me. Landed the job at Thompson—where I ended up running the Burger King business, as you know.

"Couple of lifetimes later Paul and I reconnect, over beers. They've grown to a fabulous midsized agency by now, and we simply had to get back together! We did, 'partners,' in theory, and now I've got the biggest job in the agency—unless they want to make me president."

"Maybe they should..."

"If it were up to me...but, Paul's not ready to go, not even close. So, there's nothing left for me to accomplish there. Time to move on."

The waiter's back with our main courses—strozzapreti for Linda and the seared scallops pour moi.

My iPhone's in my pocket, and vibrates with a text message. Of course, I ignore it.

"Another question: what's the biggest mistake you've made in this business?"

She's good.

"Oh, man, where to start?" I say, which evokes the laughter I was hoping for. "The *biggest* mistake? Giving up box seats for the 2007 Super Bowl, when the Giants, the wild-card team, come all the way back and beat the undefeated Patriots! The Eli Manning fourth-quarter comeback. The David Tyree one-handed helmet catch?"

"What the hell were you thinking?" she asks, wearing a teasing grin from ear to ear.

"Gave 'em to a client—and the asshole puts us in review six months later. Sure wasn't thinking about that!

"But seriously, folks...a few years ago I had a chance

to hire David Hale, and didn't. He went on to semi-greatness, as you know, and it could have been with us. Woulda, coulda, shoulda—but I regret that one to this day."

"Hard to see untapped potential sometimes," she says. I note the empathy.

"The chemistry just wasn't there, then," I answer. "And sometimes that's everything."

"I feel a good chemistry here, though," I hear her say. Which means she can't tell my heart is beating a hundred miles an hour.

She signals for the waiter, and the check. Another iPhone text vibration...

"I'm looking for a partner, someone capable of helping me run the agency. There's a couple of other people I want to talk to, but I definitely want to reconnect with you. And soon. You've got a lot to offer."

"Fantastic!" I say. "Thank you. Want to split the check?"

"Oh, please," she says, with a laugh.

Back out on 9th Avenue on this stunning fall afternoon, the sidewalk's alive with New Yorkers acting as if they've got places to go, things to do.

So do I.

"I've genuinely enjoyed meeting you," she tells me, "and look forward to seeing you again soon."

"Same here. And count on it!"

A firm, eye-to-eye handshake, and we part company on a great note. Her driver pulls up for her and she climbs in the backseat.

I hail a cab and check my texts. They're from Chris Berardo, our creative director:

Where the hell are you?

And . . .

You need to get your ass here NOW!

CHAPTER 6

"EAST 11TH STREET, between Third and Fourth," I tell the cabbie.

Marterelli & Partners' office is across town in the East Village, south of Union Square Park. It's a classic New York neighborhood, and Union Square is a great place to hang out during lunch, or for other stuff.

What the hell is Chris so excited about?

We reach 11th and Third and my stomach drops when I see a cop car parked sideways at the intersection with his red and blue lights flashing, blocking the entrance to 11th Street. There's yellow tape stretching all the way across, from one side of the street to the other.

This looks bad. Real bad.

"Far corner," I say, and pay the cabdriver.

I approach the officer sitting in the driver's seat and explain who I am. He lets me through after I show him my agency ID and driver's license.

Halfway down the block I can see *four police cars and*

an ambulance double-parked in front of our building, lights flashing.

Jesus. It's worse than I thought.

Looks like the entire agency is outside, on the sidewalk or in the street.

I get there just in time to see two medics jump out of the ambulance, open the rear doors, and pull out a wheeled gurney. Oh, God—they're headed inside the agency building!

As soon as I'm in front of our brownstone, a dozen coworkers are surrounding me.

Maureen, our receptionist, is shaking like a leaf, crying. Middle-aged, widowed, pleasantly overweight, with a face that's usually beaming, Mo's the agency den mother. I take her hand and pull her in close. She leans on my shoulder and loses it.

"What the hell is going on, Mo?"

"It's awful. Unbelievable." She's sobbing.

I spot Chris Berardo out in the street. Lanky, shoulder-length hair pulled back in an attempt at a ponytail. He's white as a ghost. He shoves his hands up in the air and looks at me as if to say *It's about goddamned time you got here!*

"What? Jesus, talk to me, Mo!"

"There's somebody up on the roof. *Dead!* Somebody who lives next door saw the body and called the cops. They got here about an hour ago and cleared the building, and still aren't allowing anyone back in. . . ."

"Oh, my God!"

"And for all they know the killer's still inside!"

Paul Marterelli's down the sidewalk, beyond the building entrance, with a reporter and a cameraman. I recognize Chuck

Esposito, the Emmy Award–winning crime reporter from the local NBC affiliate, Channel 4. Damn—bad news travels fast in New York. Paul looks like he's shaking his head more than he's talking.

"Hang on, Mo, let me see what I can find out."

A couple of plainclothes cops are standing on the top step, blocking the front door, eyes fixed on the crowd out front.

Nearest one says, "Sorry sir, we cannot allow entry just yet."

I introduce myself. "I'm second in command here, and I'm just trying to find out what's going on. I'd like to be able to reassure my coworkers that they're in no danger."

"Understood. But you're going to have to wait with the rest of them."

"Do we know who it is?"

"The victim has been identified, but until we can notify the family, we cannot release the identity. I'm Detective Peter Quinn, with the 13th precinct, over on 21st Street. I'll be in charge of this investigation. This is the second officer in charge, Detective Scott Garrison."

A reluctant silence has settled over the crowd, which has grown with neighbors and passersby.

I see nothing but deeply worried looks on my colleagues' faces. I'm still on the steps when some of them move in a little closer to me—for some kind of reassurance?

"Oh, Tim," Mo says. "I'm so glad you're here now. We all are." She pulls a couple of the agency women in against her, an arm around each one.

"All I can say is, we'll find out what's going on together. I'm sure we're in good hands," I say, trying to reassure them, with no visible success.

Soon one of the police officers pushes through the front door and holds it open for the medics.

And here comes something I haven't seen since Fallujah, and never wanted to see again. A gurney with a medic on each end moving the victim, this time to the rear of an ambulance, to load it up for transport to the medical examiner's office.

Esposito and his cameraman are getting it all.

You hear about murders all the time in the news. It's awful, impossible to imagine, but you give it a thought and then life goes on for the rest of us.

Well, not for me. Not anymore.

The body is motionless, a stiffening corpse. Completely covered with a white canvas sheet. The gurney's wheels collapse under its frame as the medics slide it against the rear deck and into the ambulance, where it's locked into place and secured with straps.

The driver closes the back doors. Our eyes meet for an instant before he climbs into the front. I offer a grim salute in appreciation, and he points a forefinger at me to acknowledge it.

The flashing red lights are back on and they head down the street. No need for the sirens anymore.

"Mr. Marterelli, can you come up here for a minute?" It's Detective Quinn, from the top of the steps.

Paul gestures to me to join him, and I do. Quinn assures us that everything's under control. We're allowed access to the agency, but not the roof, which has been cordoned off while they continue to search for evidence.

And—it is somebody from the agency. *But who?*

Now Paul turns around and faces the crowd; WNBC's

Esposito points his mic at him, and the cameraman next to him is shooting all of it.

"Okay, people, listen up. The police officers have secured the building. It is safe to reenter, and so I'm going to invite my colleagues to return to their workspaces and any area in our office—except the roof, which the police have secured while they continue their search for evidence.

"And hear this, this is important: if any of you, for any reason, are not comfortable coming back in today, I completely understand.

"Just know that we are assured that the killer, or killers, is no longer on the premises."

A killing. And not just one of those random killings you read about in the *New York Post*. It's somebody I know.

CHAPTER 7

FOUR MORE POLICE officers come out through the front door and down the steps, where they gather on the sidewalk and then spread out into the street.

Detectives Quinn and Garrison come back over. Paul and I lean in close.

"In strictest confidence, here's what we can tell you." It's Quinn. "We've already acknowledged that the victim is an agency employee, but need to notify the immediate family before we can share further information on that. You guys will figure it out soon enough, I'm sure. But know this—it was no accident. The victim died from a single gunshot to the back of the head, at close range. Likely premeditated.

"We are looking for a murderer. We will keep you fully advised, and please let us know if you hear anything. Anything."

Paul and I share a look between us that comes from someplace deep and dark, like we're both thinking the same unspeakable thing.

He takes a deep breath, thanks the officers, and turns back to the crowd.

"Okay, guys," Paul announces to the agency multitude, waving both hands above his head. "Let's regroup." He holds the door open, and people begin to file back in with no idea what they might find after an actual murder has taken place right here in our building.

The officers out in the street keep a close eye on our people as they pass by on the way in. The one at the door is asking the women to open their purses. And anybody with a shoulder bag. Even me, and mine. Not taking any chances.

I'm opposite Paul, on the other side of the door where I can connect with my fellow employees as they walk between us, gripped by a shared silence. Nothing to be said, aside from probing eye contact. A lot of them look to me as if they're searching for answers, but there aren't any I can offer. I do my best to assume a posture of confidence and reassurance.

Mo passes through with the same two agency girls, still arm in arm for mutual support. She looks at me, teary-eyed, and starts to say something—but can only exhale what must be a long-held breath, laden with sorrow. And fear.

Bonnie Jo Hopkins, one of the long-time Marterelli creatives I work closest with, lingers just a bit longer, making familiar eye contact so that I feel her concern.

Two cop cars pull away with four officers inside. No lights flashing. No longer necessary for them, either. I follow Paul back in after the others.

Quinn is following us in. "We need to talk to your people," he says. "Might as well start right now." And Garrison falls in behind him.

I assume there are still more cops up on the roof, and that police will probably be in and out of here for days.

We're met with nothing resembling order—nobody's going back to any kind of actual work. How could they? For all they know, it could be one of their coworkers who's been murdered, and everyone is trying to figure out who's missing.

There's an elevator, but few take it, opting for the stairs in the back. Many linger in the main reception area on the third floor, still trying to fathom what the hell just happened.

I make it up to my office, or, more accurately, my expanded cubicle, in the windowed corner of the fifth floor. People are gathering around my space, peering in over the half walls, and I suddenly feel like the eye in the middle of a storm gathering around me.

Madness. And not the typical ad agency madness, either. This is the bad kind.

"Oh, man," says David Gebben, a senior copywriter. "What the hell?" and plants himself with a deep sigh in one of my chairs. Here comes Bill Kelly, one of our best art directors. Slouches on the couch. "Talk to us, Tim! What's going on?"

"Look, guys. I don't know much more than you do, but I'm sure we're going to find out soon, and then we'll deal with it together."

"*Semper fi?*" I hear from Julie Reich, who's out in the hall.

My catchphrase in the office. "That's what I'm talkin' 'bout." And I get a couple of nods in semi-agreement.

Another text . . .

What terrible timing. It's from Tiffany Stone, an actress we cast in the first CrawDaddy Super Bowl commercial way back when I first joined Marterelli out of the Marines. The first

CrawDaddy girl—buxom, bawdy, and naturally funny, with some...interesting past video experience. I met her on the shoot, she's stayed in touch over the years a bit—but now she won't leave me alone.

I need to see you!

I ignore it. This is absolutely the last person I want to deal with right now.

I have to think about my 150 agency colleagues who are about to find out that one of our own has been murdered. And this is no accidental killing. This is a gunshot wound to the back of the head.

Madness.

CHAPTER 8

PAUL SENDS A company-wide e-mail asking us to meet him in fifteen minutes, at two o'clock, in the big third-floor reception and kitchen area, where we can talk.

The cops are hardly gone and here it comes. Some of the shit that I'm trying to make sense of is about to go public, and I know it's only going to make it worse for me.

Each of the three floors at Marterelli & Partners is wide open. Workstations stretch side by side nearly the whole length of the floor, flush with computers, laptops, printers, scanners, and the like. At each end are a handful of cubicles for some of the senior people. There are open conference rooms on the third and fourth floors with sliding glass doors and drapes for private meetings and presentations. The fifth floor is the top floor, with easy access to the roof. The reception and kitchen area provides the biggest open space and makes it possible for most of us to close in around Paul, who's standing behind the counter.

He asks me to join him.

"Free lunch?" from one of the creative wise guys. Gallows humor that stirs a few hesitant snickers.

"Okay, here goes," and Paul clears his throat. Twice. He speaks louder than usual, choosing his words carefully. "It is as bad as you can imagine. We have lost one of our own."

An audible gasp erupts from the crowd. *"Oh, no!"*

"Oh, my God!" moans Mo.

"I'm afraid so."

"Who, for Christ's sake! Who?" demands David.

"We've lost...Ramon...our beloved Ramon...one of our finest."

Cries of *"No! It can't be!"*

Ramon is one of Marterelli's earliest employees. He's our self-taught tech guy, keeping us online and interconnected. Making sure the creatives' Macs were humming, up-to-date, loaded with the latest software. He was the best.

I actually helped Ramon get his job at Marterelli, but that's another story....I'm going to miss this guy something awful. A genuine compatriot. A wonderful guy. A friend to everybody.

"Shit! My computer's down! Now what?" we hear from another wiseass trying to lighten the load, I guess. A few more reluctant smirks. But more people are crying.

"Who the hell would want to kill Ramon?" Chris demands to know. "And why? *Why?*"

"Amen, brother," is all I can say. This murder is starting to turn my entire world inside out.

And there's two more to come.

CHAPTER 9

I CALL JEAN at home. "Honey, you won't believe what's happened here."

"Yes, I would—it's on the news already. *Somebody got murdered there?*"

"Yeah, terrible. A guy named Ramon. Ramon Martinez, our tech guy. Great guy. Cops found him up on the roof, dead. Shot in the head sometime last night."

"Wow, honey, that's unbelievable. You okay?"

"Not exactly. I'm getting out of here. I'll be home early, okay? Bye for now."

"Sure, love. I'll be here. Bye."

It's only three thirty, but there's no damned reason to hang around work. For me or anybody else. And anyway, it's Friday. I'm outta there, on my way over to the Union Square subway station when I pass by Fanelli's Café on Prince Street, one of the oldest pubs in New York City.

What the hell? I turn around and head in for a beverage. I never drink before dinner, except on the agency roof, but God knows I could use one now, given all the shit that's coming down around me.

The bar is abuzz with classic New York characters. I squeeze in and order a Ketel One, soda, lime. Fifteen minutes later I'm a lot braver, so I pay up. Time to head for the 6 train up to Grand Central, where I can catch the 4:47 to Croton-on-Hudson. But not before I cab it down to the bank again. Can grab the 6 from there.

At the Croton-on-Hudson station I climb in my car and head for our house, which is only five minutes away. It's a big, five-thousand-square-foot 1920s Spanish Mediterranean, called Twin Eagles; there's a stone sculpture of an eagle, wings spread, on each side of the driveway. And it's twice as big, and twice as expensive, as we need.

But Jean and the kids love it. We've been here eight years.

I pull up around the circular drive in front of the house. The last thing I want is the kids—or anybody—to see me upset. So I honk the horn. *Surprise!* Here comes Brady racing out the front door, and jumps all over me. His sister, Ellie, follows out behind him. "What's up, Dad?"

They stay with me, like kids who know their father loves them. We head out toward the pool.

Then I see Jean up on the porch.

"Oh, Tim, I hope you're okay," she asks, as I park the kids in the front hall and head for the kitchen. "Have to say I'm glad you're here, but what a terrible way to get you home early."

The kids head upstairs and Jean follows me into the kitchen.

"You look terrible, Tim. Talk to me."

"Not sure I've ever told you about Ramon. I helped him get his job at Marterelli's. Our IT guy. One of the sweetest, nicest people you'd ever meet. Everybody loved him. It's like... ripping a hole in the agency's heart. Everybody seems in shock."

"And how about you, love?" she asks.

"You know, I guess I'm okay, all things considered. Truth is, I've seen worse, as you probably know.

"Remember when I'd call you from over there, in Iraq, when I was in the middle of all that mayhem and violence?"

"Yes, I..."

"Well, I tried to make sure you couldn't feel the horror. I suppose it was some kind of warped preparation for all this.

"This is definitely tough, this murder, so close to home, but I'll be fine. Got to be. Agency's counting on me for support."

"Oh, honey. I know they can. You're the best." I'm even more thankful than usual for my wife's love.

CHAPTER 10

SATURDAY MORNING I grab Brady and take him to his soccer game down at Croton Point Park, which juts out into the Hudson and offers gorgeous views of Rockland County on the other side of the river, a few miles south of West Point.

Soon as we get there Brady jumps out of the car and runs off to join his teammates. The eight- and nine-year-olds are all dressed up in their Croton Kickers T's. I think, what a gift this boy is. And his sister, Ellie, three years older.

Jean and I got married after college, where we dated for the last three years. I joined the Marines that fall. We got hitched after Parris Island and Camp Lejeune—right before I shipped out to Iraq! A hell of a move for two young people. She insisted. And she was right. Hey—she's smart!—and wears the kind of beauty and presence that is ageless. One of those independent souls that doesn't depend on others for her own internal happiness. If you didn't know better you'd think we lived an idyllic life. If you didn't know better.

But I do.

"Hey, Tim!" It's Charlie Raffin, a neighbor. We've shared

many a dinner with Charlie and his wife, Jennifer. Their son, Andy, is on Brady's team.

"Wasn't that murder yesterday at your agency? Saw it on the news last night. Jesus."

"Awful. Just awful," I say. "Lost a great guy. How the hell does a freakin' murder take place in your office? It's like something out of a movie."

"Hope you're managing okay."

"I'm okay, actually...truth is, I'm waiting to hear about a possible new job. A job I really want—just between you and me."

"Of course," Charlie assures me. "Mum's the word. Good luck on the job!"

A cheer erupts from the crowd of parents across the field. Brady's team's just scored a goal, and the boys are yelling and hopping all over the place. Coach blows his whistle and lines them back up for the kick-off.

I live in the highest-taxed county in the country—Westchester. I own a five-thousand-square-foot house, a cottage on the property, a fifty-foot pool, the works—with property taxes approaching $40,000 a year. Well, I don't actually own it. The banks do. Had to take a second mortgage on it a couple of years ago to pay down some other debt. Robbed Peter to pay Paul—the other Paul—and still am. Constantly bouncing dollars from one bank account to another—including the one Jean doesn't know anything about.

And now, I'm buried in all of it. My credit cards are pretty much maxed.

I see Diane Elvin, who Jean and I play tennis with every Sunday morning. I get my best game face back on.

"Good to see you, Di. You and Joe ready for tomorrow?"

"We'll see." She winks. "Tim, it's just so terrible, the murder at your agency. I am so sorry."

"Appreciate it, my friend. Thanks. Best to Joe."

For all Jean knows, we're fine. She has no reason to think we're not. That's how secretive I've been. I'm not proud of it.

And we're not fine. If I don't get this new job, we are done with Westchester. The house, the neighbors, these soccer games, the kids' friends, Jean's girlfriends. They would all be devastated. So would I.

I can almost see the freakin' moving trucks in the driveway. The situation, along with the murder, is weighing on me like a ton of bricks.

But I'm getting ahead of myself . . . .

My phone rings. It's Barbara Lundquist, the recruiter. On a Saturday?

"Hey, Barb, what's up?"

"Hi, Tim. I know it's Saturday. I figure you're with your kids or something, but I thought you'd like to know."

"Know . . . what?"

"I just talked to Linda Kaplan."

And I can feel some of the weight lifting off my back.

Soon enough the game's over, and Brady and I head home to Twin Eagles. Jean's in the kitchen, fixing lunch. Ellie's helping.

"Guess what, baby? Just heard from the recruiter. That interview I had yesterday went great. She's got me number one on her list! Wants to see me again, soon."

"That's fantastic, honey. I hope it's something you really want?"

Want? Hell, I *need* this job. *We* need this job. Bad. If she only knew just how bad.

"Absolutely, love. It's a great opportunity!"

Meanwhile, I send those movers on their way, out of my head, trucks empty. For now.

CHAPTER 11

IT'S A BEAUTIFUL fall night. Sun's dropping down out over the Hudson, full moon's following it up behind us. I roll the BBQ grill down by the pool and fire it up. Fillets for Jean and me and burgers for the kids. Poolside with the family is my favorite way to dine.

The kids are inside, doing whatever kids do, so I pop open a bottle for Jean and me. We love champagne, especially Dom Perignon, and have special flutes for nights like this one.

I fill our glasses, pouring just right to minimize the bubbles, and offer a toast: "Here's to life, our lives, blessed with good fortune and good health. And here's to us and our partnership, warmed by our love and devotion. . . ."

We raise our glasses in a mutual, loving gesture. "L'Chaim," she says, and I subconsciously inhale mine smack empty. No effervescent mouth feel on this one.

Jean can't help but laugh, a sympathetic chuckle. "My love!" and pats me on the shoulder. "Hope it helps."

After dinner, the kids disappear into the house somewhere and Jean and I are enjoying the last of our champagne. Very mellow, damn near at peace. It's like I'm sitting here in a protective bubble, isolated from the madness of the real life that swirls around me. My thoughts drift to Ramon, and that last night...losing him...painful...

"Now I am the master!" A growly voice lances my universe. There's a small, hard cylinder at the back of my head. I hear my champagne glass crash to the ground. Jean lets out a yelp and I spin around in my chair, sick with fear.

"What—"

It's Brady, in his Darth Vader Halloween costume. He drops his light saber and erupts into tears.

"I'm sorry, Daddy. I'm sorry!" he says, and I gather him up in my arms. We're both shaking.

My bubble has burst.

CHAPTER 12

WE CLIMB OUT of bed and roust the kids. Time to get ready for church—like I've always said, I need all the help I can get.

For the past nine years, we've belonged to Union Church of Pocantico Hills—a nondenominational protestant church that counts John D. Rockefeller among its founders. I even served on the board of deacons for six of those years, serving communion occasionally to David and Laurance Rockefeller, before Laurance died.

We pile in the car after breakfast and head for church. The small sanctuary is beautiful, lined on both sides with nine magnificent stained-glass windows by Marc Chagall—each one a depiction from the New Testament—and a large rose window up front designed by Henri Matisse, one of his last works. Nothing like a Rockefeller connection.

The preacher consistently delivers learned, insightful, and sometimes acerbic sermons.

This morning I hear him quote from Ecclesiastes 5, Verse 10: "Whoever loves money never has money enough; whoever loves wealth is never satisfied with his income. This, too, is meaningless."

Which is about the last thing I need to hear.

Reminds me of something George Carlin said: "Don't give your money to the church. They should be giving their money to you." That's more like it.

We're meeting the Elvins for dinner tonight at the Chappaqua Tavern.

I'm in a damned-near good mood, basking in what I heard from Barb yesterday. Diane and Joe are already at the bar when we get there, so we order a beverage to catch up: Ketel One, soda, lime for me, and a glass of chardonnay for Jean.

The TV's on over the bar. Chuck Esposito from NBC is on camera, in front of the agency. I hear him say:

—murder at the Marterelli and Partners advertising agency in lower Manhattan. One of their employees, Ramon Manuel Martinez, of Brooklyn, was found dead early Friday morning up on the roof of the Marterelli offices, with a bullet to the back of the head. Police and city detectives continue to look for clues. Thus far, they have none. This is Chuck Esposito reporting from downtown Manhattan. Back to you, Stacy...

"Unbelievable," Joe says, shaking his head. "So they really don't know anything about it yet?"

"Far as I know," I say. "They've got the roof off limits while they continue to search for any clues. And of course they're talking to everyone at the agency, including me."

"Sure hope they find this guy," Joe says. "So what else is going on, anything?"

"Yeah, actually, there is. Between us folk, I'm getting some great feedback on a job I'm after, a really great job."

"Fantastic," says Diane, and Jean puts her arm around my back with a loving squeeze.

"Yeah. Don't want to jinx it, but it could be good."

We're seated for dinner, and the conversation flowers among us friends, budding into lighter subjects, thank goodness. Imagine. Life could be good, if only...

Diane orders their oven-baked penne, Joe likes the grilled skirt steak, Jean splurges with fish and chips, and for me, the drunken salmon with bourbon cream sauce.

To go with the drunken salmon I order a bottle of limited edition Seyval blanc from St. George, a local winery up in Mohegan Lake. After the server pours it all around, I offer a toast.

"Here's to good friends and the wonderful lives we share," I pronounce, with a great deal of hope against hope.

"Hear! Hear!" and soon dinner is served, in the midst of animated chatter all around.

After dinner we share a round of vintage port and I ask for the check.

"Let's split it, Tim," Joe offers.

"Nah. Let me, I've got it." I hand the server my MasterCard.

She's back in five minutes and tries to be discreet. "I'm sorry, sir. Your card is refusing this charge."

Jesus! It's that bad. . . .

I get a look from Jean.

"Must be because I've been traveling. Sometimes the banks go overboard with their security precautions."

Yeah, right.

"Hey, Tim, no sweat. I'm sure it's a tech malfunction or something. Let me get it," and Joe hands her his card.

Is there no escaping this shit? Well, actually, no, there isn't.

CHAPTER 13

MONDAY MORNING...AND I'm back at it. 7:20 express, gets me in to Grand Central at 8:08, time enough to read the *New York Times* on the way in. Then I grab the 6 train downtown to 14th Street and walk over to the office.

In I go, and the weekend has not helped anybody calm down much. The office is still in a state of jangled nerves, preoccupied would-be workers, and general chaos.

Mo's at the front desk. "Hey, Tim, *good morning!* Welcome back."

"Yeah, I guess," I say.

"Those detectives, the two of them, were back. Waiting at the front door when I got here to open up. They're all over it. And us. Interviewing everybody," she tells me.

"Turns out they've been in the area most of the weekend...."

"Well, there's been a murder. I'm grateful they're here. Did they talk to you, Mo?"

"Sure. Asked me all about Ramon, what I knew about him, his personal life. His family. Who he hung out with here at the agency. All I could tell them was how much we all loved him."

I head up to my cubicle. Quinn's at the top of the stairs... waiting for me? Well-dressed, mid-forties, close-cropped, graying hair. Fit.

"Mr. MacGhee, sorry we didn't get to talk on Friday. We hear you're the man. Got a few minutes?"

"Absolutely. Why don't you step into my...cubicle? And please, call me Tim."

"And call me Pete...."

He spots my Marine eagle, globe, and anchor plaque on the wall before he can sit down.

"Seriously? *Semper fi?*"

"Damn straight! You?"

"Hell, yes! Desert Storm. 2nd Marines. Purple Heart."

"Amazing, my brother. You beat me by a few years. But who's counting? Here we are! And thank God, I didn't win a Purple Heart. Please, have a seat, Pete, let's talk." He settles into the couch.

"Thanks, Tim. So, this is a tough one. Not a random murder out on the streets. This one's in a place of business, in downtown Manhattan, full of what seem like good, professional people who care about each other. The victim is someone who is clearly well respected by everybody, near as we can tell. It just doesn't make any sense. Not that most murders do, but still..."

"I get it, Pete. Please, how can I help?"

"So far, nobody we've talked to knows anything, not really. Or at least they're not willing to say they do, yet. And they all say the same thing: *Talk to Tim. He knows more about the agency than anybody else here.*

"But I've got to tell you, so far we're getting nowhere. I'm hoping you can help."

"Absolutely. Anything."

"What can you tell me about Ramon?" he asks.

"Well, he's one of those self-made guys. Started in the old mailroom we still had. But every free minute he was on somebody's computer. Got good at it. Soon enough he was our tech guy. A self-taught tech expert, monitoring computers, making sure everybody had the latest software, figuring out how to reboot when they crashed. All that stuff...

"I didn't see him that much, day to day, but he sure made himself irreplaceable."

"Did Ramon have any enemies that you know about?"

"Oh, man," I tell him, "I cannot imagine anybody here having anything against Ramon. Zero. He would probably be voted most popular guy in the agency."

"Damn. Sure makes you wonder who would murder this guy—and why—and how they would get up to the roof after hours," Quinn says.

Sure does, I'm thinking.

"Understand completely, Detective," I tell him.

"Look," he says, "just do us all a favor and keep your eyes and ears open. Everybody talks about you like you're the one most likely to hear anything. Here's my card. Please call me if you do."

"Absolutely. You have my word."

I have a feeling I'll see Peter Quinn again.

CHAPTER 14

"YO... *DUDE!*"

Jesus, it's Lenny Shapiro, poking his unkempt head into my space. Creative guy, writer—or supposed to be. Seems half stoned all the time. I can't remember the last time he made any kind of significant contribution to anything at the agency. Remember Sean Penn in *Fast Times at Ridgemont High*? That's Lenny.

And now here he is, leaning his big head of hair around the corner, working to make glassy-eyed contact. He's looking bad.

"What's up, Tim? Did you hear..."

"Of course I heard, are you serious? You don't look so good, man. You in some kind of pain?"

"Naw, man, I'm cool. It's just—who the hell would kill a guy like Ramon? Unless it was somebody here, like, at work..."

"Why the hell would you think something like that?" I'm all over him.

"Well, Ramon helped us out, a lot of us. Who like to, well, imbibe..."

"What the hell does that mean, Lenny?"

"You know...weed...hash...sometimes a little upper. What I'm saying is...we buy our stuff from Ramon. Us creative guys. At least we used to."

"Are you shitting me?"

"Maybe he cut somebody off. Maybe somebody owed him money...you know?"

"Lenny, you look like shit. And it's not even lunchtime. Why don't you take your sorry ass home and crash?"

"Okay, okay. Later, bro."

And I'm thinking, Lenny just qualified himself as a prime suspect. He better keep his mouth shut.

Bonnie Jo Hopkins, the group creative director, sticks her head in just as Lenny's stumbling out.

"He looks totally wasted. What's going on?" she asks.

"BJ, you know as much as I do." I shrug, smiling, almost. As always, I'm a little struck by how damned hot she is.

"Whaddya gonna do?"

"Hey—you do what you gotta do," she says, like the New Yorker she is, and shrugs back at me with one of those lingering, flirtatious smiles.

Bonnie Jo Hopkins turns around and walks her beautiful self back to her cubicle, making sure I get a good look on the way out.

There's guys out there who would kill for some of that.

CHAPTER 15

"HEY, LOVE. I'M jammed. Got to work late again, so don't wait up for me. I'll grab something in Grand Central and eat on the train." I'm on my cell to Jean, with a story she's heard all too often.

There's a huge new business pitch end of this week, and I'm buried in it. It's for Weight Watchers, a prospect I've been after for months. I've been cultivating them through e-mail, agency highlights, and successes, then took the top two guys out for drinks and dinner a couple of times—the latest last week. We had good chemistry. And they've finally agreed to visit the agency, to test my promise of some new insights into their business.

I'm damned good at this stuff.

But now this pitch, on top of everything else, is threatening my sanity.

Bonnie Jo sticks her head back in. "Hey, a bunch of us are going up to Hill Country after work. Chris's band is playing. Why don't you join us?"

What the hell. I'm already covered at home. "Sure, I'm in. I'll see you guys there."

Soon I pack up my laptop and head downstairs. It's a beautiful night, and I've got to clear my head, so I decide to walk up to Hill Country, on 26th Street between Sixth and Broadway. I want to take the city in, feel the energy, remind myself of why I'm here.

And here's Chuck Esposito from WNBC out on the sidewalk, and his cameraman's with him, again! So much for clearing my head.

The cameraman points his camera at me and starts rolling.

"Sorry to bother you, Tim, but we just…"

"Hold it, hold it! And please turn that damned thing off." They do.

"Look. I respect what you guys are after, and what you do, searching for the truth, you know? It's just that I've got nothing to say, nothing to add to what you already know."

"We've talked to Detective Quinn, who said he was impressed with your knowledge of the agency and all the people who work here. That if anybody knew anything it'd be you…"

"Flattering, I guess. But I don't. And if you'll excuse me, I'm meeting some folks. …"

"Okay, sure. But we'll likely contact you again and…"

I'm headed down the street before he can finish his sentence. Give me a break!

Down at the corner I can finally take in a deep breath. *Exhale.* Helps. I'm making my way across Union Square up toward the Flatiron Building when I see a couple of guys I vaguely recognize. "Hey, buddy," one of them says to me, with a slightly forced smile.

"Hey..." Who the hell are these guys?

"Hope you're well. Don't remember your name. But I know you were friends with Ramon. Terrible about Ramon. Fucking terrible."

"Sure is," I say, eager to move on.

"Got that right. Anyway, sorry. I know you guys were close."

Which is totally weird. "Sure, thanks. Take care," and I head on up to 26th Street.

This is getting crazy.

Hill Country is rockin'. Chris and his Desberardos are playing downstairs, and their music reaches up to the street. I can hear Chris blowing his harp, and that's our Bill Kelly backing him up on guitar. Down I go, and spot a group of agency types over by the bar.

Bonnie's out on the floor in front of the band dancing, and I join her. It's a rockin' tune, but I pull her in close for a spin, and drift off into fantasyland. The song's over much too soon, so I release my grip on her and we head back to the bar.

"So, Tim..." David Gebben, the copywriter, speaks close to my ear. "If I didn't know better, I'd say you and BJ were getting it on."

"Oh, Jesus, no. Not saying I wouldn't like to, but, you know, never dip your pen in company ink...."

"Right," he says, utterly unconvinced.

By the time I walk through the front door at home, Jean and the kids are upstairs, fast asleep.

I tiptoe into the kids' rooms, first Ellie's and then Brady's, pull their covers up and steal a late kiss good night. Ellie cracks one eye open. "Hi, Daddy..." Brady's out like a light. Jean rolls over as I'm approaching our bed and moans something loving. She's at peace, for now.

If she only knew....

A soft kiss good night and I'm back downstairs to pour myself a glass of pinot noir, Signaterra 2012. Then I settle into my chair in the den and drift off into thoughts about the life I'm living.

Up until a few days ago, it was semi-perfect. Or at least it looked that way to the rest of the world, including Jean and the kids. A good life. Great family. Comforts. Peace and love. Church. All of it.

At the bottom of my second glass of wine I can only agonize over a pipe dream. If only it could stay just like it is, forever. But it can't.

I drag my raggedy ass upstairs and climb into bed with Jean. If she only knew....

This damned murder has already made any semblance of a normal life impossible.

And it's only the first one.

CHAPTER 16

SAME 7:20 EXPRESS Tuesday morning and I'm back in the city. I wave at Mo on the way in to the office. "Hey, Mo!"

"They're baaaack," she says, and she's not talking about the poltergeist.

I grab a cup of coffee in the kitchen and head upstairs to my cubicle. Surely the cops have turned up every bit of so-called evidence that would be here in the office. Why the hell do they keep coming back every day?

Do they think somebody here did it?

I get into my e-mails and see one from Paul to the entire office, subject line: *A wake for Ramon.*

To my dear colleagues:

I've been informed there's a wake for Ramon tonight at the St. Bartholomew's Church, 1227 Pacific St (at Bedford Ave), Brooklyn. 6-9p. A or C train, Nostrand Ave stop and walk a couple of blocks. I know his family, loved ones, and friends will appreciate our support. Hope to see many of you there. Paul

I click Reply All.

Absolutely Paul, I'll be there.

Before I can finish my coffee, Detective Quinn stops by. "Hey, Tim, how's it going?"

"Morning, Pete. If it wasn't for this murder business, things would be pretty good. Just found out there's a wake for Ramon tonight, over in Crown Heights. Of course I'm going."

"Good to hear. You guys have a nice shop here. Lots of solid people. But I've got to tell ya, I'm getting a weird vibe from some of your creative types."

"Whaddaya mean, Detective?"

"Well, best I can put it is, we don't speak the same language. And worst case is, they know something and they're not telling me."

"Weird. Yeah, they're unique, that's for sure. Have to be to work in this business. You know, the more you act out in this business, the more creative you appear to be, the higher the rewards. Where's the disconnect? What's going on, Pete?"

"We've talked to most of them. People who have worked in the same, relatively small company together for a good while, and know the deceased, one way or the other. But they're not saying shit. It's almost like they're protecting somebody. And why the hell would they? Based on what you're telling me about Ramon, what's to protect?"

"Beats me," I say, avoiding the obvious. For now. "But this is a crazy business. I've got a good feeling about most of these guys, for what it's worth."

"Understand. But I'm not getting the feeling that I can

count on what little they're telling me. We're really counting on you to keep your ear to the ground. Because so far...we're clueless."

"I'm keeping my eyes and ears open, Detective," I promise.

"I'm sure I'll see you again," he says, on the way out.

Can't wait.

CHAPTER 17

"OKAY, NOW WHAT?" It's Bonnie Jo, back at my door as soon as Quinn's gone.

"Oh, man," I say. "I'm seriously convinced they suspect somebody here at the agency. And I've got to tell ya, he's asking me all about you creatives."

"What! Why us?"

My iPhone vibrates with a text. Jesus, it's Tiffany again. . . .

I must see you! Please respond!

"Jesus, BJ, take a look at this." I show her the text and am instantly sorry I did.

"Tiffany? Tiffany Stone? From our CrawDaddy spot all those years ago? Why the hell is she texting you?"

"She's looking for work. Thinks I can help her. Why the hell isn't she after *you* about work, Bonnie, instead of me?"

"Good question." There's a look on BJ's face I haven't seen before.

"I mean, first of all, it's you guys who cast the talent, not me," I say. "I'd love to help, but I'm not a creative. Has she ever been after you?"

The emerging look of suspicion on Bonnie Jo's face is unmistakable. "Is there something you want to tell me?"

"What? You think I'm hiding something? C'mon, you know me better than that."

"Well, I thought I did. Just let me know if you hear anything else, okay?"

"Definitely. You going to the wake?"

"Of course," she says, and, as always, I watch her turn around and walk away.

In no time Lenny's back at my door, looking only slightly better than he did when I sent him home yesterday.

"Hey bro, everything good?" he asks. Instead of the glassy-eyed smile, I get one that's decidedly twitchy.

"Far as I know, Len. Have the cops talked to you yet?"

"No, man, why?" For him it's rapid-speak. "Feels like they're leaving me out for some reason."

No wonder, I'm thinking. You're half stoned all the time.

"Just curious. I know they're talking to all the creatives. Which shouldn't be a surprise based on what you told me yesterday, should it?"

He's clearly nervous, shifting from one foot to the other. He could sure use a couple of hits to mellow out.

"Guess not," he admits, rubbing his ass, which is no doubt getting tighter by the minute.

"Take it easy, Lenny. Be cool."

He starts to leave, but stops at the door and looks back at me. And what do I get from this drug user and now murder suspect?

A thumbs-up. *Seriously?*

My cell rings. It's Bob Nardone, my tax accountant for the past ten years. A guy who has helped Jean and me through more financial shit than you can imagine.

"Hey, Bob, what's up?"

"Well, I'm looking at the paperwork you sent over the other day, and it's not looking so good. There's no way I can get you guys into a tax return scenario. You've got more coming in than you can apply expenses to...."

"Damn, Bob, you sure couldn't prove it by me."

"I know, Tim. And you know I'd do anything within my powers to make it better, but I'm afraid I can't this year. Looks like you're going to owe approximately...twenty thousand dollars...."

"*Are you serious?* I don't have that kind of money right now. Oh, Jesus—Jean has no idea this kind of shit is possible."

"I understand," he says. "I know you all too well, both of you. Look, there will be options. First of all we'll get the maximum extension. And then we can file for extended monthly payments over time, like up to six years, so it should be manageable at least. Not pretty, but manageable."

And I'm wondering what else can go wrong in a world that is coming apart at the seams.

My world.

CHAPTER 18

IT'S SIX FIFTEEN, time to get over to the wake. There's still a handful of people at their laptops as I pass through the third floor, where most of the creatives are.

Chris's packing up. "Hey, Tim. Got any thoughts about all this madness?"

"No more than anybody else, Chris. Have they talked to you yet?"

"Yeah, why?"

"Heard from Quinn they started with the creative guys. You must know about Ramon, right? What he was up to?"

"Well, you hear stuff. Won't say I haven't."

"Exactly. You know damned well the detectives have heard the same stuff by now. Just between you and me, my guess is they actually suspect somebody here at work killed Ramon. We haven't seen the last of these guys, you can count on that."

"For sure. You're going to the wake, right?"

"Absolutely."

"Want to grab a beverage on the way to the train?" he asks.

The last thing I want to do right now is hang out with this guy. Or anybody else.

"Sorry man, I've got to make a stop on the way over." I grab my shoulder bag and head straight for Fanelli's to disappear into the bar crowd, to try to gather in a few minutes of sanity. Ketel One, soda, lime.

Then I'm off to Crown Heights to honor Ramon's passing. Grab the downtown 5 to Fulton Street and the A over to Crown Heights. The walk to St. Bartholomew's helps clear my head, and it needs clearing, that's for damned sure.

On the way over I call Jean, like the broken record I am.

She answers before the second ring: "Now what?"

"Look, baby, I'm on my way to a wake for Ramon, over in Brooklyn. I know you'll understand that I have to make an appearance. Won't be too late, but you probably shouldn't wait for me for dinner."

"Okay, I do. And I won't. And don't be too late."

"Later, love. Bye for now."

CHAPTER 19

IN TEN MINUTES I'm climbing up the stairs into the St. Bartholomew church and the sanctuary. Damn near half the agency's there, most of them with coffee in hand, chatting quietly in a handful of groups. And probably another fifty or sixty others, mingling at the side, near one of the naves. Obviously family and friends; I don't recognize any of them.

I see Ramon's casket up front, sitting between the two altars, isolated, bathed in glorious flowers. It's an open casket, which I didn't expect. Catches my breath.

Paul comes over. "Hello, Tim, we all sure appreciate you coming over."

We're speaking in subdued, respectful tones, like everyone else.

"Of course, you know I loved and respected Ramon as much as anybody. Had to come. Now, if you'll excuse me..." and I walk down the center aisle to the coffin.

There's sweet Ramon, placid, pallid, at some kind of peace.

His hands folded over his chest. For the first time in all the years I've known him, here he is in a suit and tie.

Needless to say, there's no visible evidence of a gunshot wound. Thank God.

I set my shoulder bag down, and with one hand on a casket handle for support, I kneel to the floor and share a silent, very private, and personal message with Ramon.

When I stand up and turn around a young woman is approaching me, Hispanic, dressed in black, including a black scarf covering her head, and wearing a pained, miserable look on a beautiful face, with searching black eyes.

Tears are streaming down her face. "Pardon, sir. You Mister Tim MacGhee?" I get an inquiring, hopeful look.

And it hits me. "Why, yes. Yes, I am. And...you must be Juanita...."

"*Sí, señor.*"

This is the woman Ramon has lived with for seven or eight years. He talked about her all the time.

I pull her in close and offer some kind of condolence, and then extend my arms so I can look at her. "I am so, so sorry for your loss. Ramon has told me so much about you. He is...was...so proud of you and loved you so much. He made that very clear to me over the years.

"We all loved Ramon, very much."

More tears, which she wipes away with an overused handkerchief.

"And...*por favor, amiga*...don't call me sir. *Mi nombre es Tim, mi amiga.* Okay?"

"*Sí.* Okay. I just want you know how much you mean to *mi* Ramon, and so much he respected you and your business.

Ramon always glad he know you so good." Her broken English interspersed with more tears and more dabs from her handkerchief.

"Thank you so much, Juanita. That means a lot to me. And here, please, take my card. If there is ever anything I can do for you, will you please call me?"

"*Sí. Gracias.* Thank you." We hug again, although she's oddly a little distant this time, and I start back down the aisle.

"One thing," I hear her say, and pause in my steps to turn around and re-approach her.

"Sorry, *señor* . . ."

"No, please, what is it, Juanita? Anything."

"Well, couple weeks ago Ramon tell me that . . . when anything happen to him . . . I should come to you."

"Ah . . . yes," I say, bracing for something I had not expected.

"Sorry, *señor,* but Ramon pay for apartment. Without him, *mi madre y yo, esta nada* . . . he said . . ."

And suddenly, in this church, in the midst of a wake for this woman's longtime live-together mate and our beloved colleague, I'm being confronted with the same kind of bullshit I've been getting for days. Especially from Ramon.

"Oh, *señora.* What can I say? It pleases me that Ramon thought enough of me to tell you that, but . . . I'm just in no position to offer that kind of financial help right now, much as I'd like to."

"*Si, señor.* Forgive me for saying. It's just . . ."

"I understand, Juanita. *Yo entiendo.* Do not worry. And you have my word, if things change, and I'm in a position to help, I certainly will."

And I start to pass her to go back down the aisle. But she's holding her place.

Suddenly there's some kind of bad vibe hanging in the air. I can damned near taste it.

"No, *señor.* No." And now I'm looking at a different Juanita. Much of her accent is gone, replaced by what sounds like assertion. Her posture stiffens.

"No. *Mira,*" and she's got this piercing look in black eyes that one minute ago were bottomless wishing wells, and are now ablaze with anger. I actually rock back on my heels.

"*Mira,* I know about you and Ramon." She actually gestures to his corpse. "I... *know.* He told me all about it. Your business together. Your *moneymaking* business. So, you want to... help me? So I say nothing? Then, share. *Comprende, señor?*"

I swallow hard. And I don't need a translator.

"Look, we're in a church. We're here for Ramon's service, for Christ's sake." It's all I can do to keep my voice down.

"Share Ramon's business with me. Or, *no se* what happens."

Only one way to put an end to this shit, for now.

"Okay, okay. I will make some arrangements. Tell me how to reach you and I will do something. I am sure there are many people at the agency who will want to help, too."

"*Aqui,*" and she hands me a crumpled piece of paper, obviously prepared for this moment. I open it and there's a Brooklyn address scrawled on it, barely readable, with a cell number.

"Send money order. Then we see. Juanita Cisneros. C...
I...S..."

"Yes, yes, got it. Okay, I will. Count on it. I...want to help. I do."

And I'm looking at another metamorphosis. She's reassuming the humbled look of a law-abiding illegal alien who has just suffered a painful loss, and is once again unclear about what tomorrow will bring....

"Muchas gracias, señor." She imposes another hug, and I see now we're being watched by some of the agency folks down by the coffee urn.

"De nada" is what I say, but not what I'm thinking.

I'm almost sympathetic, because of my relationship with Ramon.

Ay dios mio!

CHAPTER 20

I WANT TO join some of the agency folk for a minute before I go—now more than ever. As I'm walking back down the aisle...*there's Detective Quinn,* sitting in the last pew, way over on the far side.

I walk down behind the pew to greet him. "Pete? I didn't expect to see you here."

"Hello, Tim. Yeah, it's an opportunity for a look at Ramon's world, his people, his friends. I spoke with his father outside, and he welcomed me in."

"See anything, Detective?"

"Tim, that's out of order here. You take care of your people. I'll be leaving soon."

"Absolutely. Sorry. I do appreciate your diligence on all this." I turn to cross over to where my agency people are clustered in small groups. I'm getting no eye contact, although I catch a glance from Chris and continue to the coffee urn, where Bonnie Jo is refilling her cup.

"Hey, Bon. Sorry to have to see you here, that's for sure."

"For a whole lot of reasons. Right?"

"What's that supposed to mean?"

"*Shhhh*...hold it down, Tim. Not the time or place. I know everyone's glad you're here."

"Really? Sure doesn't feel like it."

"Well, they can't help but notice that the detectives seem to be talking to you more than anyone else."

"Gee, Bonnie, I wonder why? I'm second in command, they know that I know everyone, and they assume I know everything that goes on at work. Which, of course, I don't."

"Sure, I believe you. You just better hope the others do." She walks over to one of the groups.

I fill my cup and head over to Paul, standing there with Mo, Bill, Julie, and Chris. Mo breaks the awkward silence. "Hi, Tim, thanks for being here."

"Of course, Mo. Of course." My phone vibrates and I look down to see that it's Tiffany *again*....

Tim!!!!!!!!!!

I sign the guest register on the way out. Is nothing sacred?

CHAPTER 21

BY THE TIME I get up to Grand Central, the schedule monitor next to the ramp to the lower level shows an 8:29 express to Croton-on-Hudson, track 119, downstairs, so I head down the ramp past the Oyster Bar—and *here's Tiffany Stone,* leaning up against the wall like she's waiting for me.

Of course. She *is* waiting for me. How the hell did she know I'd be here?

"Oh, Tim!" she bleats. "I am so glad to see you. I really need to talk to you!"

"Listen, Tiffany, I'm so sorry, but I've got to get home and don't want to miss my train."

"No, you listen to me! I'm scared. Scared to death. It's awful what happened to Ramon."

"How the hell did you know Ramon? I just came from his wake, for Christ's sake."

"I connected with Ramon one time when I was at the agency, and then I got weed from him sometimes, just like everybody else. I even resold some of it every once in a while. Now Ramon's dead. And I'm wondering who's next?"

Only way to describe the look on her face is somewhere between pain, fear, and anger. Which somehow makes her even more sexy.

"Look, Tiffany. I'd love to help if I could. But I can't, not now, anyway. Not tonight."

"Tim, if I didn't know better I'd say you were trying to avoid me! After all these years!"

Shit. I can't leave it like this...who knows what she'll do next?

"Okay, I can see you're in rough shape. Tell you what. Let's grab a cocktail. Come with me. This will help, I promise," and we head down to the Oyster Bar.

"Okay thank you, *thank you.*"

By the time I'm done with Tiffany it's the 9:54 I catch, barely. At home, this time everybody's long asleep.

I crawl into bed with Jean. Her back's to me. I sense she's awake. But no acknowledgment I'm here.

I take the hint.

CHAPTER 22

NEXT MORNING I'M walking back through Grand Central to catch the 6 train down to work and there's cops all over the place. A hell of a lot more than usual.

My blood pressure spikes. I instinctively pull my carry bag a little closer. *What the hell's going on?*

"Excuse me, sir," I say to one of the cops standing next to the terminal clock. "Can't help but notice you guys have, like, tripled up in presence here. Is something going on?"

"Can't say, sir. Please move on. Have a nice day."

Now what? Maybe it's some kind of terror threat....

I try to figure out what's going on the rest of the way to work.

"Morning, Mo," I say as I pass by her desk into the office.

"Oh, Tim! The detectives are back talking to us again. *There's been another murder!*"

"Oh, sweet Jesus, Mo! Who? Has the entire universe gone mad?" She shakes her head.

I head up to my cubicle and Quinn's sitting there waiting for me.

"Good morning, Tim."

"Morning, Detective. Hardly good, though. I hear there's been *another* murder?"

"I'm afraid so. But first things first. How are you doing?"

"Truth? Not great. This murder stuff is way too close to home. It's seriously getting to me."

"I'm sure you're feeling it more than most, given your history and standing with Marterelli's."

"And now there's been another one, Pete?"

"I'm afraid so."

"So what's this latest murder got to do with us?"

"Tim, a woman was murdered in Grand Central Station last night...."

My knees start to buckle. Wonder if it shows? No wonder there were so many damned cops there this morning.

"She was an actress. And the reason we're back here is she was a person a lot of you guys worked with a good while back."

I suck in my breath. Here it comes....

"Her name is Tiffany Stone...."

"Oh...my...God! The original CrawDaddy girl! The one we put in their very first Super Bowl commercial?"

My world is officially fractured. The devil himself has decided to fuck with me.

"They found her in the basement of Grand Central Station— with a bullet through her mouth."

I collapse against my desk, trying to collect my wits, and make some sense out of all this insanity.

But I can't.

The second person I know has been murdered.

CHAPTER 23

QUINN'S NOT DONE with me yet. I sit on my desk for some stability.

"I feel your pain, Tim. You must have known her pretty well." Is he trying to empathize with me?

"Not really. But I was on the CrawDaddy shoot back then, the first time I was with Paul. She was great. Hung out. Everybody loved her. Funny. Smart. Bawdy—in a good way. Hell, she ad-libbed half her lines in the commercial. It's not right. Just...not...right."

"So, Tim," he looks me in the eye, "that's two murder victims with connections to the Marterelli agency. Any thoughts?"

"Okay. It occurs to me that there's something that could be helpful. Look, we're a downtown, independent New York ad agency. Nearly two hundred employees. Highly creative. Break a lot of rules.

"So it shouldn't surprise you that a lot of these guys smoke some marijuana every once in a while. Some of them a lot."

He's nodding his head. "No surprise there."

"For all I know they're into other stuff as well..."

Another nod. And insistent eye contact. Not exactly comforting.

"I'm not saying I was one of them. But what I hear is most people got their stuff from Ramon. I think Ramon might have been the office dealer, the guy they went to for their weed. And who knows what else? Everybody loved Ramon. Maybe that's why."

More nodding. He's not saying so, but I can tell he's still not surprised. These guys know more than they're letting on.

"That's fairly serious stuff, Tim. Why didn't you share this with us earlier?"

He's got me. "I should have, I guess. I really didn't know for sure until just yesterday, and it didn't make any sense to me at first."

Is he buying it?

"Look, Tim. None of these things ever make any sense. Until they do . . ."

Yeah, but not before one more person in my quickly collapsing world gets murdered.

"Listen, Tim, I really appreciate your input. Rest assured, you've been a big help. I know we can count on you."

"Absolutely, Pete, anytime."

"Now I've got some things to follow up on." We shake hands and he's off again.

CHAPTER 24

I SIT DOWN and open my laptop so I can send out an agency-wide e-mail to see if we can raise some money for Ramon's family.

"*Lenny?*" He's back. This time with Chris. Chris has got his blues hat on, which pushes his now unleashed locks close against his face, and he looks like he's twisted as tight as Lenny. Unusual for him.

"Chris, you okay?"

"Well, Tim, not exactly. Not really. You sure are talking to the dicks a lot. You and this Quinn guy have really buddied up. What's that all about?"

"Yeah, dude," pipes in Lenny. "What's going down with that?"

"Guys, what's the deal? Don't you trust me?"

"Well," Chris says. "You know, we're all in this together, right? You know pretty much everything that goes on here. It's no wonder these detectives keep talking to you."

These guys are losing it. So am I.

"So, what exactly have you been telling them?" Chris wants to know.

"I'm not telling them shit. Don't have to. They already know. They know guys here at work smoke weed. And worse. They know most people get it from Ramon. They know that. So back off, guys."

Two guys I thought I knew really well are standing there facing me like total strangers. Pissed-off strangers.

Then Chris blows me away: "Tim, don't take this the wrong way, but you should know...I'm carrying...." and he pulls open his jacket to reveal some kind of pistol stuck in the inside pocket. He's staring me down, fully intending for me to take it the wrong way.

"What the hell is that, Chris? This is insane. We're friends, for Christ's sake. I was just at your gig Monday night. What the hell?"

"I'm just sayin'," Chris says.

Lenny's got this smirk on his face. "Yeah, you know?"

"Saying what, that you'll *shoot me* if you see me talking to a law enforcement officer who has come to my desk, in full view of the office, to ask about a murder that happened right here?"

"Whatever, man," says Chris. "Just thought you should know."

What I know is that Chris has now got to be the number one suspect.

I take a deep breath. Back to my laptop...

I'm reaching out to my agency friends and colleagues to join me in honoring the passing of our dear, beloved Ramon. Some of you met Juanita—the love of his life—at the wake last night. She's a strong and dedicated woman who loved and supported Ramon for many years. And now she's left to confront life's challenges without him—which is going to be difficult. So I'm setting up a website so we can pool our efforts. Please go to www.ramonmartinezpm.org and you'll see the easy steps to contribute something. I know Ramon and Juanita will appreciate any help we can provide. I certainly do,

    Tim

And tap Send...

My phone rings. "Tim MacGhee," I answer.

"Tim, this is Chuck Esposito, WNBC, New York...."

"Ah...sure, how can I help?"

"Well, there's been another murder. Tiffany Stone, whom your agency hired several years ago for a CrawDaddy Super Bowl commercial...."

How the hell do these guys get this stuff so fast? "Yes, we..."

"Would you care to comment, Tim? You were with Marterelli's back then, right?"

"No. Well, yes, I was. But no can do, Chuck. I'm sure you'll understand. Again."

"Not exactly. But of course it's your option. I may call again though."

Damn, these guys are persistent. Lucky me.

CHAPTER 25

I'M SITTING HERE in my desk chair still trying to get a grip on what's happening when my cell rings again. This time it's Bonnie Jo.

I tap Accept. "Hi..."

"So hey, Tim. Thinking about you..."

"Where are you, BJ?"

"I'm home. Playing hooky."

And then she says, "Why don't you come on over?"

Okay, I admit it: Bonnie Jo Hopkins and I have a...relationship. And I'm not talking about the one at work.

I'm not exactly proud of it. But with the stress I'm under...damn, it's good.

"I don't know, baby...."

"C'mon, things are nuts there. That's why I stayed home. And I've been thinking of you since I woke up this morning."

My temperature's starting to rise. She has that way about her.

"Get your sexy self over here and maybe we can help each other forget all about it...."

That's all the encouragement I need.

"Meeting Steve Zimmerman for early drinks and dinner," I tell Mo on the way out the door, explaining why I'm leaving work at five—a final meet with the new business prospect from Weight Watchers before our pitch Friday.

"Got it. I know you'll be your usual charming self," she says. "See you tomorrow."

Bonnie Jo lives over in Tudor City, First Avenue and 40th way over on the East Side, near Turtle Bay, in one of the co-op apartments. A classic neo-Gothic building, it was the first residential skyscraper in the world. Fabulous old apartments. BJ's is renovated, with a spectacular bedroom view of the UN headquarters and the East River from the twenty-sixth floor.

I grab a taxi out on 11th Street. Don't want to waste a minute getting up there.

CHAPTER 26

THE SECURITY GUY behind Bonnie's reception desk recognizes me and waves me on to the elevators. Up on twenty-six I ring BJ's doorbell and there she is, opening the door, slowly, to reveal her full, gorgeous, sexy...naked self.

Takes my breath away. Always does.

"Hi, Timmy," and she leans in to me with a soft, lingering, open-mouthed kiss. "How nice to see you."

"How nice to see *you*, too," is all I can come up with.

"Come in, love, I have something I think you'll enjoy," she says, and leads me by the hand over to the couch where we sit down. She torches the weed in her pipe, takes a toke, and passes it over to me.

"It's some of Ramon's finest...." she reminds me.

Perfect.

We're in no hurry. No need to be. Besides, there's nothing like making love when you're high.

I'm about to be saved by a beautiful, talented woman, who will make us both forget the madness around us. Nothing else will matter, for a while anyway.

We kiss. The high is taking hold. Mouths open, tongues searching. We kiss again, and she unbuttons my shirt and caresses my chest. Has me totally under her spell. Then it's my jeans, and the rest of it, and there we both are, fully revealed.

This time I lead her by the hand, into the bedroom. We turn down the covers and lay facing each other, and pull the other close. There's a rush of blood and a flash of light until finally, we lay back on the bed, gazing into each other's eyes.

She lights up her pipe for another hit and passes it over to me, and we linger in the moment for a while. I'm starting to think none of this tragic shit matters, that it will all blow over.

A delusion that's only going to last another few hours...

CHAPTER 27

BONNIE JO ROLLS her naked self back over to me. "Hey, love, why don't you just stay here tonight, with me? I really don't want you to go."

"Neither do I." She's absolutely irresistible. "It's almost eight o'clock. Let me see. I'll be right back."

I grab my cell phone and step into the kitchen to call home, without a stitch of clothes on.

"Not again," Jean answers.

"Afraid so, honey. We are totally jammed on this new business pitch. I'm not going to get out of here until who knows when. I'm afraid I won't even get to leave until two a.m. or something, so I'm going to grab a room at that bed-and-breakfast down the street."

"Oh, dear. Good thing they're paying you the big bucks."

"Thanks for understanding, baby. I hope. Anyway, kiss the kids good night for me—tell them tomorrow night we'll have dinner at that place they love, Pizza Pizazz."

"Okay. Be careful. We'll be here. Love you."

"Love you. Bye for now," and on the way back into the

bedroom I get a text from Barb Lundquist, the recruiter—
she's sure no nine-to-fiver.

Hey Tim—Linda wants to see you again, 8 AM tomorrow! Possible? Landmark Diner, Grand/Lafayette. Let me know ASAP when you get this.

Can't say it's perfect timing. But I tap a quick response....

Count on it. Thanks.

By midnight Bonnie Jo and I are spent, physically, emotionally. No more weed. We climb in the shower together and hold each other there for a good while, close and soapy under the steaming hot water.

She gets out first and is drying herself when I absolutely blow it: "Hey Tiff—*Bonnie!*—hand me a towel, baby?"

"What the hell did you just call me? Fucking Tiffany?"

She totally loses it, shrieking, with fire in her eyes.

"You two-timing asshole!"

Now I've blown it. How do I tell Bonnie Jo that she's not the only other woman?

"Jesus, baby...we were just talking about her, it was a slip of the tongue."

"Bullshit!!" She's not buying it. "You goddamned *psycho!*"

It takes everything I've got to calm her down. And now I'm stuck here the rest of the night.

I sleep on the couch. Doesn't help.

CHAPTER 28

MY IPHONE ALARM buzzes at six thirty. Set on vibrate. No sound.

I slip off the couch, headed for the shower, trying not to make any noise. I see through the cracked open bedroom door that Bonnie hasn't moved a muscle since I left her in bed last night.

Showered and shaved, I put on a fresh shirt and underwear out of the hall closet, where I keep a few things for just such occasions.

Normally I'd leave a note or something. But after the blow-up last night we are by no means normal, so I slip out the front door and take the elevator down to the lobby.

The Landmark Diner is back downtown, below the agency. I take a cab to save time and Linda's already there, waiting for me. We have another great chat over breakfast and I insist on picking up the check this time.

At least, I feel like it was great. But truth is I don't remember a whole lot about our conversation. My fight with Bonnie Jo is weighing heavily on me; we've never had that kind of trouble before.

To think that I could possibly lose her hurts like hell.

CHAPTER 29

I GET TO the agency by nine thirty, close enough, but not before I go by the bank, again.

Up on the third floor Mo greets me. "Morning, Tim. Paul wants to see you right away. He's in his office." The president is after me early.

"Hey, Paul, good morning," I greet him, sliding open the glass door.

"C'mon in, Tim, and close the door, okay? We need to talk. These murders are terrible, unbelievable. The only way we're going to be able to deal with it is by being frank with each other."

"Of course, man. What's up?"

"I need to know what you know about Ramon. God rest his soul."

Here's a guy who founded and runs a successful, midsize New York ad agency, and he's basically clueless about a lot of the people who work for him.

"Okay, look. You know some of our creatives use a little—"

"A little what?" he asks. Seriously? He doesn't know?

"Marijuana, Paul. Weed. A lot of them smoke it. You know that, right?"

"Well, sure, I've heard there's some grass around...."

"So..." I tell him, "Ramon is the guy they were getting it from. And other stuff, too. Who knows?"

"Oh, my God. It's worse than I thought. Much worse. Do you think that had anything to do with him getting killed?"

"Of course I do. And I think the cops do, too. Which is why they're all over the agency. And Tiffany's murder only makes it worse. Apparently she was getting her drugs from him, too."

"My God—what has become of my agency? And I have to tell you, Tim—you're making it *worse* yourself."

"What the hell are you talking about, Paul?"

"I know you're looking for another job."

Oh, shit. Should have known that kind of thing doesn't stay secret.

"Paul...that was before all this. It's not that I'm unhappy here...."

"Look, we've worked too long and too close together to tiptoe around," Paul says. "This happens in our business, but I like you and so does everybody else here. We'd hate to lose you. And the timing absolutely sucks."

He pauses, then says, "So, how's the search going?"

I fumble for a response and say, "Well, yeah, got a couple of possibilities...I...."

"Good! Glad to hear it," he says. Really?

I take a deep breath. "Thanks for your understanding, Paul.

And for your support." What else can I say? Nothing, so I reach for the door handle.

"By the way, Tim," Paul says, "Bonnie Jo's not at work again. Any idea what's going on with her?"

CHAPTER 30

HOME, FINALLY. LATE again, near eleven o'clock. New business pitch is tomorrow. Of course the kids are asleep, and surely disappointed we didn't get to Pizza Pizazz, as promised. What about Jean? I pour myself a glass of wine from the bottle of Signaterra from Monday and find her in the family room in her nightgown and robe, reading. Or acting as if.

"Hello, love. Can I get you anything?" and she finally looks up at me with an expression that is hard to read. It lingers somewhere between forced attention to the book in her lap and a question, probably about what the hell is going on with me.

"No, Tim, I'm fine. Well, not fine. But here I am, which is more than I can say for you lately."

"I know, baby. What are you reading?"

"Jesus, Tim, who cares?"

"What's the matter, love? Is something bothering you?"

"Hell, yes, something's bothering me. Everything's bothering me. Lately I'm with you like six hours a day, all of it after dark and most of it sound asleep. Or trying to be.

That's no life. At least not the life we planned on. Or I hoped for.

"And now another murder is all over the news. Another one—connected to your office! Did you know this woman?"

"I know, it's terrible. Well, she was in our first CrawDaddy Super Bowl commercial, and I was on the shoot. So sure, I knew her from that, a long time ago.

"I know it's been a little crazy these days, for us. I didn't plan on it being this way, either. The advertising business is crazy. And where Marterelli is right now is even crazier. Especially with these murders."

"To say the least," she says.

"Plus, we need new clients, big time, and that's on me. So I have to put in these insane hours to try to help give us a shot. To make shit happen—for myself, and for us, too. Which is what I told Linda Kaplan in our interview the other day.

"It's a great job at Kaplan-Thaler, by the way, one that I really want. One that . . . we really need."

"Define *need*," she says.

"Fair enough," I answer, and take another sip of my wine. "Look, my days at Marterelli are numbered. I'm done there. Paul knows I'm looking. It's time to move on. And this job offers huge financial upside, which is always a good thing. . . ."

"Of course it is," she says.

"Yeah, but there's more to it than that. Which is what I mean about the need thing. So let's be honest—*we need the money*. This house is a huge financial burden. And, well, our credit cards are maxed, too. Property taxes are due just around the corner."

"So is our income tax. . . ."

"All of it's piling up, making me nuts, and it's about to bury us."

"Define *bury us.*"

"Oh, baby. I'm just saying that with our debt, and taxes, if I can't generate some more income, well, worst-case scenario, we might even have to . . . move . . . to a less expensive location. And trust me, I don't want that to happen any more than you do."

"My God, Tim. I had some sense of all this, but not to this degree. You're scaring the hell out of me."

"All I'm saying is we need the higher income this new job will get us. Then we'll be fine. I want you to count on me, just like always," I say, which I know by now is wishful thinking.

I set my glass of wine next to the lamp on the side table, kneel down in front of Jean and look into her eyes. "Listen, my love, I will never, ever, put you in a situation that's not good for you. Not good for both of us."

How the hell can she buy any of this?

"From the bottom of my heart, you have my word. My commitment."

But maybe she is. She's relaxing a bit. Her eyes soften, and with that I take her head in my hands and lean in and plant a loving kiss on her lips, hoping she'll accept it. She does.

"Why don't we take this conversation upstairs, you know?" It's the moment of closeness we've needed.

"Okay," she says. I click off the table lamp, take her hand in mine, and up the stairs we go, with a peek into the kids' rooms on the way by. Once we're in our bedroom she takes off her robe, I shed my clothes, and we climb into our king-size bed.

Lights off. And while I'm still trying to figure out what else I can say to reassure my wife of nearly fifteen years, she pulls her nightgown up over her head and offers herself to me with a lingering, loving kiss. The kind of kiss built on a history of marriage and family that's lost none of its flame or desire.

It's not sex we have. It's pure love. Which instead of being good for me, breaks my heart.

I toss and turn awhile, half awake....

Where is all this shit going?

...And finally drift off into a reluctant sleep.

CHAPTER 31

ANOTHER DAY, ANOTHER dollar, thanks to Paul, for now. Back at work.

The day of the pitch, and first a quick run-through before Zimmerman and his colleagues from Weight Watchers come to the office and dare us to amaze them. And we've got to. We need this business.

I've promised Steve some innovative, top-line insights into their business, and we'll use some of the agency's work to demonstrate how we've successfully addressed similar challenges for other clients. Weight Watchers has had, like, six agencies in the last ten years. Nobody can get it right, at least that's what they think. But we can. I'm sure of it—with groundbreaking work that produces results.

That's what a lot of agencies lose sight of—*the work has to work!* If it doesn't sell the brand, or something relevant—it's a waste of the client's money.

I'm up in my cubicle, grabbing some stuff I need for the rehearsal, when I get a text from Barb Lundquist:

Congratulations! You've got the job! Linda loves you!
Call to discuss details.

Yes!!! In the middle of all this chaos, all this horror happening around us, this lights me up!

Will do!! I text back, then head downstairs to the third floor and walk over to the meeting room. I've got our heavy hitters set up to participate in this one: Chris Berardo, our top creative guy—overlooking his bullshit from the other day; David Gebben, the copywriter; Bill Kelly, our best art director.

I'm taking the lead, as usual, and Bonnie Jo is set to partner with me on this one. So far everybody's here except her.

Guess the smile on my face is obvious, because this is what I hear from Chris: "Tim, what the hell are you so happy about all of a sudden?"

"Something personal, but thanks for asking. I'll let Paul know we're ready for the run-through," and I head over to his office while they set up.

I rap a knock on my way in and he looks up. "Paul, I know the timing on this totally sucks, but since our talk yesterday...you need to know...."

"Know what?"

"I got the job."

"Wow. Who's it with, if I might ask?"

"It's with Linda Kaplan, at Kaplan-Thaler. I'm going in as a partner and president!"

"Well, shit, fabulous! I'm actually happy for you. Seriously. Hate to lose you. You're irreplaceable. But opportunities don't come along every day, and when they do, you need to grab on to them."

"Thanks Paul, you're the best . . . I . . . "

"And now for some more reality, Tim, and I know you'll understand this: We're going to need you to leave right away. There's no sense in you leading the Weight Watchers pitch when you're on your way out the door. And word travels fast; I don't want the others seeing you still here, knowing you're leaving—which they'll find out soon enough. Even worse when the client finds out, and they will, too. I'm still good for the two weeks' severance pay, but that's it."

"Fair enough, Paul. I understand. Can't say I blame you."

"Yeah, well, everything else is coming apart at the seams, this just pours a little more gasoline on the freakin' fire. Like . . . *an inferno* . . ." which he manages to say with a half smile.

"Needless to say I'll step in on the new business pitch, although you're a hard man to replace," he says, generous to the end. "Tell the guys I'm on my way over."

"Will do," and I stand up and shake his hand, which is awkward, and he collapses right there in his chair, head in hands, scratching the hair on his head and rubbing his eyes. He's actually moaning.

CHAPTER 32

I'M BACK IN the conference room. "Guys, listen up. Got something to tell you. And this ain't easy."

I get mixed looks from David and Bill, an agitated glance from Chris.

"After five great years here, for which I'm grateful to all of you for making possible, I am leaving the Marterelli agency for a much-needed change of scenery. I know you guys can appreciate that, and..."

"Wow! Who's it with, Tim?" Bill asks.

"Kaplan-Thaler, you know, with Linda Kaplan."

"Damn, she's cool, that's for sure. And she's built a great agency," David says, and even Chris is forced to nod in agreement.

"Yes, she is. And indeed, she has. Now, the thing is, Paul, who has been incredibly supportive through all of this—for all of us—well, he's asked me to pack up my stuff right away and get out of everybody's hair. Which I totally understand.

"So I'm heading upstairs, and will stop back by on my way out. Meanwhile Paul is on his way over and will take the lead on this. You're in great shape, and I'm sure Weight Watchers is going to be impressed." This time my smile is ear to ear, and genuine.

And then it is absolutely crushed. Mo practically crashes through the sliding glass door before David can pull it open for her.

She's hysterical.

"Oh, my God! Oh, my God!"

She's bawling, struggling to get a sentence out, and when I hear it my life is officially upside down.

"Bonnie...is d...d...dead! Bonnie Jo is dead! Murdered. They found her in her apartment, dead!"

CHAPTER 33

STUNNED SILENCE. GROANS. Gasping breaths. Faces twisting into sorrow, and anger. Bill buries his face in his hands. Mo collapses into my arms, and I gently sit her down.

The new business pitch is instantly forgotten. I can hardly breathe.

Chris looks up toward the ceiling. "Sweet Jesus, what in the world is going on?" and shakes his head, unconvincingly. I've never heard him talk like this. Gebben picks up a chair and slams it against the wall, to shrieks from the others.

I've got to see if I can do something, anything, to help. Can't leave my mates like this.

"Okay, guys. Okay. Let's try to get a grip here. This is insane. Awful. And scary. And weird. Clearly somebody has it in for us. But we've got to try to keep our cool—otherwise they win." I'm trying to create some calm, but it's just barely working.

"Tim. *Tim...*" Mo says. "What should we do? What *can* we do?"

I know one thing I can do, something I should have done yesterday: call Quinn about Berardo and his gun.

"Hang on, guys, give me a minute." I head for the third-floor restroom, where I can call Pete.

"Detective Quinn," he answers.

"Pete, it's Tim. Sorry to bother you...."

"No problem, Tim. No problem at all. What's up?"

"Now this thing with Bonnie Jo is simply beyond the pale. Insane. Madness. I—"

"It certainly is, Tim. Certainly is. And needless to say it just puts Marterelli's deeper under the microscope. What the hell is going on over there?"

"Damn good question, which is why I'm calling you...and Jesus, I feel like a traitor...but I know you guys are counting on me and something happened late yesterday that I think you need to know about."

"I'm listening...."

"Right before I left work last night, I had a visit from Chris Berardo, our creative director."

"I know who Chris is."

"Well, and I don't know quite how to say this any other way...he's carrying. He's got a pistol. Showed it to me, and I have no idea why."

"Are you sure, Tim?"

"Absolutely. And of course with an all-points out for a murder suspect who's killing people with a gun, a pistol, and now Bonnie Jo, well..."

"Absolutely, Tim. Would have liked to have known about this last night—but you've done the right thing, thank you," he says, and hangs up.

CHAPTER 34

I RUN SOME water in the sink. Splash some on my face and take a cold, hard look at myself in the mirror.

I don't recognize the guy looking back at me.

Who are you, MacGhee? Who the hell are you, really? Where does all this madness go? Where does it end? And why? Why is this shit happening now? And what does it mean for me?

No answers...not yet...

I dry off with a couple of paper towels, brush my hair back, take a deep breath, and head back for the conference room. Chris is looking at me, determinedly, like he's searching for answers, too—a different kind, no doubt—and I'm wondering if he thinks he sees a look of betrayal on my face.

"Tim. What can we do?" It's Mo again.

Before I can come up with anything, I see Detective Quinn and his partner through the glass wall, quick-stepping it past Mo's desk, headed for a conference room where Paul is waiting.

That didn't take long.

Then Paul sticks his head in and, despite our conversation just twenty minutes ago, asks me to join them. I follow him over to the conference room.

My friend Pete doesn't look quite as friendly anymore, standing there, straight as an arrow, arms folded.

"Detective," I nod. He nods back, expressionless, like a stranger. Like he was trained to be.

"This is so awful, so sad. So impossible to even believe, much less deal with," Paul says.

"Tragic," I say. "Absolutely tragic. Ramon was bad enough. And Tiffany. But Bonnie Jo Hopkins? The brightest light in this agency. An inspiration to everyone. What a terrible, *terrible* loss...."

"And what a wicked coincidence, isn't it?" Quinn says. "Three people murdered, all of whom had a relationship with this advertising agency. We sure are missing something here, that's a damned definite."

I have to sit down.

"I know you guys will get to the bottom of this," I tell them. Surely they can see the devastation written all over my face.

"Count on it," he says, leaving no doubt he'll be talking to me again.

"Understand, Detective, absolutely. But you need to know something that Paul and I have just discussed. I am leaving the agency as of today, at my own initiative, and going to work with Linda Kaplan over at Kaplan-Thaler. Great opportunity. Due to start Monday. But of course you can contact me there, and you have my cell and e-mail info."

"Understand," says Quinn, looking down at the floor, and then back up at me. "We've got a lot more talking to do with people here, too, so we're going to get back at it. But before I go there's something you both should know, and it's based on the input we just got from MacGhee: Chris Berardo has been seen carrying a weapon, a pistol, inside the office—we don't know for how long—so we're taking him in for questioning."

"*Are you serious,* Detective?" It's Paul, in an extended state of disbelief.

Then he looks over at me.

"Slam dunk, based on what MacGhee's telling us. Want to get him away from the others to talk. But you need to know because that's where we're headed right now, and that's why he'll be leaving with us."

Paul and I watch as the detectives approach the meeting room and gesture for Chris to step outside. There's twenty seconds of detective speak from Quinn and then they turn him around, place his hands up against the wall and pat him down! Surreal.

"How did you know about the gun, Tim?" Paul wants to know.

"Don't ask, Paul. You wouldn't believe it anyway."

All anyone can do is stare in disbelief. Gloved, Quinn removes a pistol from Chris's inside jacket pocket, drops it in the evidence bag Garrison's holding, and pulls Berardo's hands down behind his back to cuff him. As they escort him out I get a satanic stare from Chris that would pierce a granite wall.

He's not looking for answers anymore. He knows.

At least now the cops have a lead suspect. . . .

CHAPTER 35

THE AGENCY IS completely unwired, just like when Ramon got killed. No, worse. The sooner I get out of here, the better.

Quinn's across the way, and his eyes follow me as I cross the third floor and head for the back stairs, tracking my every step. What the hell?

Bill Kelly approaches. "Tim, oh man, I am so, so sorry for all of this. And look, I just want you to know how especially sorry I am for you and...Bonnie Jo...I..."

"Why, man? I mean, we all loved Bonnie Jo. I worked very closely with her over the years. Just like a lot of you."

"Just wanted you to know, that's all," he tells me, with what amounts to a knowing look.

Jesus, what else do people know about me?

I grab a couple of empty boxes from the kitchen storage room and head up the back stairs. And here's Lenny smoking a joint! "*What the hell, Lenny? Have you lost your freakin' mind?*"

"Want a hit?" he says.

"No, I don't," I lied. "Put that thing out and get the hell out of here!"

Yeah, it's time to go.

I'm crossing over the fifth floor to my cubicle and pass Clay Caulkin's workspace. He's one of our top account guys. "Hey, Clay, you okay?"

"Yeah, I guess," he says. For the first time I see the old *Adweek* column, "Making Stuff Happen," actually framed and hanging on his wall.

"Clay, I can't believe you've still got that old *Adweek* column on your wall. So do I. No wonder you're so damned good."

"Whatever," he says. He looks defeated, and I don't blame him.

There's nobody around when I get to my cubicle. Got one more thing to take care of, so I pull out the note Juanita gave me.

"*Como?*" she answers on the second ring.

"Juanita, *buenas tardes*. It's Tim MacGhee, and I have some good news for you. We've been able to collect some money for you...."

"*Bueno...*" is all I get.

"Sure, so I'd like to bring it to you after work tonight. Will you be at home?"

"*Sí.*"

"And will *tu madre* be there, too?"

"*Sí.*"

"Okay, good. I will try to be there by seven. Is that okay?"

"*Sí.*"

"Good. *Bueno.* I'll see you then," and hang up.

Takes me just fifteen minutes to pack my stuff. I spend

another minute catching my breath. Five years, five more good years here, and boom, it's done. It's hard to be excited when my entire universe has caved in on me. I've got one chance to make it right, and that's the new job at Kaplan-Thaler.

Thank God for minor miracles, I think, and head for the elevator.

But no quick escape—because Detectives Quinn and Garrison are there *waiting for me.* How the hell'd they get back here so fast?

"Pete?"

"Let's make it Detective Quinn, MacGhee. And I'm afraid we've got some more questions for you."

"Well, sure. What else can I tell you? Let's go back to my cubicle where we can talk."

"No, not quite. We're going to need to take you down to the station, where we can be sure our conversation is completely private."

"Seriously? Well ... of course, if that's what it takes. As you can see I'm in the process of leaving the agency."

"Yes, like you told us. And we want to make this as easy as possible, and attract as little attention as possible. So first, we're going to ask you to drop off your things back in your cubicle. And then we'll escort you downstairs to our car."

"And I'll take that bag," this from Detective Garrison. I hand it to him. Nothing in it except my laptop.

Jesus—is this their way of showing me how valuable I am to their investigation?

By the time we head back to the elevators the entire fifth floor is watching us, with a range of expressions—curiosity, surprise, some smirks. Mary Claire, Julie Reich. All of them.

Clay stands up and I get the raised fist and arm slap of indignation—the old Iberian finger, which Ramon would appreciate.

Downstairs we pass Mo on the way out. I can't bear to look at her, but I can see she's clapped her right hand over her mouth in genuine concern.

"It's okay, Mo. We're just going to find a more private place to talk."

Out on the street, Garrison locks my bag in the trunk, opens the front door, gets into the driver's seat of their unmarked car and cranks up the engine. Quinn opens the back door so I can climb into the backseat. *It's caged,* with no way to open the doors from the inside.

What the hell is going on?

CHAPTER 36

OFF WE GO.

"I'm a little confused at why all this security stuff is necessary," I ask.

"Not to worry, MacGhee. Just official procedure. We want to get you away from the office so we can get down to business."

"Got it . . . I guess. What'd you do with Berardo?"

"Sent him with two other officers."

We pull up in front of the precinct office on East 21st Street. Quinn opens the door for me and walks me inside. Garrison gets my bag out of the trunk and turns it in at the front desk.

"Coffee? Water?" Quinn offers.

How 'bout a cocktail?

"Ah, water's fine, thanks."

"Come with me." I follow him over to the watercooler and then down the hall to a private . . . *interrogation room?*

"Have a seat, MacGhee. My partner will be here momentarily."

I take a seat and Quinn sits down on the other side of the table. This room has no windows, bare walls, a table, and four chairs. Just like the interrogation rooms you see on TV.

Two knocks on the door and Garrison joins us without waiting for a response.

"Detective Scott Garrison, 21st Precinct." A formal introduction again, and this time he presents his badged credentials to me.

Quinn sets his Samsung smartphone on the table, taps one of the apps and then taps it again.

"I'm going to record our conversation, MacGhee. Understand?" He slides the phone toward me, so it's in the middle of the three of us.

"Okay, sure…"

"Okay, let's get down to basics." Here it comes. "There's been three murders connected to the Marterelli and Partners agency, where you've worked for more than five years, this time around, and earlier, for some sixteen months when you first started with them back in 2004. By all indications, you are the main man there, the one with the best connections to and relationships with just about everybody there."

"Well, sure, you know, five years is long enough…" but I'm interrupted.

"Correct. And of course that includes Bonnie Jo Hopkins."

My gut tightens.

"What exactly is your relationship with Bonnie Jo Hopkins?"

"You know this, Detective. I've worked with her ever since I got there, most recently, and she was already there back when I started with Paul right out of the Marines. She's the key, hands-on creative in the agency, so she's involved in virtually every aspect of our advertising, from writing, to production, and including new business pitches. So I work with her all the time."

"Right. What about after work hours?"

"Well, sure, we have long days, a lot of times. Sometimes some of us unwind together at a local pub or something. In fact a bunch of us went to hear Chris Berardo's band just, what? Monday night."

"What else?"

"I'm not sure what you mean, Detective."

"What else does your relationship with Bonnie Jo Hopkins involve?"

"Nothing, really. I mean, sure, we're close. We share a lot of things, professional and even personal...."

"Have you ever been to her apartment?"

My tightening gut twists its way up to my throat, which I have to clear.

"No, no. Well, wait. There was this one time when I helped her get a bunch of art bags home for an out-of-town client trip she was taking the next morning, but..."

"That's it? That's the only time you were at her apartment?"

"Yes."

"MacGhee, we've checked the LUDs from her cell. And there are dozens of calls from you, and from her to you, most of them after hours. What's that all about?"

My pulse is quickening.

"Like I said, we're close. The agency business is 24/7. We had lots of stuff to talk about, all the time."

And I realize my right leg is pumping under the table at a hundred miles an hour, and I hope he's not seeing it.

"Put that aside for the moment...Now, I want you to have a look at something." He picks up his phone, swipes it a few times, and holds it out to me. Video starts playing.

Jesus!

"This is the lobby in Bonnie Jo's apartment. As you can see, the lobby monitor has you entering her apartment building. This one's from two weeks ago."

Yup, there I am.

The video cuts to the next piece—me leaving.

"And, as you can see from the time/date code, you're leaving her building some three and a half hours later. Can you explain that—since you've just told us you were only there once, to drop some stuff off?"

"Right..." I gulp. Hard. "Forgot. We had to crash on a new business pitch, so I hung around so we could work together, till the wee hours, you know?"

"So you say. There's more. But I want you to look at this one. As you can see from the time/date code, this is from two nights ago...."

Holy shit!

"The last time anyone saw her alive..."

"Okay, look. Yes, we had a relationship. We had an affair, actually. For a long time."

"Obviously, MacGhee. We've searched her apartment. We've got pictures. The hall closet is filled with clothes that are your size, that will no doubt have your DNA all over them. The bathroom is loaded with men's toiletries, presumably yours."

"Oh, my God. Fine. We loved each other. And yes, I was there Wednesday night. She was alive and well. Anything that happened, happened *after I left*."

"Really? Here's the lobby video from the next morning. You were there until seven forty-five a.m."

"Exactly! And we found out at work a *day* later that she had been murdered. Which of course is plenty of time for the killer to do his deed *after I'm gone*."

"The medical examiner's report on time of death isn't going to support that," Quinn tells me.

"Detective—ask my colleagues—I was crushed, shocked, heartbroken when we found out. Jesus Christ, I wouldn't kill her. I loved her!"

"A strange coincidence, all of this, don't you think, MacGhee? But that's okay, you don't have to answer that. Now I want to ask you about Tiffany Stone, the actress who was killed in Grand Central Station Tuesday night, the night of Ramon's wake."

"Can I have some more water?" I need a minute to try to bring some order to the utter chaos in my head.

The detectives leave me alone in the room. It is a very long time before they return.

CHAPTER 37

I AM ABOUT to be hoisted by my own petard, by the kinds of cruel coincidences that get the wrong guys accused. I search for some corner of my spinning head that can respond with plausible answers to these determined detectives.

I gulp down my water and ask for more.

"Yes, clearly I knew Tiffany . . . I hired her for that CrawDaddy commercial way back when." *Shut up, asshole. Just answer the questions.*

"And just how well did you know her?"

"Not well. Honestly. She knew the creatives better, since she was in the business. She knew Bonnie Jo." *Uh-oh. Too much information!*

But of course, if they know about me and Bonnie, they probably know about me and Tiffany.

"I mean . . . I knew her . . . but I didn't really know her, if you get the drift . . ."

"Would you be surprised to learn that we know otherwise? We've talked to people. Clearly you had an extended, ongoing *relationship* with her, too. It's obvious she was in love with you, MacGhee. Even CrawDaddy's CEO knew all about it."

"Sure. Parker Roberts and I stayed in touch for a while after the shoot. He was cool." I babble on. "First time we met Tiffany out in LA he takes one look at her boobs and says, 'Are those real?' She goes, 'Real *expensive*.' From then on it was like a match made in heaven."

"Stop the bullshit, MacGhee. How could all of that be if you didn't know her well? Really well. Can you answer that?"

It's time to come clean. Past time. I've got my fists clenched in full view... *relax!*

I take a deep breath.

"Actually, yes. I plead guilty. I have a weakness where women are concerned. Not especially proud of it... but I'll own it. Tiffany and I stayed in touch over the years. Or more accurately, she stayed in touch with me. Anyway, we'd see each other from time to time, you know. Get together. *Long lunches...*

"So it's no wonder she would feel like this was the real deal." I try a joke. "I can tell you from experience those boobs were worth every cent she spent on them..."

"C'mon, MacGhee. Let's make this easy on both of us. Enough of the bullshit..."

"This isn't a crime. Grounds for divorce, maybe, though I hope my wife doesn't have to know. But not a crime..."

Detective Quinn isn't listening anymore. His eyes pierce mine.

CHAPTER 38

I'M SWEATING BULLETS. I stand up and take my jacket off. I suck down more water.

"Listen carefully, MacGhee...." Quinn says.

"Is all this really necessary? I..." and I get the unmistakable stare that says *Yes, it is, so shut up and listen.*

"You have the right to remain silent, and refuse to answer any questions. Anything you say may be used against you in a court of law. You have the right to consult an attorney...."

"Detective, please. I know this stuff. I..."

He raises an open hand to shut me up: "If you cannot afford an attorney, one will be appointed for you. If you decide to answer questions now, without an attorney, you have the right to stop anytime and request one. Knowing and understanding your rights, are you willing to answer my questions without an attorney?"

I nod yes.

"I need to hear you say it, MacGhee."

"Yes, of course, I am willing to answer more questions."

"The other day you told us about Ramon. You told us

he provided drugs to people in your office, presumably for money."

"Yes."

"What about you? Did you get drugs from Ramon?"

"Some occasional weed, yes, I admit it."

"You did two years in the Marines before you started in the business...."

"Yes, and damned proud of it."

"We checked your records. Good marks all around. Guess what else we found out?"

"I can't imagine." I'm hoping against hope....

"Ramon served in the Marines, too. With you. In Iraq. He was in your battalion. *In your squad.* Ramon Martinez was in the same Marine Corps squad in Iraq that you led. You must have known each other a hell of a lot better than you've admitted to so far."

He's got me there, for sure. "Yes, we served together. That was before the agency business. Didn't think it mattered...."

And my mind wanders, believe it or not. I'm out on checkpoint Foxtrot with Ramon, dug in between the corner walls of a decimated building on the outskirts of Fallujah, deep into the night before we are to launch Operation Vigilant Resolve to retake the city from the insurgents. Our orders were to prevent anyone from entering the city, or leaving it, and our responsibility covered some twenty-five meters to either side. The calm before the storm. I'm scoping the landscape with night vision binocs. No action out there so far.

And so we drift into Spanish. Ramon and I were close and I wanted to learn his native language.

"*Mi amigo...*" I hear Ramon say...and then...

"You're not supposed to think! Christ, MacGhee, you even helped Ramon get his job at the agency back when you first worked there! And we know this: you were in the drug business with him."

God help me. They've got it all. At least, they think they do.

"What's that got to do with his murder? Why would I murder an old friend? A brother?" I'm desperate for anything.

"Well, while you were panicking on the way over here we searched the boxes you were taking out of the office, and found this." He nods over, and Garrison holds up a Ziploc bag of coke. *Shit!*

"Yeah, okay, I did some blow every once in a while. But it's not..."

"That wasn't a question, MacGhee. But this is: what was your specialty in the service?"

"I..."

"Never mind. We know what it was. MOS 8541. US Marine Corps Scout Sniper, especially trained in marksmanship with an M40 sniper rifle and an M9 pistol. Ring a bell?"

I'm speechless. And not by choice.

"In fact, your entire squad was sniper qualified, and that included Ramon. You guys were brothers in arms. No wonder you worked the drug business together. And you clearly knew how to handle a firearm."

Holy shit. Maybe they do have it all.

"Now, my partner has a couple of questions. Detective Garrison...?"

"I do. We also found this in your boxes." He holds up a key. "You know what this is, right? It's the key to a safety deposit box. Yours. Bank of America, down on Canal Street. Separate bank from your family checking accounts. Guess what we found in it?"

I start to stand up.

"Sit down, MacGhee," commands Quinn, in a distinctly military voice.

"This is a Marine-issued M9 pistol. Yours. With the barrel threaded for an Airsoft suppressor. This one." He holds that up, too.

And then Quinn says, "What do you think the odds are that the bullet slugs we found in Ramon, in Bonnie Jo Hopkins, and in Tiffany Stone will all match this weapon?"

CHAPTER 39

SO NOW, HERE I sit, helpless. I hear talk down the hall....

"Remember the end scene from Psycho? *You know, Mrs. Bates's boy, Anthony Perkins, sitting in that jail cell, with this sick, haunted stare? That shit-eating grin on his face, like he's sitting on some dark secret, and enjoying it?"*

"Yeah, I do. Only it sure as hell wasn't a secret."

"Exactly. Well, that's that guy sitting down there in the ding wing, cell block number 9. Scary, man."

How did I get here?

Being in the advertising business is like being in a pressure cooker. Got to get it right, every time—only none of those final decisions are yours. They're the client's—it's his money—and you can only hope they make the right decisions. If they don't, it's your damned fault, not theirs. It's your ass. Every time. They can always fire the agency, before they get fired themselves.

Big-time stress. Enough to make you nuts.

That's one thing.

Plus, I was in way over my head financially. Big house. Big mortgage. *Two* mortgages.

Obscene taxes. Credit cards maxed. Spending out of control. Switching money from one account to another to cover checks, if only temporarily. Sound familiar? Maybe not. But that's where I was. Where *we* were, thanks to me. Although Jean never complained much about any of it. So...you look for some relief from all the freakin' pressure. Extracurricular activities. A cocktail. Or three. A little weed. More weed. Xanax to cool down. Or oxycodone, if you can get it. Maybe some coke to pick you back up.

Most nights after work, me and the guys would end up on the agency roof passing joints around before I went home, or wherever. Last time I saw Ramon was the night he was murdered, up on the roof, where we were sharing a joint after work. And that's where they found him, with a bullet to the back of his head.

We'd get all this stuff from Ramon. Congenial, connected Ramon. Our dealer. Cash money. A lot of it. How else would a lowly tech guy have a nice big brownstone apartment in Brooklyn? He was our source, and he did well for himself.

Then...I ended up partnering with Ramon. He knew where to get all this shit. I didn't, and I never asked. But I had the contacts, the connections, inside the agency and beyond. I was the man—which the detectives finally figured out.

We made a good team, Ramon and me. And some money. For a while.

I tapped my secret bank account and gave Ramon extra money so he could expand his supply. Investment capital, so we could both benefit from growing demand.

But pretty soon he's asking me for more capital. And more. And then he's not asking—he's demanding. I ain't got it anymore—but he's not buying it.

So he starts threatening me, more or less. And then more. Unacceptable. Got out of control. Had me in a corner....

I had a great time with Tiffany over the years. She stayed hot, in every way imaginable. Her Super Bowl commercial put her on the map. Hell, a year later she's on the cover of *Playboy*! Fully revealed inside. Like a dream come true for this guy. Every guy's dream—never comes true. Except it did, for me. Had me a Playmate! For a while. We'd...see each other.

I loved her. Well...I loved...being with her. But she didn't love me. She was using me because she thought I could help her career.

And worse, she was seriously into junk on her own. Turned out she was getting hers from Ramon, too, after connecting with him through some creatives. Then she's leaning on me to get her more stuff—and pay for it! Which got to be unacceptable and it freaked me out, knowing the cops might soon be onto us.

But what led the cops to me? When I think about it, maybe some of the creatives started getting suspicious. Lenny? That was a joke. And Chris was never a serious suspect, either. And once the detectives figured out my connection to Ramon, I'm buried in this. Fried.

I ended up being the prime suspect.

Sure, I have a Marine-issue Beretta M9, fitted with a threaded barrel to accommodate a suppressor. So what?

Semper fi!

CHAPTER 40

LOOK, I'M A guy who was confronted with tough, unbearable situations that left me with no options. My world completely caved in—in the space of a single week! I was drowning in the pressure of it all.

What's a guy to do?

I had to do something about all of it. And I did.

Tiffany had rigged my iPhone text settings to "share my location" one night while I was in a postcoital shower at her place. Which is how she was waiting for me in Grand Central Station that night.

We did second cocktails, and then a joint was a natural next step. So I took her down to the sub-basement—M42 it's called—a totally secret space that houses all of Grand Central's AC to DC converters. You won't find it on any public maps. Ramon took me there one night to trade copious amounts of dope for serious cash.

And that's where they found her body. Her gorgeous body. With a bullet wound in the back of her head.

And Bonnie Jo?

I was seriously falling in love with Bonnie Jo Hopkins. The real deal, which was bittersweet because I'm already in love with another woman. My wife.

But our sex was...genuine. Intimate lovemaking.

We were genuine partners at work, too. BJ helped cast Tiffany for the CrawDaddy spot, and was on the shoot.

Bonnie was a social user. Just weed, really. She got hers from Ramon, just like everybody else. Always had some when I came over. Cool. Then she finally put two and two together, and was convinced she knew what really happened to Ramon.

And then in a world record slip of the tongue, I damned near called her Tiffany that night. Close enough. And that was it.

Our last night together—the all-time high and the all-time low in the space of a few hours. We experienced lovemaking like neither one of us ever had before, ever. Not even close.

And never will again.

It's no coincidence these people were found dead right after the last time I saw them.

I murdered all three of them.

CHAPTER 41

RAMON WAS TOUGH. My foxhole buddy. My partner. But he had to go. Squeezing me too hard.

I waited for the roof to clear the other night. He was leaning against one of the chimneys on the roof of our building, lighting a joint. Facing to the back, toward the alley, which helped. I pull my M9 out of my serviceable attaché, suppressor already mounted, place it to the back of his head, and pull the trigger.

I ease him down to the rooftop, brush his eyelids shut, straighten his legs out and fold his arms over his chest. *Semper fi,* my friend.

Tiffany? Much easier. There we were in the depths of Grand Central. I mean, hell, she's already on her knees, preoccupied. I've still got my bag over my shoulder, pull my gun out, pull her besotted head back and slide the suppressor tube mounted on my M9 into her mouth, and before she realizes what it is, she flops over backward, knees buckled underneath her, wearing a stunned look of disbelief on her beautiful face.

And Bonnie Jo? That one hurt almost as much as Ramon. But she went ballistic on me, and who knows where that goes? I mean, she knows I'm a dealer. I'm afraid she's got me pegged for Ramon. So when she was fast asleep, I did it.

Felt all clear then—except for Juanita.

She's lucky. The cops saved her life the night they arrested me.

CHAPTER 42

I'M A KICK-ASS New York adman, Madison Avenue, yada yada. A wife who loves me. Two wonderful kids. I'm a family man.

Like I told Linda Kaplan: I'm a guy that makes shit happen. And I did.

I'm a guy who was confronted with tough, unbearable situations that left me with no options.

Like they say, "Judge not, lest ye be judged."

Jean and the kids are on the way over for a visit. They still love me, and their husband and father loves them more than simple words can describe.

Can't wait to see my guys!

"MacGhee." It's one of the jailers.

"Yeah?"

"Your family's not coming."

"Not again! The fourth goddamned time, for Christ's sake!"

I hear some guys down the hall in front of a TV. "Hey!" one of them says. "Check this out. Shh! Quiet!"

"…*Esposito, for WNBC, with exclusive, breaking news. New York City police have just confirmed the arrest of their prime suspect in the triple homicide case that has had lower Manhattan on edge for the past week. His name is Timothy James MacGhee, and he is a senior partner at Marterelli and Partners, the advertising agency that all three victims were connected to. MacGhee's being held at the Manhattan Detention Complex on White Street awaiting arraignment.*

"Here's Detective Peter Quinn, lead officer on the case for the 21st Precinct. Detective Quinn, what finally led you to Timothy MacGhee?

"These advertising people are crafty, I'll give them that. He didn't make it easy, that's for sure. But…"

And the guys down the hall erupt into spontaneous applause, just like my client did the other day.

So, here I sit in this godforsaken jail cell. Successful New York adman. Family man. Husband. Father. Churchgoer. An upstanding member of the community. And now my family is deserting me.

You know what? Fuck 'em.

Besides, if you saw me sitting here now, you'd have to say "…*why, he wouldn't even harm a fly.…*"

STINGRAYS

JAMES PATTERSON
WITH DUANE SWIERCZYNSKI

CHAPTER 1

THE GIRL

IMAGINE SHE'S YOUR SISTER.

Smart, shy, six feet tall—and she has absolutely no idea how beautiful she really is. Her fellow students at St. Paul's Prep gravitate toward her. They like her sweet nature and silly sense of humor. Her closest friends have the twin impulses to protect her and maybe corrupt her a little, because it's just too much fun. *Come on, have a smoke. Let's shotgun a beer!*

Now, your sister's never had a drink before—not even a secret sip of Mom's wine at the Thanksgiving dinner table. So she almost always says no, thank you. Or takes the faintest puff or smallest sip, just to appease her friends.

Your sister's a good kid.

But when her two best friends invite her to a very private beach party on Turks and Caicos during spring break—all expenses covered—she can't help herself. She feels like a kid who was denied sweets growing up and one day stumbled into Willy Wonka's Chocolate Factory.

Of course she grew up hearing the usual advice about partying smart, pacing yourself, and keeping your hand over the top of your drink so nobody slips a roofie into it. And she believes in that advice. But she's also never been invited to a party like this before. Someone has spent a lot of money to lay out an array of culinary delights, yet everybody seems to ignore the food. Instead they drink and dance to throbbing electronic music under strings of lights and palm fronds. Or steal away to a quiet corner for a more intimate conversation.

Your sister's best friends from school, an adorable pair of twins, press a cocktail the color of a bruised sunset into her hand and encourage her to take just a sip. *C'mon, just one!* So she does.

And it tastes…*amazing.* Nothing like the cheap beer they'd sneak on campus. Before she knows it, she's finished her first and the twins are handing her another. And she downs that, too. Easily, and it's as refreshing as a glass of orange juice.

And after the second drink the twins manage to drag their normally shy friend onto the dance floor and begin to twirl under skies so beautiful she can hardly believe this is real. Any of it.

Of course, the men notice her because there's no one else at this party quite like her. In a sea of bodies trying too hard, she is an effortless beauty, full of laughter and light.

First comes the handsome Italian lifeguard, just a few years older than your sister, but much more experienced in the ways of the islands. So he's not entirely surprised when he's nudged aside by a trust fund kid with a yacht—and this kid mentions the yacht *a lot.* Soon your sister and her twin friends are tipsy enough to agree to go see the yacht, a Squadron 60 (whatever that is—your sister doesn't know), anchored just off the beach.

Once they're on board, however, the yacht's captain cozies up to your sister. He's in his forties, but the captain is charming enough to make your sister fall for him just a little, even though a voice in the back of her mind screams, *He's twice your age!* But he pours her shots of clear, sweet rum between dances, and she kind of loves how she feels in his muscular arms. . . .

Sometime after midnight, the party is broken up by local cops. It's not so much a raid as a gentle shakedown, in which the trust fund kid is expected to fork over a tiny sliver of said fund. When your sister looks around, she realizes the twins have already left the yacht, pretty much abandoning her.

One of the cops is kind enough to offer her a ride back. He's very friendly. So friendly, he insists on a good-night kiss before she goes home. She offers him one. He pushes things further. She pushes back. He gently insists with the manner of someone who is used to hearing no, but also used to completely ignoring it. . . .

Now imagine your sister coming to her senses a little. Those old warnings from Mom and Dad are nagging at her, so she parts ways with the cop and decides to go for a walk to clear her head. Sand beneath her feet, ocean spray on her face, and all that. This was a nice diversion to fantasyland, but now it's time to return to reality.

But it's darker on the beach than she realized. And before she can make it back to the party—hands reach out from the darkness and grab her.

She fights back. With everything she's got. Deep down, at

the animal instinct level, she knows: this person means to do her harm.

But the stranger's hands, they're too powerful, and she's had too much to drink. They pull on her wrists and she's brought down to her knees, then tumbles down onto the sand.

Still, she refuses to give up. Whatever those hands want with her, it can't be good. She punches, she kicks, she scrambles up to her feet, and she thinks she's just about to make it when...

She's tackled, hard—her face smashing into the beach. She inhales to scream and sucks coarse sand down her throat.

Her attacker does not care. The hands, so incredibly powerful, drag her choking body down to the water's edge. She tries to hold on. Struggles to undo the mistakes she thinks she's made tonight. If she can only hold on a little longer...

But the tracks from her fingers, as they claw at the beach, will be erased by the tide the next morning.

CHAPTER 2

THE STINGRAYS

"PAIGE RYERSON'S BODY WAS never found," Matthew Quinn says, continuing his tale as he sprays the inside of a Teflon pan with coconut oil.

The five of them, as usual, gather in the oversized kitchen where Quinn is cooking breakfast. His $7,000-a-month Cambridge loft has plenty of other places where they can gather, but they prefer to talk about their cases over a hot meal. In this instance: the Sunday morning omelet station.

The other four take in the details of Quinn's story as the pan heats up.

"That last bit is your theory, of course," says Theo Selznick, who is standing at Quinn's immediate right. The stocky, clean-cut man has known Quinn the longest, and he expects to be served first.

"My theory?" Quinn asks, as he cracks an egg over the side of a silver bowl.

"You know, the part about the hands grabbing her out of the darkness and all that. The last person to see her alive was the cop with the sweet lips, right? As far as we know, Paige Ryerson is still alive and well somewhere in paradise. Oh, and no cheese in mine, please."

"It's not an omelet without cheese," Quinn says.

"You've known me since college," Theo replies. "When have you ever known me to give a damn about the rules?"

Quinn cracks another egg. "Kate? How about you?"

Kate Weber, standing to Quinn's left, has a stormy look on her thin face. "If she were my sister, I'd be rounding up the lifeguard, the rich kid, the captain, and the cop and work them over hard until I learned the truth. Maybe twice, just to be sure."

"No," Quinn says. "On your omelet, I mean."

"Oh," Kate says. "Just egg whites, please."

"That's also not an omelet, either," Theo says. "You know, according to the *rules*."

Quinn expertly cracks three eggs and separates the yolks from the white by using the two halves of the shell. His movements are fluid, relaxed—almost sleight-of-hand. He admires Kate's Spartan tastes. She was the same way in the US Army, when they briefly served together. No muss, no fuss. Just get the job done.

"Believe me, Kate," Quinn says as he works. "There's nothing I'd like better than to gather those men in a room and squeeze them until they pop. But you know how we work. We never let—"

"—*our targets know they're in our crosshairs*," says Jana Rose, who has positioned herself directly opposite Quinn. "We know, Matthew, honey. Maybe you could have that embroidered on a quilt."

Quinn smiles at Jana, who has the classic beauty of a stage actor from another era. She's the only one who dares to tease him like this. Even Theo—whom Quinn has known since they were roommates at Harvard—knows there are limits. But Jana knows Quinn more intimately than anyone else in this room. Or the planet, for that matter.

"And what would you like, Jana?" Quinn asks.

"Now, you know I don't like eggs," she says.

"Which is why you'll find Greek yogurt and a small fruit salad in the fridge at knee-level."

Jana's face lights up. "Wonderful."

From the other side of the kitchen comes a sigh. "I guess it's up to me, then."

The fifth member of the team, Otto Hazard, is perched on the kitchen counter, apart from the group. As usual. Otto met Theo in "finishing school"—the US Penitentiary at Leavenworth—making him the only member of the team without a direct connection to Quinn. So he constantly tries to earn his place, with a curious combination of bravado and laid-back disinterest.

"What are you thinking, Otto?" Quinn asks.

"That I'm gonna be the only one who will order a *real* omelet. Six eggs, plenty of cheese, mushrooms, onions, ham, and the hottest peppers you have. You've got habanero sauce somewhere in this place, right?"

"Check the pantry behind you."

As Quinn cooks and Otto searches, Kate shifts impatiently. "I don't know what we're waiting for. Let's vote and get moving on this one."

"Hold on a sec," Theo says. "We need to know a little

more. For starters, which agency is interested? The feebs? The CIA?"

"Nope," Quinn says. "Private party."

Which is unusual for the group. Their particular set of skills—creating elaborate stings to entrap those who believe they're above the law—are usually in demand by various government agencies. Not ordinary civilians.

"Huh, that's weird," Theo says. "The girl's parents?"

"I don't want that to cloud our judgment," Quinn says. "We always evaluate cases on their intrinsic merits alone."

"What's our objective?" Jana asks.

"We've been asked to find Paige alive—or catch her killer."

"And she disappeared . . . ?" Kate asks.

"Two nights ago. Friday evening."

"So the trail is going cold fast," Theo says.

The others consider this. Even Otto stops searching for the habanero sauce and turns to face the group. Meanwhile, Quinn finishes the three omelets cooking in three separate pans, then glides them onto waiting plates.

"What do you think, boss?" Kate asks.

Quinn says, "I think that Paige Ryerson is probably dead. I believe that I may know who did it, and I believe I know how the girl died. But right now I have no idea how to prove it."

"So who did it?"

"No shortcuts," Quinn said. "You find the evidence and bring it to me . . . then I'll tell you. Shall we put it to a vote?"

"I'm in," says Kate. "We either bring her home safe or give her a proper burial."

"Sure," says Theo. "I could stand a little island action."

"Absolutely," adds Otto through a mouthful of omelet.

"You wouldn't have brought this case to us without good reason," Jana says. "Let's do it."

"Actually, I don't think we should take this one," Quinn says. "But it's four to one, so consider us officially engaged."

The rest of them stare at Quinn, trying hard not to express their surprise. Their boss can be mercurial, but they've all learned it's better to just roll with it. You don't play chess with Matthew Quinn. You play five games of chess simultaneously, and you just have to accept that you won't be able to see all of the pieces (or the boards, for that matter).

Instead of ruminating further, they simply eat the breakfast he prepared for them.

"What about your omelet?" Jana asks.

"I ate earlier," Quinn says, pulling a file folder from the side of the omelet station. "Now here's the plan...."

CHAPTER 3

THEO (THE TRADER)

THE FLIGHT DOWN TO Turks and Caicos is smooth as can be expected, and within minutes of clearing the gate I have a drink in my hand. (Which is kind of awesome, actually.) The sun is shining, the freezing snows of Boston are just a memory, and I'm carrying a bag full of bait that will hopefully catch a killer. What better way to spend a Sunday evening?

My target is the lifeguard—one Paolo Salese. The first one to dance with Paige Ryerson.

I'm looking forward to a spin around the dance floor with him, too.

A private car takes me to one of those sprawling resorts north of Grace Bay Road. This is where Paige Ryerson and her girlfriends stayed, and this is where Paolo works during the day, guarding the Olympic-sized pool. Usually, I'd expect him to be on the prowl at one of the five bars on the property. Most likely, the watering hole with the greatest percentage of underage ladies.

But not tonight.

Tonight there's some serious global heat on Paolo the

Playboy, so he's probably going to fade into the background like a local. Takes me a few drives (and a few fat tips), but somewhere around 9:00 p.m., I find his location: a glorified shack bar not far from the beach, but far from the path that tourists care to wander. It's the kind of place where the bar top can be lifted off its moorings and hidden away come daylight. The kind of place where guys like me (in a suit) aren't usually welcome.

Like I give a damn.

Paolo's hunkered over a shot of something brown and a cheap island beer. Guessing by the sticky rings on the wood beneath his arms, he's had more than a few.

"Hey there, Paolo."

Paolo spins, takes one glance at me, and tags me immediately. I'm wearing a suit and carrying an expensive leather valise, which means I'm one of Them. The Establishment.

"No comment," he says, waving me away. As if he'd been harassed by Anderson Cooper all day. Then again, maybe he has. Paolo Salese *is* the prime suspect in the murder of Paige Ryerson, featured in media reports all around the world.

"Look, buddy, I'm not a journalist. It's even worse—I'm a lawyer! Let me buy you a drink."

Paolo shakes his head. "Piss off."

I sit down next to him anyway and give him my best lawyerly pitch. (I actually *am* a lawyer, so I'm pretty good at this.)

"I've got a client who will pay half a million dollars for closure in the disappearance of Paige Ryerson."

The look on Paolo's face tells me that he may not know the definition of the word "closure." So I try again.

"My client wants to know what happened. No strings

attached. No blame, no fault...and certainly no cops or courthouses, you understand? Completely off the books."

Paolo says nothing. Takes another shot of whatever amber fluid is in those glasses. I gesture to the bartender to give him another round.

"All I need," I say, leaning in close, "is a body."

The playboy lifeguard freezes in his tracks momentarily, then quickly recovers. Ah, *body,* that magical word. Makes everybody feel uncomfortable. I love deploying it at just the right moment.

"I don't even need that much," I continue. "Point me in the right direction, and it ends here. You walk away from this bar half a millionaire."

Finally, he turns to look me in the eyes.

"Not interested. Now seriously... *piss off.*"

He almost spits the last two words in my face. Classy.

Paolo goes skulking away from the bar-shack (don't get me wrong, I'm sure it's Zagat-rated), and I take my bag and follow him. He walks faster. I match his pace. If this is going to escalate into a chase sequence, it'll be one of the more absurd ones I've been involved in. Lawyer in a Suit vs. Tanned Lifeguard Dude, kicking up sand all the way to the ocean.

"Forgive me, Paolo, but I find it hard to believe you'd turn down this offer. How many friends have you got on your side? I'm willing to bet you don't have five hundred thousand of them."

The lifeguard continues walking, but his pace slows a little. Maybe my words are sinking in to that handsome skull of his.

"I'm telling you, Paolo—I don't give a damn what you did,

or didn't do, or any of that. I'm not a priest. I'm just a guy hired to ascertain a simple answer to a simple question. No matter what it takes."

Paolo stops, turns in his tracks, then sneers at me. "You're not a priest. But you're *definitely* a cop or a reporter."

"Oh, yeah?"

I smile, then gently toss my valise at Paolo's feet. "Go ahead. Open it."

CHAPTER 4

THEO (continued)

PAOLO GLANCES DOWN AT the leather case as if there might be a metal bear trap inside.

"Geez, Paolo," I say. "You pull kids out of shark-infested waters for a living. You can't possibly be afraid of my carry-on."

But Paolo doesn't trust me. Not. One. Bit. He's made it this far by keeping his head down and not talking to anyone. The media has given him the usual promises about "protecting his identity" and "being on his side." But what they *haven't* given him is what's in my leather case.

"Go on."

Paolo opens it. His eyes widen when he sees what's inside.

"Take it," I tell him. "It's yours."

He reaches in and pulls out the modest stack of crisp hundred-dollar bills bound with a paper wrapper.

"That's twenty-five grand," I say. "Consider it good faith money."

Paolo looks at the stack in his hand, feeling the weight of it. "You said half a million, Mr. Lawyer."

"What part of *good faith* don't you get? You point me in the direction of Ms. Ryerson's body, and the next time you'll need a bag to carry all of your money away. Unless you prefer a check?"

"No, cash is good."

Of course it's good. Money is an abstract thing until the moment it's sitting in your hand.

"So we have a deal, Paolo?"

Finally, the spell of the greenbacks dissipates. Paolo looks at me as if he's still trying to figure me out.

"You can't be a cop, because giving me this money would be entrapment or something like that, right?"

I squelch my inner lawyer, who wants to shout, *You idiot, that's not how it works!* But I'm here to find the truth—not give this playboy free legal advice.

"You know how little cops make in a year? They aren't usually in the habit of bribing their way to a murder confession, Paolo."

"I'm not confessing to anything," he says, suddenly defensive.

"I told you, all I want to buy is some information. Do you have anything you want to share right now?"

"I know what *good faith* means, Mr. Lawyer Man. It means you have to give me some time to think it over."

This is wonderful. I can practically see him doing the mental calculations as he speaks.

"You're absolutely right, Paolo." I hand him a fake business card (eggshell, Romalian type) with a real cell phone number on it. "Call me when you're ready. But my client would like closure as quickly as possible."

Again, Paolo looks down at the stack of cash in his hand, already lost in his plans for the next few hours. "Yeah, I get it."

And so do I. A few minutes later I'm calling Quinn in Boston. "I'm really liking Paolo for this."

"That's promising to hear. But can you prove it?"

"It's only a matter of time, my friend."

"Then...have at it."

"Of course, but what do *you* think? You suspected him all along, right?"

"I think you should go with your gut, and I'll go with mine."

I've known Quinn for two decades now and he hasn't gotten any easier to read.

CHAPTER 5

JANA (THE ACTOR)

OH, MY DEAR MATTHEW.

You send other Stingrays to the sunny tropics, yet somehow I end up here, in snowy New Hampshire. Sometimes I think you have it in for me.

(Or is it that you wanted to keep me close at hand?)

Even worse: I'm at an elite New England prep school. I didn't much enjoy school back when I was *required* to attend, and I'm certainly not in the mood to be here now.

But the two young ladies who invited Paige Ryerson to spring break have returned to St. Paul's Prep, home to the high-school-age children of the international elite. Hannah and Brooke Clee have resumed their classes and are presumably showing off their tans and resuming their ordinary lives.

Unlike Paige Ryerson.

Today I'm playing the role of a midlevel federal agent pulling down $68,933 a year, so I have to dress the part. I want the Clee girls to feel superior to me but also fear me, because I could be one of those idealistic, low-paid FBI agents who can't be bought. All of which means I have to pull a slightly hideous pantsuit out of my wardrobe—one I last wore in an off-Broadway production of *Catch Me If You Can.*

The things I do for this team!

After the usual bureaucratic nonsense (ID checks, phone calls), I make my way to the dorms, where I'm told the girls will be studying. The Clee girls share a room in Brewster, a girls' dormitory known for the rooster perched over the entrance. This fowl theme is carried into the hallways, where each door is marked with paper roosters—made from the handprints of the students—that are adorned with the names of the residents. It doesn't take long to find Hannah and Brooke's door birds.

I knock, but there is no reply.

So much for studying, eh?

Five minutes later, I find the Clee girls perched on a short stone wall behind their dormitory, smoking pungent clove cigarettes that they quickly begin to hide when I approach.

"Feel free to keep them out, ladies," I tell them. "I'm not ATF."

One of the twins, whom I recognize as Brooke from her many social media accounts, smiles at me.

"You want one?" she says, offering up a square, elegant package of some hipster brand. Brooke Clee is shorter and stockier than her sister, and she's far more social, based on her thousands of followers, friends, and fans. She is fond of late-night confessions and revealing selfies.

Hannah, meanwhile, eyes me warily. She holds up her cell phone like it's a stun gun. "So where *are* you from? Who let you onto school grounds?"

I tell them my fake name, show them my fake credentials.

"The Bureau sent me here for some follow-up questions. We're all very concerned about Paige, and would like to find her as quickly as possible."

"We spent hours with you guys already," Brooke says. "What more is there to ask?"

"You should be going through our father's attorney," Hannah adds.

"Relax, ladies," I say. "This isn't formal. I came up here to get a better sense of Paige's school life. Who her friends are, the kinds of things she enjoys…"

Brooke loosens up, but it's clear her sister isn't having any of this. "You should be down on the island looking for her, not up here," Hannah says. "I'd still be down there if my father didn't insist I return for classes."

"And where would you be looking?"

Brooke leans forward, wispy smoke curling out of her petite nostrils. "Think about it. She didn't fly home, and she didn't walk. The only other way off that island is by boat."

Hannah turns to shush her sister, but Brooke flashes eye daggers in return. "What? Are we supposed to protect that trust fund jerk? For what?"

"Does this jerk have a name?" I ask.

"Brooke, stop being a moron. This is what they do—ask the same questions over and over again and hope you say something different. I'm calling Daddy's lawyer."

Of course we know the trust fund jerk's name already. And, my dear Matthew, I know you didn't send me here to squeeze information out of these two. You sent me trekking up here in the cold snow to push their buttons and see what happens.

So I push.

"Before you call your father's attorney," I say, "you guys should know something."

Hannah's eyes narrow. "What's that?"

"We're fairly certain Paige is dead. And there's been a huge reward offered for closure on the case."

The look on their entitled little faces tells me that indeed I've pushed the right buttons.

"How..." Brooke stammers. "How can you *say* that?"

CHAPTER 6

JANA (continued)

NOW HERE'S WHERE I get to turn my "friendly FBI agent" persona into something more sinister. It's not as much fun playing the good girl, the straight woman, the high-cheekboned representative of law and order.

I much prefer the role of the woman who wears a professional face for all the world to see...until the mask slips slightly, and what's underneath is someone you'd *never* want to meet.

"The only way she left that island on a boat," I tell them, "is if someone wrapped her body in a tarp and gave her a burial at sea. No...I think she's buried in the sand somewhere. Close your eyes and picture it, ladies. Your *best friend,* at the bottom of some dank hole, while somebody shovels sand over her body. Her arms. Her legs. Her face. Until there's no trace of her."

"Stop saying she's dead!" Brooke cries.

But I'm more interested in Hannah's reaction to my little rant. She's not a bad actor herself, and she looks like she's trying really hard to keep a firm grip on the wild thoughts running through her mind.

"Fine," I say. "Maybe she's not dead. Maybe she's alive and well. Maybe you two know her disappearance is a hoax. Maybe you're even *in* on it. Maybe the whole trip to the island was just a convenient way to help your friend disappear."

And then there it is . . . the tell.

You know how when you cut yourself deeply there's a thrill of panic throughout your body, even before the pain begins or the first drop of blood is spilled?

I see that thrill on their faces now. *They know something.* They quickly recover and do their best to hide it from me, but it's too late.

So I build on it.

"Closure will happen, ladies. When the reward is large enough, nothing is kept secret for long. So I'd like you to think about that. For all I know, your time is already up."

Hannah now holds the phone to her ear. "You're not FBI. I'm calling campus security."

CHAPTER 7

SECURITY

THE GUARD APPEARS WITHIN seconds—which is what they're paid to do. When you have a campus full of the offspring of the world's elite, you'd better be sure that your security is top-notch and ready for action at a millisecond's notice.

Hannah and Brooke Clee relax the moment they see the familiar uniform round the corner of the dormitory. To most students, the guards here at St. Paul's are like glorified baby-sitters with badges whom you can easily bribe to do your bidding. Did your car break down when you're trying to sneak beer on campus? Heck, they'll have it towed to a garage *and* store the cans in your minifridge for you. The guards aren't here to tell the students what to do; they're here to keep the scumbags out.

Like this fake scumbag FBI agent, who Hannah probably assumes is just another tabloid reporter looking for a scoop. Absolutely shameless.

"My daddy is going to destroy you," she hisses at Jana. "There won't be anything of you left."

Jana Rose, meanwhile, says nothing. She simply slips the bland professional mask back over her face as the burly guard approaches.

"You're going to have to come with me, ma'am," the guard says.

Jana blinks. "*Ma'am?* Do I look like a *ma'am* to you?"

"Please, you're not welcome here."

"Clearly," Jana says. Then, to the girls: "This isn't over. You'll be seeing me again very soon."

"No," Hannah says, with the certainty of an umpire calling a strike, "we won't."

Jana doesn't reply. Instead she allows the guard to guide her by the arm back around the dormitory building. Once they're out of eyesight and earshot, Jana and the guard relax.

"They definitely know something," Jana says. "I could see it on their faces."

The guard, who is actually Otto Hazard dressed in a stolen uniform, shakes his head and smiles. "You think everybody knows something. You're suspicious of the whole damn world."

"That's because almost everyone is guilty of something," Jana says.

"Oh yeah? What am I guilty of?"

"Calling me *ma'am.*"

"To these kids, we all look ancient."

"Maybe *you* do. My lifestyle choices ensure that I will always look younger than the age that can be ascertained from my birth certificate."

"Yeah, and that's why mine is forged," Otto says, as he leads her back past the entrance of Brewster. "Anyway, what makes you so certain the Clee girls are hiding something?"

"I floated all possibilities by them, one by one, to see which would strike a nerve. They were good actresses when it came to Paige's possible death. They were shaken a bit when I told them about the huge reward offered for information about their friend, explaining that it would drive out the truth soon enough. But the mention of the possibility of a conspiracy—one that would point a finger directly at them? Well, that pushed the Clee girls right over the edge. So much so that they called you."

"Speaking of, I need to dump this uniform somewhere."

"Not yet," Jana says, stopping in her tracks and forcing Otto to stop, too. "I want to push one more button."

"What's that?"

"You stole a pair of keys along with that uniform, right?"

CHAPTER 8

JANA (THE ACTOR)

OH, THE LOOK ON their faces, my dear Matthew.

I'm not sure what shocked them more—the fact that I was sitting in their dorm room, their precious inner sanctum, or that a campus security guard was lounging on Hannah's bed, feet up, lazily thumbing through a copy of *Vogue*.

"You..." Hannah shouts, as if she's about to have a seizure, "you can't be in here!"

Poor Brooke, meanwhile, has turned as pale as nonfat milk. She stands behind her sister, hoping that her sibling's sheer rage will act as a force field.

"I know what you both did," I tell them calmly, "and I want you to know that you're not going to get away with it."

This is a lie, of course—I don't know their role in this conspiracy quite yet. But perhaps pushing this final button will reveal something.

It's just like improv. If you sense an opening, you take it and see where it leads.

But like any decent actor, I know when to stop pushing and make my exit. I'm sensing Hannah is headed toward a total meltdown and will do something rash once she gets there. I nod at Otto, who grumbles a bit about climbing back out of bed—I think he would have kept reading there all afternoon if I'd let him.

This time, Hannah knows better than to summon another security guard…*because they might be in on it, too!* The cell phone in her hand—which she ordinarily uses to overcome any small impediment to her otherwise perfect life—can't help her now. Daddy's too far away, *and there was a security guard lying in her bed!*

"Cock-a-doodle-doo," I whisper as we pass by.

Suddenly, this trip to snowy Concord isn't so unpleasant after all.

CHAPTER 9

THEO (THE TRADER)

I CAN SMELL PAOLO'S room even before I pick the lock and slip inside. Damn, this kid uses a lot of cologne. It's so thick in the air, I practically have to wave my hand around so I can see.

For a guy in hiding, he's already made a mess of this squalid little dump. Skinny jeans and shiny shirts and over-sized grooming products and sticky beer bottles and, weirdly, random pieces from board games are scattered all over the place. Guess he likes to lure his underage prey back to his place for drinking and a few rounds of *Sorry!* (And, boy, will they be.)

With all of this chaos, I have my work cut out for me. I only have a few minutes before Paolo returns, and the sting will be over if he catches me in here.

There are two items on my must-find list.

I trailed Paolo (and our money) back from the beach bar to this room. I knew he didn't need time to "think things over." No, Paolo wanted to take the good faith money and book passage off this island immediately. Rio would be my guess.

But he wouldn't book a flight online (too easily traced). He'd need to book something in person. And if he's doing that, he wouldn't be foolish enough to bring the $25,000 in cash with him. He'd stash it somewhere in this dump for safekeeping.

So I'm standing here now thinking: *I'm a playboy lifeguard about to go on the run. Where do I hide my windfall?*

Now, I knew a lot of guys back at Harvard who did some small-time dealing from their dorm rooms. They needed places to hide their product and their cash. As a work-study/ scholarship kid who occasionally found himself a little short, I got to know those dealers and their hiding places very well. (Hey, I only stole from criminals. It didn't make me a criminal; it made me friggin' *Robin Hood*.)

The usual places—inside an envelope taped to the back of the toilet, inside an aspirin bottle, taped to the bottom of a dresser drawer—wouldn't work with twenty-five large. Paolo needed to hide those thick stacks somewhere clever in a hurry.

The fridge—no. Freezer—no. Drawers—no. Luggage— no. Beneath a pile of clothes that reek of cheap cologne—no.

Come on, where, *where,* Paolo?

The best hiding places are often in plain sight. And when I step over a dented and scuffed board game box, I realize that Paolo knew this, too.

I check one game—nothing. Another—nothing. But the third box feels heavy. I lift the lid and check under the little cardboard insert that keeps the cards and tokens and whatnot in place. And yep, there it is.

Our "good faith" money.

You've got some brains after all, Mr. Playboy Lifeguard.

I shove the money into my jacket pockets, knowing that without it, Paolo will be staying put for the foreseeable future. Now, the other thing on my must-find list.

The clothes he was wearing the night Paige Ryerson disappeared.

From the looks of this place, our man's not much for the Laundromat or dry cleaner's. So they must be here somewhere.

My reference is a photo posted on social media from the night of the party. The light wasn't very good, so I can't tell if I'm looking for an off-white or a light-blue button-down shirt. But the swimming trunks are unmistakable: pink, with silver tarpons all over them. As if to subliminally tell the ladies that he's a real catch?

After a few minutes of methodical searching, I start to wonder if Paolo has been as clever about his garments as he was with the good faith money. Maybe he thought ahead and threw them away or had them destroyed....

I hear footsteps in the hall. Time's up.

CHAPTER 10

QUINN

MATTHEW QUINN APPROACHES THE reception desk, where he finds a bored security guard who's making $13.50 an hour to protect a billion-dollar skyscraper.

The guard glances at Quinn's forged ID card, then up at Quinn's face. He sees exactly what Quinn wants him to see— a white guy in his early forties, tired eyes, not exactly looking forward to a long day of hanging from a harness while he squeegees the grime off a pane of glass thirty stories above the pavement.

The guard nods. Quinn walks through.

He heads to the service elevators, because right now he's dressed like one of the service people nobody notices. A few hours ago Quinn scoped out a blind spot not covered by security cameras and studied its dimensions until he could imagine them as clearly as his own living room.

He slips into that blind spot and begins to shed his khaki skin, walking as he transforms, swiftly and expertly. The khaki uniform goes into a black satchel that's already strapped across his torso. It's a Montblanc—most businessmen around here carry them or something just like them. The messy hair beneath his work cap is smoothed and parted neatly into a fashionable rakish look. Quinn's posture changes from that of a slight, exhausted workingman to a confident, broad-shouldered businessman.

This takes all of seven seconds, tops. Quinn's moves are as polished as a stage magician's. Truth is, Quinn doesn't even think about any of it very much at this point. His movements are hardwired into his nervous system.

On the other side of the blind spot, Quinn emerges as a completely different man—a handsome up-and-comer who's got a very nice suit and even nicer bag and probably a spectacular dinner reservation somewhere this evening. He also looks nothing like the real Matthew Quinn.

Up on the thirty-sixth floor, the office suites of Paul Clee & Partners are modern and hip. There's a falling-water display in the lobby, which is both pleasing to the eye and the source of a comforting white noise that practically forces visitors to keep their voices hushed and respectful, as if they were in church.

Somewhere down the hall Paul Clee himself is expecting Quinn, but Quinn is not going to see him.

Not yet.

He glides past the receptionist, who's actually not a receptionist but a college intern filling in during the lunch break, which is why he chose this particular time to meet. The intern has only been here a week, so employee faces are still a little fuzzy. Quinn nods confidently and waves as if he works here; the intern nods and thinks, *Crap, I should know that guy's name, but I can't remember....*

Quinn places himself in the conference room and dials Paul Clee's extension.

"Mr. Clee? This is Matthew Quinn."

"Where are you...wait—are you calling from our conference room?"

Quinn hangs up and waits. He learned a long time ago to keep his movements secret. To disguise his true identity. A person like Paul Clee may present himself as a potential client only to lure Quinn into a death trap. Better to keep them guessing at all times.

Clee appears in the doorway a few seconds later. "How did you get in here?"

"Good afternoon, Mr. Clee. Have a seat."

Mr. Clee, to his credit, does. "I wasn't sure you would ever respond to my message. Friends told me you and your team were...picky."

"Why reach out to us in the first place?"

"I was worried for Hannah and Brooke—they're still in shock over the whole thing. And I was extremely fond of Paige. We just want to know what happened to her."

"So does the FBI," Quinn says.

"And they seem to be dragging their feet. Look, I'm not a man who's used to waiting. If you want something done, you hire the best and get it done."

Quinn stares at Clee. No visible emotion on his face, no reaction to the ham-handed attempt at flattery.

"Well?" Clee asks after a few uncomfortable seconds. "Are you going to take the case or not?"

"Yes. My team is already engaged."

"Hey, that's great!" he says, clapping his manicured hands

together. "But, uh, we haven't discussed terms or anything. How does this work?"

"We'll take care of the details later. If you couldn't afford our services, you would have never heard from me. But I am curious about one thing, Mr. Clee."

"What's that?"

"Why were you so fond of Paige? I mean, you've never actually met her."

Clee stiffens. "She is a close friend of my girls, Mr. Quinn. They're absolutely heartbroken. What father wouldn't want to do everything possible to get to the bottom of this tragedy?"

CHAPTER 11

KATE (THE SOLDIER)

MATT, THINGS ARE MOVING fast and I'm 95 percent certain that Jamie Halsey, the trust fund kid with the yacht, killed Paige Ryerson. And if that 5 percent chance is right and he didn't do it—I'll bet anything he knows who did.

I caught up with Halsey's Squadron 60 yacht (named *Hostile Wake-Over*) at the El Conquistador Marina in Puerto Rico. Halsey thought he was being clever by altering his itinerary at the last minute, slipping down to PR instead of following the reservations his corporation had filed with various marinas in the Bahamas.

But I don't track marina reservations. I track boats directly by GPS transponder. Easy enough to do when you pick up the right piece of software on the dark web.

As we discussed, my forged State Department credentials were enough to gain me complete access to the hotel and its marina. When I arrived, Halsey's yacht was in the middle of the docking process, and his suite was still being prepared. So I headed in to the 35-slip marina to welcome him personally.

"Hey, I'm looking for Jamie," I said, with the brightest smile I could muster. As if I was just a girl, looking for a cute boy I'd met. "I thought I'd surprise him."

But the crew wasn't having any of it. Clearly, they were used to "girls" stopping by for their boss.

"He in the Bahamas," one of them mumbled.

I laughed. "Bahamas, huh? Well, then he's going to miss one hell of a time in room 223, where I'll be waiting for him. In bed."

The crew glanced at each other, for a moment wondering if I was telling the truth. Room 223 was indeed where Halsey would be checking in—the front desk confirmed it for me five minutes ago. And the boss . . . well, this probably sounded like something the boss would do.

I was about to take advantage of the confusion and push my way past the crew to look for the little punk when I saw a blurry flutter out of the corner of my eye. Damnit! Fifty feet away, Jamie Halsey was leaping from the boat to the dock and running like hell. The pedigree of my credentials didn't matter; somebody at the El Conquistador must have tipped him off.

A thick hand grabbed my upper arm at the same moment I started to bolt down the dock. I turned to look at the crew member who'd dared to touch me.

"You *really* don't want to do that," I said, by way of fair warning.

"You leave Mr. Halsey alone, he's got enough lady trouble."

Lady trouble, huh? I thought.

I'll admit it, and I apologize in advance—but the crew really ticked me off.

So maybe I twisted their arms a little harder than I should have, hit those nerve bundles with a little more force than necessary. Once they saw that I was not some silly girl, they started attacking back with serious intent. Hands tried to crush my windpipe. Fists tried hard to shatter the bones in my face.

Within thirty seconds, however, all three of them were writhing around on the deck of the yacht and I was in full pursuit of Halsey.

The kid had hopped on one of the funiculars, which was carrying him up the side of the steep hill to the main hotel. There was a second funicular, but it was still crawling down the side of the hill and wouldn't reach me for another two and a half years.

So I did the only thing I could—chased after the funicular on foot.

Hell, Matt, you and I have both hauled ass through more treacherous terrain in the army. So after a minute of huffing it I had caught up with the tram. You should have seen the look on the kid's face when I pried open the door and leaped into the car with him.

But that was nothing compared to the way his features shifted when I slammed him to the floor, hard enough to make his teeth chatter.

"Hi, Jamie," I said, catching my breath. "Got a minute to talk?"

CHAPTER 12

KATE (continued)

"I WANT A LAWYER," the kid said.

They always say that, don't they, Matt?

"Good for you," I told him. "But I'm not a cop. And a lawyer wouldn't do anything other than burn through that fat trust fund one billable hour at a time."

I think I used too many words for one sentence, because the brat looked up at me with big, blue, uncomprehending eyes. I'm sure his father told him from the time he was a little boy: *If you're ever in trouble, Daddy will send the best lawyers in the world to help you.*

"You . . . you can't do this!"

I had Halsey right where I wanted him, of course. Trapped, with no way out. Which was the right moment to throw him a little lifeline.

"Come on, get up," I said. "I'm not here to arrest you. I'm just here with some information you might find useful."

The brat relaxed a little, now that I was taking handcuffs and a perp walk off the table. "What kind of information?"

The funicular came to a stop. We disembarked and Halsey

tottered along next to me like a reluctant puppy. We found two cushioned chairs in an empty cabana. I told him where to sit. He sat. I took the opposite chair and stared at him.

"So . . . what is it?"

I continued to stare at him.

"You said, uh, that you had some, uh, information for me."

As you know, most people can't stand a long silence. They are very eager to fill the void. And the brat did not disappoint.

"Look, I know you're here about that girl."

"What girl would that be?"

"What's her name, Paige something. I'm telling you, I barely even talked to her. She came with a couple of chicks—and I didn't know them, either. Somehow word spreads about a boat, and suddenly the whole friggin' island shows up, you know? But anyway, I definitely saw her leave with her friends. So whatever happened to her didn't happen on my boat. It's not my problem."

I asked Halsey, "Are you familiar with the term *bouquet of death?*"

He blinked. "What?"

"It refers to the chemical by-products of decomposition that only cadaver dogs can detect. Did you know that the nose of a German shepherd, for instance, contains 200 million receptor cells, while human beings have barely a tenth of that?"

"Lady, I don't know why the hell you're telling me this."

"There's also ground-penetrating radar, and chemical analyses of soil and air samples. There's even this cutting-edge method involving tubes and air pockets that can detect a corpse under a concrete slab. Isn't that incredible?"

Halsey stood up to leave. "I don't have to listen to this."

I grabbed his wrist and squeezed. He winced at the sudden pain radiating up his arm.

"Ow!"

"What I'm saying is that it's only a matter of a day, maybe even a few hours, before they find Paige Ryerson's body."

"So what? I told you, that has nothing to do with me."

"I'm also hearing that there is concrete evidence linking you to her death."

"Evidence? Of what?"

My eyes bored into his. "I want you to think about this carefully, Jamie, and answer me honestly. Your freedom may depend on it. Are you sure there's nothing that would link you to this girl?"

Halsey's eyes went up and to the right. Which—as you know, Matt—is a surefire tell that he's accessing visual memories. Something he saw.

"Yeah," he said. "I'm sure. Now let me go."

I released my grip on his wrist. As Halsey rubbed it, some of the arrogance returned to his face. He was thinking he was back in charge again. A brat like him couldn't stand the idea of being bossed around by a "chick" like me.

"When I tell my father what just happened, he's going to go nuclear on you."

I smiled. "Who do you think sent me, dumbass?"

Halsey's jaw popped open. I just blew his mind. "Wh-what?"

"Listen to me, Jamie. For your own good. I know that what happened was probably an accident, and it would be very smart if you told the truth now. Things will go a lot easier on you. If you don't, and they pull that poor girl's body out of the sand...well, there's nothing even I can do for you. And let me tell you, if they sent *me,* it means your daddy pulled strings at the highest of levels."

Matt, the look on his face at that very moment is what convinced me. This little brat did it. Or at the very least, knows what happened to Paige.

CHAPTER 13

KATE (continued)

AFTER LEAVING HALSEY QUIVERING in his Armani boxer briefs, I went looking for his head employee—Captain Jacob Kurtz. Maybe he'd spill a detail or two that would cement the case against his employer.

Didn't take long to track him down. I selected the most ridiculous bar in the vicinity and listened for the sound of a man bragging. I elbowed my way through a force field of drunk women until I finally reached the bar, where Kurtz was sipping fruit juice and rum cocktails and holding court.

What is it about women and certain uniforms, Quinn? Put somebody from our old army unit in that same bar and I guarantee you he'd be drinking alone, unless there were other soldiers present.

But Kurtz? I had to fight to get anywhere near him. Yet all I saw was some overtanned blowhard in a yacht captain's uniform—complete with his white cap tilted to one side, like he was going to be performing with Toni Tennille later that evening.

He noticed me right away, though. At first I thought it was

because he sensed I wasn't like the other women looking for a little vacation fling.

"You, young lady, embarrassed the hell out of my crew," he said. "I think we ran out of ice tending to their bumps and bruises."

"Where were you, Mr. Kurtz?" I asked. "Kind of wish you'd been part of the action."

"Belowdecks. I'm a lover, not a fighter. A seafarer, not a war-wager."

Oh, boy. I decided to get to the point or we could be here all night.

"But are you a killer, Mr. Kurtz?"

The captain smiled. Genuine amusement lighting up his eyes. "Oh, I like you. I had no idea government agents could be so much fun. Come, let's go somewhere a little more private."

As Kurtz led me to a half-circle booth in the corner of the bar, I thought about the half-dozen ways I could incapacitate him if he tried anything. Kurtz offered me a drink. I got to the point.

"I'm here to give you a heads-up. Paige Ryerson's body is only a few hours away from being discovered. If you want to jump off your boss's sinking ship, now's the time to do it."

"But the yacht is completely fine, Miss...? Or is that Mrs.? I'll be honest, it doesn't matter to me either way. Marriage is just a piece of paper."

"If that body comes up, and it has your forensics anywhere near it, it'll be too late to help you."

Kurtz smiled. "I can think of some ways you can help me, Kate. Some very creative ways."

"So you know my name. Your boss called you."

The flirtation drained from his face quickly, as if I was suddenly boring him. "Yeah, I know all about your supposed string-pulling on behalf of the kid's old man. Junior may have believed you, but you can't kid a world-class kidder, kiddo."

As I slid closer to Kurtz in the booth he flinched slightly. He probably thought he covered it up quick enough, but I saw it. Perhaps he was worried I was about to dish out some of the same punishment his crew had received.

Instead, I touched Kurtz's face lightly and looked up into his eyes. Taking a page right out of the Jana Rose playbook.

"How did it feel to dance with someone one minute," I said softly, "then help bury her dead body the next?"

"I wouldn't know," Kurtz said, refusing to break eye contact. "From what I heard around the island before we left, the girl is still alive."

CHAPTER 14

OTTO (THE CON ARTIST)

THE FIRST THING OTTO does when he lands at Providenciales International Airport is look for a place to eat.

The in-flight meal was garbage. So he stops at a place called Gilley's Cafe and wolfs down a double order of conch fritters and a lobster salad sandwich, then washes all of that down with two bottles of Turk's Head Amber.

The second thing Otto does is hop a free resort shuttle to the beach, even though he hasn't booked a room at the resort painted on the side of the vehicle. Matthew Quinn gives all of his operatives a generous expense account, but old habits die hard. Back in his grifter days, Otto took special pride in never paying for transportation. Someone's always looking to give you a lift. And just as often, a place to crash. Only suckers paid for cabs or Uber—and on top of that paid a tip. Are people crazy?

The third thing Otto does is get into character.

He stares at the photo of Paige Ryerson. No; not just Paige Ryerson. This is *his* little sister. Paige. Only eighteen years old. Sweetest girl in the world. Big Brother Otto would always look out for her. But that would change when she went off to private school in New Hampshire. Big Brother wasn't around to protect her anymore. And now look what happened.

Otto stares at the photo for so long that he begins to believe Paige *is* his baby sister. He actually feels the grief as his eyes water and his cheeks burn with rage.

I'm not leaving this island until I know what happened to her.

Only then does he consider himself ready to mix among the locals, photo in hand.

"Have you seen my sister? Her name is Paige Ryerson, and she's gone missing. Please help me find my sister!"

Otto focuses his efforts on the areas Paige visited during her short time here last week. Her hotel, the site of the beach party, the marina. Some people blow him off without looking at his face or the photo in his trembling hand. That's fine; they're not potential witnesses anyway. By now everybody on these islands has surely heard or read about the Case of the Missing American Girl. Those who don't give the photo or name a second glance are either self-absorbed or new arrivals.

"Please help me find my sister!"

The ones who do pause fall into two groups. The vast majority are people who have heard about the case and see the tearful anguish in Otto's eyes but truly know nothing beyond what they've seen on TV or read online. Some try to chat him up a little for some inside dirt.

"No, I haven't seen her . . . but is it true that she didn't drink at all before coming here to the island?"

"I'm sorry, I have no idea where she might be. How are your poor parents dealing with this nightmare?"

At which point Otto takes his grief into overdrive and

suddenly becomes too choked up to possibly continue this conversation.

But a small group—a very small group—claim to have seen the girl the day of her disappearance. For these individuals, Otto gives his complete and rapt attention, gently pressing them for more details. A few are clearly lying, reciting details they saw in the media. Others, however, sound like they're telling the truth.

"She looked like she was having so much fun. I still can't believe what happened!"

"I was on that boat, too. There was a lot of heavy drinking going on. I was so hungover the next day, it's not even funny...."

"I saw her and that cop making out. My first thought was, uh, totally gross. But later I started to think about it, and wonder if he had something to do with it. What am I supposed to do, though? Report a cop to the cops? No way."

And then come three eyewitness reports that rock Otto to his core. (And he's about as jaded as they come.) Otto can write off the first instance as a case of mistaken identity. Maybe even the second, because false sightings happen all the time. But a third?

"I'm telling you, man, those reporters have been going down the wrong path. Your sister is still alive! I saw her yesterday! I was over in this little town about twenty minutes away, and I swear, it was her. I even called the cops, but they didn't believe me."

Could it be possible? Matthew Quinn is a genius and all— probably the most impressive mind Otto has ever encountered. But maybe Quinn had it wrong. Maybe the girl wasn't buried in the sand somewhere.

Maybe she was hiding.

CHAPTER 15

THEO (THE TRADER)

WITH PAOLO STUCK ON the island (since he lost his getaway dough), I turn my attention to the next creep on the list: Nigel James, the islander cop.

Now, you have to understand something about me: I *love* messing with police. I consider it a form of karmic payback. The uniforms who arrested me all those years back took a little too much pleasure in snapping the metal cuffs around my wrists and slamming me into the nearest wall.

I was arrested on suspicion of insider trading, for Pete's sake (not that I'm admitting any wrongdoing). It's not like I was the Zodiac Killer. The violence and condescension were uncalled for.

So, yeah, I admit... I've been looking for excuses to return the favor ever since.

"Detective James! I've been looking all over for you."

Nigel James looks at me through narrowed eyes. "Who are you?"

"Ted Selznick, special investigator with the New Hampshire

State Police. While I'm sad to be down here, given the circumstances, I've gotta say it's nice to be away from all that snow for a while."

But Detective James does not want to take part in a conversation about the lousy weather in New Hampshire, or beautiful sun down here on the islands. He's all business in his lightweight suitcoat, jeans, white Oxford, loafers, and very expensive tie. Hard to believe he's here alone. The man is a dark-skinned god, impossibly handsome, and has the muscles of a man who spends more time in a gym than he does sleeping.

"What can I do for you, Mr. Selznick?"

"That's Trooper Specialist Selznick, technically, but let's not get bogged down over titles. Is there somewhere quiet we can talk?"

Mind you, James and I were standing on a fairly empty stretch of beach. Before I approached him, he was sitting on a wicker lounge chair, staring at the ocean, eating seafood salad out of a plastic container. We had all the privacy you could want. But I wanted to see if James was spending his lunch hour here for a specific reason.

"We can talk here. May I see some identification, Special Trooper Selznick?"

Eh, close enough. But I have the feeling James is mangling it on purpose. He seems like the type who pays close attention to the details.

I flip open the leather badge holder with the state ID. I'm sure James has been interviewed by more than a few federal agents over the past few days. I want to present myself as someone from an agency he wouldn't be familiar with.

"I understand you were the last person to see Paige Ryerson alive."

"As I've told countless others, Trooper Selznick, I don't know if that's true. I did meet Ms. Ryerson late Friday evening, but when we parted she was headed back to the party to join her friends. I offered to escort her, but she refused my assistance."

"And you're not the type to force yourself on a lady," I say.

James just stares up at me. I was throwing a left jab, and he took it like a pro. No reaction whatsoever.

So I pull up another wicker lounge chair and sit down. I'm facing the ocean, just like James, and pretending to admire the view.

"Damn, this is pretty spectacular," I say. "I can understand why you'd want to take your lunch breaks here."

"And I'm afraid I must return to duty," he says, then licks his fork clean.

"Hold on, Detective. I need to clear up a few minor details, and I was hoping you could help me."

James snaps the lid shut over his half-eaten salad. "Go on."

I look around, pretending like I'm a tourist getting his bearings. "Okay, so the infamous yacht party was over that way," I say, pointing to the right.

James nods. "Our marina is in that direction, correct."

"And," I say, turning my head back and forth, "if I'm not mistaken, the girls were at a beach party over there." I point to the left.

"Correct."

"So...when Paige left your company, she must have wandered down this very same stretch of beach, am I right? And if someone were to have murdered her, this would have been a very convenient place to bury her body."

James stares at me with eyes that have transformed into red-hot daggers. "Good afternoon, Mr. Selznick," he says, standing up.

Ooh, we're back to mister now. I have upset the poor detective.

"I think I know what happened, Detective. And I don't blame you. She was drunk and things got out of hand. You were just trying to calm her down, but the more you tried, the more she freaked out, and...well, you're the kind of guy who doesn't know his own strength."

Now James was walking away. But upon hearing that last bit, he turns around to face me. I get the distinct feeling he'd like to bury *me* in the sand.

"We are both policemen, Mr. Selznick, trained in the same techniques. Do you really think your wild conjectures will spark some sort of reaction out of me?"

"No," I say. "But I do think you're nervous about the idea of men with shovels down on this beach, which is why you camp out here every chance you get. And let me tell you, as a fellow comrade in law enforcement—they're coming. Somebody very important would like closure, and they're willing to pay as much as it takes to get it."

CHAPTER 16

THEO (continued)

"ARE YOU FORMALLY ACCUSING me of a crime, Mr. Selznick?" James asks.

"No, no, of course not," I say, backing off like I'm a pipsqueak who's just taken a cheap shot at the heavyweight champion of the world and needs to retreat to the safety of his own corner.

That seems to satisfy him. Until I follow up with a right hook.

"But, Detective, I *know* you were involved in Paige Ryerson's murder. Either you did it yourself, or you covered up evidence to protect the real killer. And the evidence is going to surface very soon. You're going to want to hire a top-drawer criminal defense lawyer or start running."

Finally...*finally*...that cool, finely muscled exterior begins to crack. Exactly what I've been waiting for.

"I could have you arrested," James snarls. "You're out of line, and way out of your jurisdiction, Selznick."

I hold out my wrists. "Oh, that would be great. Do it! I could use a vacation. Better a nice, warm jail cell than a cold and bitter trooper station, believe me."

"Are you mocking me?"

"No! I *want* you to arrest me, Detective. Even better, should I try and resist? Would that make it more fun for you? Or do you only get your jollies when it's a young girl struggling for her life?"

Now James's thoughts are as clear as a two-story neon sign: I VERY MUCH WANT TO RIP OFF YOUR HEAD AND PLACEKICK IT INTO THE SEA.

And for a minute, I think he's actually going to do it. I sit there mentally plotting some countermoves in case this cop decides to pounce on me. I would never forgive myself if the grand adventure that is my life were to come to a sudden end in a stupid wicker chair.

But James recovers his senses, takes a deep breath, and then turns his back on me. He walks away—away from the surf. I stay seated but turn around and watch him carefully. *You're going to do it, aren't you? You're not going to be able to resist. The weight of it is too much.*

And then he does—he glances back one last time.

Not at me.

But at the sandy beach, where I'm now certain we're going to find Paige Ryerson's body very soon.

When James is gone, I call Quinn to update him on everything.

"Mark my words," I say, "it's the cop."

"Just last night you were convinced it was the lifeguard," Quinn replies.

"Well, now I'm telling you it's Nigel the cop. Maybe the lifeguard was involved. Maybe they're partnered up on it. But the cop is definitely guilty. Not only was he the last person to

see Paige alive, but he was staring at the sand like he expected
her to come crawling up out of her own grave to point an
accusing finger at him. He's gonna crack, Quinn. And I want
to be there when he does."

"I'm glad you're so certain."

I listen for a few more seconds, waiting for something.
Anything. Praise? A complaint? Something I missed, maybe?
Quinn likes to watch you weave a beautiful tapestry and then
yank it out from under your feet with a single question.

But then I hear something weird. Like an echo. Crashing
surf behind me, but also crashing surf coming from over the
cell phone connection.

"Quinn...uh, where *are* you?"

CHAPTER 17

QUINN

AS MATTHEW QUINN RAISES his hand, a waiter, clad in shorts, approaches. Quinn wordlessly gestures down to a pair of empty glasses with moisture beaded on the sides. Then he makes a peace sign. The waiter nods and whisks away the empties.

"I'll see you this evening, Theo," Quinn says, then disconnects the call and turns to face Jana. "I presumed you wanted another cocktail?"

"As if you read my mind."

"Good."

"This is much better than New Hampshire," she says with a slight purr in her voice. "Apology accepted."

"I missed the part where I said I was sorry."

"Don't worry, Matthew, dear. It's understood."

They're sprawled out on reclining chairs right on the beach, mere yards from the crashing surf. Quinn and Jana flew down to Turks and Caicos separately. They booked rooms in hotels a mile apart. They weren't supposed to see each other, in fact, until this evening at six, when all of the Stingrays were gathering in person to discuss strategy.

But then Jana texted: Meet me for a quick drink?

Ordinarily, Quinn prefers to spend his time in a dimly lit climate-controlled room with white noise or classical music playing in the background as he considers the clues, eye-witness accounts, and narrative elements of the case at hand.

But then Quinn read those six words again and thought about Jana's playful smile as she thumbed them into her cell. So he replied: Cocktails on the beach? Because why not combine some relaxed case meditation with a little daytime drinking?

Drinking for Jana, that is. Quinn never imbibes when he's in the middle of a case. She doesn't know that Quinn pulled the bartender aside when they first arrived at the beachfront cafe and instructed him to mix proper cocktails for the lady, virgins for himself. She was the type who could only relax when she thought everyone else around her was relaxing, too.

"Let's go for a swim," she says suddenly, gently nudging him in the ribs.

"But we have drinks on the way."

"You mean you'd rather sit around and sip juice than jump waves with me? I know you never drink on a case. Which is why I asked the bartender to serve us both virgins."

"Hmmm. So we're paying full price for fruit juice."

"Appears that way. I knew that if you thought I was relaxing you'd take it easy, too, for a change. So come on, my love. Last one to the beach pays for the wildly expensive fruit juice!"

Naturally, Jana beats him to the crashing waves. Quinn

dives in after her, but she's a fraction of a second ahead of him. He sucks down foaming surf as he falls, then comes up laughing, despite himself. She leaps over a wave. The same wave smashes into Quinn, nearly knocking him off his feet. She laughs. Only she can do this to him. Take him back to the giddiness of being twelve years old. Even though twelve was a particularly rough year for Quinn.

In carefree moments like these, Quinn can be fooled into thinking that he and Jana could have a life together. What more do you need than sand, water, laughter, and expensive fruit juice? She soothes the turmoil in his soul like no one else alive.

But the effect is temporary. Jana is a brilliant actor, but she can only keep up the facade for so long. They tried it once. Living together. It was destined for failure, because whenever Quinn's obsessed with a case, he has one default setting: *brood*. At first Jana played the role of the supportive partner, letting Quinn have his space. But she quickly tired of it, because it turned out that Quinn needed his space almost all of the time. Actors, like most people, need someone else in the scene.

Dripping wet, Quinn and Jana make their way across the hot sand to their chairs. Part of Quinn wishes he could remain in the playful state, but it never lasts longer than a few minutes. Something always taps him on the shoulder and reminds him of the people who need him. Like the schoolgirl who may be somewhere along this beach, buried under the sand.

Crying out to him.

"Look at this, our fruit juice is waiting for us," Jana says.

"We'd better drink up," Quinn says. "We have a lot of work to do this evening."

Jana reaches over, takes his hand. "Not quite yet. We have some time."

At first Quinn tenses at her touch, but then he remembers her sweet laughter in the water. She's right. There's some time. He squeezes her fingers gently.

CHAPTER 18

THE STINGRAYS

"LET'S GET TO WORK."

There's no omelet bar this time, even though Quinn has rented a penthouse suite with a well-stocked kitchen. He believes in feeding his operatives at the beginning of a case, then celebrating with them at the closing. But now, in the thick of things, it's all about take-out food (jerk pork tenderloin and curried shrimp from Coco Bistro), along with coffee and adrenaline.

"Theo, you're up," Quinn continues. "Tell us what you've got."

Theo Selznick stirs his heaping bowl of shrimp and rice. "I'm thinking Paolo Salese and Nigel James are working together to cover this up."

"The playboy lifeguard and the suave cop?" Jana asks.

"Both clearly know something. Paolo took our bait money with a promise to lead me to the burial site. And as for Nigel James, I'm pretty sure he's our doer. We had a little talk earlier today and I started pushing buttons. I really thought he was going to try and do me."

Through a mouthful of jerk pork, Otto mutters, "We're not that lucky."

"Why would James suddenly snap and kill a tourist?" Kate asks. "I'm sure Paige isn't the first pretty schoolgirl he's encountered on this island."

"This cop is extremely vain. I could see him playing the role of the good guy, offering a ride home, and then putting the moves on her. Only when Paige doesn't play along, Nigel gets rough."

"And you think Paolo the lifeguard saw it?" Jana asks. At the same time, her cell phone vibrates. She looks down at the screen and grins.

"No doubt," Theo replies. "Maybe the lifeguard was lovestruck and followed her around all night. Saw something he wasn't supposed to see."

Kate finishes her mouthful of curried shrimp. "I don't know. I'm liking Jamie Halsey for this. At first he denied everything, no doubt thinking that Daddy's lawyers would make everything all right. But when I convinced him that Daddy had in fact sent me to help him, he got very worried."

"Yeah, but witnesses saw Paige leave the boat and then meet up with Nigel James on the beach," Theo says. "What, did Halsey and Kurtz wait an hour, then sneak around and ambush her right there on the surf?"

"Then again, the Clee girls thought Halsey was to blame," Jana says. "Brooke Clee said something about protecting a trust fund jerk. She also seemed to think that Paige was still alive and island-hopping with her new, rich friend."

There's a sudden muffled sound that startles the others. They turn to see Otto, his mouth chewing on a sizable piece of jerk pork. He holds up a finger, *hang on a sec*. The group waits, resisting the urge to roll their eyes.

After a small eternity, Otto swallows his food and then speaks. "Paige Ryerson is still alive. I have proof."

CHAPTER 19

THE STINGRAYS (continued)

"SO YOU JUST LET us go on and on?" Kate asks. "Why didn't you say something earlier?"

"I was hungry," Otto says.

Kate's eyes narrow to a kind of laser-beam focus. *Are you jerking us around or what?* Otto is the one team member she knows the least, and that worries her. Theo looks angry, too—and those two shared a jail cell for a while. Jana, meanwhile, shakes her head and smiles softly, which is what she always does when she's frustrated and doesn't want it to show. She types something on her cell phone.

"Hey," Otto says when he sees the look on his teammates' faces, "you guys seemed so excited about all of the hard work you've been doing. I didn't want to interrupt."

Quinn says, "Let's hear your proof, Otto."

"Okay. So I spent most of the day impersonating Paige's older brother. She doesn't have one, but whatever. Most people don't know that. I wanted to see if anybody else had eyes on her while she was here. And I found three people who saw Paige Ryerson on three different occasions on three different parts of the island. And this was over the weekend, after the Clee girl first reported her as a missing person."

"Why didn't they call the police?" Kate asks.

"They told me they did but never heard anything in response," Otto says.

Theo frowns. "Who are these witnesses, anyway?"

Otto points at Quinn's laptop. "I did some quick background checks on all three, and they're solid citizens. I uploaded it to your secure folder, Matthew. You can do your deep web magic from there, but I'd be shocked if they were anything but legit."

They all knew that Matthew Quinn was an expert at surfing the so-called deep web, the murky underbelly of the internet that lies beyond search engines and passwords. It is the kind of digital underworld that takes a skilled navigator to operate.

"I'll check them out," Quinn says. "What did the witnesses say Paige was doing?"

"They all said she looked like she was feeling no pain—either tipsy or maybe even a little stoned. This is, after all, the tropics, man."

"And somehow this drunk or possibly stoned girl was able to evade an island-wide search for her?" Kate asks. "Sorry, I'm not buying it."

"Why would these people lie?" Otto asks. "It's not as if they came forward with this information on their own. If I hadn't gone digging, chances are they wouldn't have told another soul."

Theo hurls his fork into the sink like a petulant child. "So what I'm hearing is that everybody's guilty, or nobody's guilty, because our so-called victim might be off on a bender somewhere."

"So where does this leave us?" Jana asks. "And what do we do next?"

"For one thing, we don't take our frustrations out on innocent cutlery," Quinn says, cocking an eye at Theo. "This also means that the next phase of our investigation will require great care. Whether Paige is dead or alive, I believe we're dealing with a conspiracy—not the passionate mistake of a single perpetrator. And if they're smart enough to form a conspiracy that's eluded the feds, they're smart enough not to get caught. The clock is ticking. Our ruses may have kept the suspects close at hand, but that won't last forever."

"I guess this means no dessert," Otto says.

Jana is the first to rise, straightening her cocktail dress with a few tidy, precise movements. "I don't know about the rest of you, but I'm dying for a drink."

CHAPTER 20

JANA (THE ACTOR)

I PROMISE YOU, MY dear Matthew, my desire for a cocktail has nothing to do with our wonderful afternoon at the beach sipping overpriced kiddie juice.

But like you said, the clock *is* ticking, and I don't want to let certain opportunities slip away.

As predicted, Jamie Halsey decided to return to Turks and Caicos along with Captain Kurtz. Before our 6:00 p.m. meeting with the rest of the group, I paid a visit to the marina and recruited a couple of confidential informants who were more than happy to text me when the *Hostile Wake-Over* made an appearance. Amazing, the information you can glean with nothing more than a crisp hundred-dollar bill and a knowing smile.

One of my informants texted in the middle of our group meeting with a bonus piece of news: Jamie Halsey was apparently headed straight to his favorite watering hole, the Infiniti Bar at the Grace Bay Club.

The name is not misleading. The main feature of this bar is a ninety-foot stretch of black granite that runs all the way out to the water. Not quite infinity but close enough, I suppose. I weave around the well-heeled travelers snacking on ceviche and sipping $18 cocktails until I find Halsey. He's doing shots of Grey Goose and flirting—badly—with a pair of glistening young women who are either twins or friends who aspire to look exactly alike.

I hate to see a young man flirting badly. I decide to show him how it's done.

You know how I flirt, my dear Matthew. I'm irresistible.

Especially when I do nothing except order a drink and look like I have the kinds of problems that only a rich young man can solve.

"Hey, what's going on?"

This is his opening gambit. *Snooze.*

I say nothing but give him the tiniest of openings—a brief glance, followed by a facial expression that's somewhere between *You're Going to Disappoint Me, Dear Boy* and *I Might Be Bored Enough to Let You Try*.

"This your first time here at the Infiniti? Crazy, right? I just love the ocean breeze you get out here. Best bar on the island."

"It is nice," I allow.

"I'm going to buy you a drink," he says, emboldened.

Notice there's not even a question. It's a bald statement of fact. He's going to buy me a drink. And presumably this is going to mean I owe him something.

The glitter twins long forgotten, Halsey lowers himself into the seat next to me as he signals to the bartender. I've barely had the time to sip my first drink, but now I have a backup coming. I understand the strategy: he's trapped me here for at least two drinks. After which...well, I'm sure he'll suggest something.

We do the usual *What's your name?* and *Wow, such a lovely name* and *You're an actress? I would have guessed model* and so on until he finally builds up to his bold suggestion: *You know where you can catch the best ocean breezes? On a boat.*

"You're right," I say. "I love the open seas."

"Then you're in luck, because I happen to own a boat. A yacht, in fact. Squadron 60. You ever been on one of those? It lives in that sweet spot where bad-ass meets luxury."

Pretty sure he's quoting the man who sold him the yacht right now.

"I'm not sure I'm dressed for a boat ride, Jamie."

"That's the beauty of a yacht, sweetie. You can wear anything you want."

Wait for it....

"Or nothing at all," he continues.

I scrunch up my nose a little and turn my attention back to the dregs of my first cocktail. I have to let him know that he's just stepped over the line. Not a deal breaker, necessarily, but I'm not some strumpet who will strip naked at the mere suggestion of a spin around the bay.

Halsey, to his credit, senses this and immediately turns it down a gear.

"You're right, though. That dress is too pretty for a cruise. How about we take a stroll down the beach? My family spends the holidays down here every year, and I could show you some places the locals don't even know about."

"Could you," I say.

Is this what he told Paige Ryerson? *Meet me later, I'll show you a place the locals don't even know about*—*like six feet under the sand.* For a brief moment I wonder if he's a thrill killer, and he's done this thing a half-dozen times before, at ports all over the Caribbean, protected by Daddy's bankroll and loyal Captain Kurtz.

I'm curious to see if he'd try such a thing with me.

But before I can respond, I hear a loud exclamation: "Brah! I didn't know you were coming back to the island!"

I swivel around to see Paolo Salese, playboy lifeguard, arms open and waiting for a hug from his pal Jamie.

CHAPTER 21

JANA (continued)

"DUUUUUDE," JAMIE SAYS, THEN wraps his arms around Paolo for a very manly yet intimate hug. There is more grunting and laughing, and there are more exclamations. For a minute I feel very much like a third wheel. Then Paolo catches a glimpse of me.

"Hey, who's this?"

"Paolo, meet my friend Jana—she's an actress."

The lifeguard takes my hand and gives it an awkward kiss, like you've seen in countless movies but never in real life. "Stage or screen?"

"Minor roles on Broadway, major ones off, you know how it is. A little television work when it's in New York."

But Paolo barely comprehends the words coming out of my mouth. He's sizing up my body like he's a costume designer. Then, upon seeing my second cocktail, makes a suggestion. "Dude, we need shots."

Shots it is. The bartender busies himself lining up the glasses while Jamie and Paolo busy themselves competing for my attention. As amusing as such a competition might be, I was more interested in hearing these two talk. How do they know each other? Up until this moment, the teams of suspects had been clearly defined: *Lifeguard and Cop, Rich Kid and Captain.* What connected the Rich Kid with the Lifeguard?

I gradually withdrew from their antics, and they sensed I was not interested in either as a nighttime companion. They focused on each other, their speech punctuated by shots of Grey Goose. Soon enough, Paolo leaned in close and whispered, "I need some help."

"What's up, man?"

The bar is bustling, and they no doubt thought they were speaking too softly for anyone to hear. But I learned lip-reading as part of my stage training years ago. To me, their conversation is as clear as a high-definition radio broadcast.

"I could use your advice on something," Paolo says. "You know any diamond experts? Like some guy who can authenticate them?"

"What, did you rob some old lady?" Jamie says, giggling. He's drunk.

"Dude, I'm serious. I've got a line on something but I need someone I can trust."

"No worries. I'll hook you up. When do you need him?"

"Tonight, man."

"Tonight?"

"I wouldn't ask if it wasn't super-important. I'm meeting this guy at ten."

Halsey pulls out his cell phone and begins thumbing it. "Done. Just texted my guy here on the island." Then he claps Paolo on the shoulder and, in his normal *brah* voice, yells: "More shots! Who's in?"

Halsey looks over at me expectantly. Perhaps through the haze of alcohol he believes he has another chance. After all, I didn't flee the scene.

"What about you, Jana?" he asks.

"I've got the lady's drinks," says a voice behind me.

Your lovely voice, dear Matthew.

I'm thrilled you came after me, but for these two brats, I still have to play the part. I put on a pout. "Oh, *now* you want to drink, Matthew. I was having a perfectly lovely time without you."

"With these two?" you say, eyebrows cocked. And I love you for it. You have no idea how badly I want to kiss you in that moment.

But before Paolo and Jamie realize they are being insulted, you whisk me away.

CHAPTER 22

THEO (THE TRADER)

"YOU GOT THEM?" PAOLO ASKS.

We're in the same backwater bar where we first met. The perfect shady place for shady business. Normally I'd suggest a drink, but the kid's impatient and jittery (and already drunk), so we get down to the matter at hand.

I open my valise and show him the uncut rocks, tilting the bag a little so they glisten. "Here they are. Now, do you have a little information for me?"

"Not yet. I have a guy coming to verify those diamonds."

"What? You don't trust me?"

"No offense, man, but I gotta look out for myself. You understand."

Oh, I understand completely. I also understand that guy is supposed to be here any minute, thanks to the intel that Jana provided. Which is why Quinn hacked into Halsey's phone and texted the diamond authenticator to cancel this evening's sudden appointment. All that remained was figuring out who would take his place on such short notice.

And then I see him.

Oh, boy.

"You the guy? Yeah, I'll bet you're the guy," Otto says with a rapid-fire cadence, making him sound like Martin Scorsese on uppers. Then he points at me. "Who's this? I don't know this guy. Halsey said it would just be you. I don't know this guy."

"Take it easy, man," Paolo says. "This is my business associate, uh..."

"Ted," I say, shaking Otto's hand. *You glorious fool.*

Just you wait, his eyes reply.

"Ted, huh? Well, yeah, good to meet you, Ted, you the guy with the stuff? I haven't got long, Halsey said this was an emergency. I've never known an emergency that concerned diamonds, but there's a first time for everything, I suppose. Let me see the stuff, Ted. Come on, break it out."

I know what Otto's doing—taking the attention off me. By the time he's through, Paolo is going to consider me an old trusted buddy compared to this twitchy weirdo. Which is exactly where we want him.

Otto's performance is kind of inspired, I must admit. He balances his manic Scorsese with a bit of Laurence Olivier from *Marathon Man,* taking his time when it comes to examining each (very fake) diamond from the stash I've brought. He *tut-tut*s. He looks at the same facet twice, three times, then a fourth just for good measure. He strokes his chin. He talks to himself. By the time he's ready for a verdict, Paolo's practically jumping out of his skin.

"They're real, kid."

Paolo exhales.

"Halsey told you about my cut, right? No? Well here's the

deal, I take five of these off your hands. I don't negotiate because before me, you didn't know if you had real diamonds or stuff that ladies use on their purses and jackets, what's that called, when you put bright little pieces of clear plastic on something....?"

"Bedazzling," I offer.

"That's exactly right, Ted! You could have been bedazzled by Ted, but thanks to me, you weren't. You got a problem with me taking five?"

Paolo says he has no problem with that. Otto nods, takes great care to scoop five pieces of worthless glass into a velvet pouch, and then takes his leave. Paolo is so rattled by Hurricane Otto that I have to nudge him back to the business at hand.

"So . . . you've got your payoff. Now what about the girl?"

"Yeah," Paolo says, sounding like he has the weight of the world on his shoulders. "I'll take you to her."

CHAPTER 23

THEO (continued)

THE KID IS NOT entirely disarmed. He has the presence of mind to ask for my gun, then searches me for a wire. It's a rather sloppy search, though. I've had more invasive pat-downs from TSA. There are any number of places I could have hidden a wire.

But I'm not here to secretly record Paolo. I'm here to see if he actually knows where Paige is buried, or if he's trying to scam me.

As he leads me all over the island, I begin to suspect it's the latter. Paolo acts like a kid who forgot he was supposed to deliver an oral report to the class and is making it up as he goes along. *Not too much farther now. Sorry, I get a little turned around in the dark. I've only been here in the daytime. I swear, just a few more minutes...*

I say nothing, because I'm looking for signs of an ambush. That's the only thing that makes sense to me—some of Paolo's hidden buddies waiting to pounce on me. And by the time I wake up in the hospital, the lifeguard will have long fled the island. That's if I'm lucky. If I'm not, I'll end up under the sand, just like Paige Ryerson.

"It's right over here."

We're at an empty stretch of beach that nobody's gotten around to developing yet. Good palm tree cover, and an empty shack. No other inhabited buildings within shouting distance. If I'm going to be jumped and dumped, this would be the ideal place to do it.

Question is, how many punks am I going to be fighting? I'm counting on Paolo being either cheap (and hiring only one or two people) or not having many friends.

Paolo stops to turn around. "You coming, or what?"

Gradually I realize that this is not a trap, and that this life-guard may actually know something. Paolo scans the beach, which is littered with beer bottles and cigarette butts and plastic cups—the aftermath of a party.

Paolo points at the one beer bottle that's upside-down and sticking perfectly straight out of the sand.

"She's here."

Which instantly depresses me. A beer bottle for a grave marker on a strip of dirty sand? A sweet girl like Paige Ryerson didn't deserve this. Quinn's voice is in my head: *Imagine she's your sister.* I make a silent vow to avenge her, no matter what.

Paolo looks at me expectantly. As if I'm just going to say, *Don't worry, buddy, I'll take it from here. You go on back to the bar and have a few cold ones for me.*

"I need confirmation, Paolo."

"You didn't say anything about digging her up."

"Considering the number of uncut diamonds I've just

given you, I was hoping you might throw in that service for free."

Paolo sighs, then drops to his knees and begins to reluctantly claw at the sand with his bare hands. He's in no hurry to dig up whatever is down there, so I get down there, too, and start helping. The sand is rough and burns my skin. But I don't care. The faster I dig, the faster Paolo digs—he's the kind of guy who can't help being competitive.

We're only a foot deep when the smell hits me. There's no doubt—there's a corpse right below us.

CHAPTER 24

THEO (continued)

SHE'S BENEATH A PLASTIC tarp, about three feet under. The stench is overwhelming. I take shallow breaths. I'm endlessly creeped out by the knowledge that smell is transmitted by tiny microbes flying through the air and attaching themselves to the olfactory cells in my nose.

In short: I have microscopic pieces of Paige Ryerson's dead body in my sinuses. I may never forgive Quinn for this.

After I blink the tears out of my eyes, I hold up the flashlight app on my smartphone to take a better look. (Though I would really, *really* rather not.) Mentally I try to compare the picture of Paige Ryerson to this...being under the tarp. I have a hard time reconciling the two. The girl has been under the sand for over a week now and the elements have not been kind.

"So...we good?" Paolo asks.

"This could be anybody," I say.

"What, do you think I'd bring you to some random dead body? This is the girl, I'm telling you, man!"

I don't say anything because I want to see what Paolo does

next. Is he going to stick around to see what we learn about the body? Or is he going to flee the island like the guilty little jerk that he is?

I also use my phone to take a series of quick photos and text them to Quinn. (Hey, why should I be the only one having fun?) Quinn must have been waiting by his phone with breathless anticipation, because he pings me back almost instantly.

Need confirmation, he texts.

OK. Tell me how, I reply. After all, I'm no forensic science expert. I'm barely qualified to tell someone if the milk in the fridge has gone bad. Dead bodies are Jana Rose's weird little hobby.

Look for jewelry, Quinn texts. Specifically a watch and a ring, given to Paige by her parents.

As I peel back the clear plastic tarp, Paolo starts to fidget. "What are you doing? You shouldn't be touching her, should you? I mean, if it's a crime scene?"

"You watch too much TV, buddy." The plastic is cold and clammy under my fingertips. I do wish I'd brought plastic gloves, just like the ones on those TV crime shows I was mocking. But on the corpse's left wrist is indeed a sensible Marc Jacobs watch—the kind of watch proud, middle-class parents might buy for their daughter at the end of an outstanding academic year. I snap a photo and text it to Quinn.

And on the ring finger of her right hand is a petite platinum ring with a ruby heart at its center. I think about how happy and proud she must have been when she first slipped it on.

And then I think about the human monster who choked the life out of her, dragged her to this cold stretch of beach, and then chose to mark her grave with a dead soldier.

Within seconds of my sending the second photo, Quinn responds: Got your location on my phone. We'll be right there.

The anger must be showing on my face, because Paolo is looking increasingly nervous. He's brushing the sand from his hands and knees, slowly backing away from the scene of the body dump.

"So we're all done here...right, man?"

"Why? Are you in a hurry, sport?"

Emotion is getting the best of me, I know. Quinn definitely wouldn't approve. But you know what? Quinn's not here right now. He's not staring at Paolo, who's been more than happy to profit from this young girl's death. I want to take the same raw, sandy, bare hands I used to dig up Paige's grave and squeeze his neck until his head pops off.

"Don't look at me that way," Paolo says. "We had a deal."

I point at the grave. "And she had a life."

Paolo realizes that sticking around isn't the smartest option at this point. He jogs away, looking over his shoulder every few yards to make sure I'm not coming after him. Believe me, I'm tempted. But my job now is to keep vigil over Paige, buried among these beer bottles and plastic cups. I sit down and stare at the ocean, trying to calm myself. I think about the cases we've handled as a team. Not one of them feels as heavy as this one does now.

Quinn and Jana arrive. They don't bother to say hello; they see the lost look on my face. Jana peers down into the open grave, and genuine grief washes over her face. Quinn, as usual, keeps his emotions buried deep within a lockbox in his mind.

"Paolo split a few minutes ago," I tell him. "We can still catch up with him. Pound the truth out of him."

"No," Quinn says. "Let him go."

"Why?"

"Because he didn't kill Paige."

CHAPTER 25

JANA (THE ACTOR)

MY DEAR MATTHEW, DO you remember the first time I told you I'd performed autopsies and you didn't believe me?

We were out for a nightcap, and I dropped that little bit of trivia on you. You said it wasn't true. I insisted it was. This was followed by a frenzied cab ride to Boston University School of Medicine, where you generously tipped our way into the cadaver lab and then offered an extraordinarily large tip (some might even call it a minor grant) for a fresh cadaver. You simply had to see me in action for yourself. It was *put up or shut up* time for me.

So I grabbed the nearest scalpel and *put up*.

At the time, you didn't know that I was once cast in a pilot for a TV show called *Flesh and Blood*, where I portrayed a plucky yet brilliant medical examiner (aren't they all). That show was never picked up, but I threw myself into the role with great élan. I took classes. I pored over texts. And soon I talked my way into rooms with real medical examiners who showed me the ropes. Or the intestines, as it were. The examiners allowed me to do a little cutting, too. It was glorious.

I'll never forget the look on your face as I glided the scalpel down the front of that anonymous corpse and proceeded to give you a tour of the dead man's internal organs.

In this bleak room now, however, the mood is much more somber.

"It's her, isn't it?" Theo asks. "I mean, there's the ring, and the watch."

"Let's not jump to conclusions," I tell him. "There are five stages of decomposition, and this body is in the second stage—bloat."

"Yeah, I noticed."

"You don't have to be in here, you know."

"No," Theo says. "I really do."

This is what we both love about Theo. Beneath that swaggering, devil-may-care exterior is a human being with a good heart, who cares until it hurts.

I begin my work.

Fortunately, my dear Matthew, you've secured us an emergency trauma center, the one erected to serve the population if a natural disaster occurs here on the island. It has the official seal of CDEMA, the Caribbean Disaster Emergency Management Agency, and all the tools I need for a speedy autopsy. You were very thoughtful to procure a set of Paige's most recent medical records so that I might make some comparisons to confirm her identity.

"How do you know Paolo didn't do it?" Theo asks.

Quinn says, "A guilty man would have long fled by now. Instead, Mr. Salese stayed around to profit from his knowledge of the crime."

"Which means he *knows* who did it—which is just as bad."

"Not necessarily. Just because you hear about a certain crime doesn't mean you're an accomplice. Besides, he's not going anywhere with those fake diamonds you gave him. I presume he's going to learn the truth very soon, and he'll come looking for you."

I interrupt the boys. "And when he does, I'd like a word with him."

"Why's that?" Theo asks.

"For a man whose alleged profession is lifeguard, he seems to have run into more than his fair share of dead people."

"What do you mean?" Matthew asks.

"This woman is definitely not Paige Ryerson."

CHAPTER 26

KATE (THE SOLDIER)

OKAY, QUINN—HERE'S THE LOWDOWN.

We arrested the trust fund kid and his captain a little after midnight, just as the *Hostile Wake-Over* was preparing to leave port.

Of course I knew Jamie Halsey and Jacob Kurtz would try to bolt. Once we allowed word to spread that Paige Ryerson's body had been unearthed, it would only be a matter of time before the rich little snot and his captain either lawyered up or decided to split. An interception of port communications revealed the pair had chosen the latter.

"Hands in the air!" I shouted the minute I set foot on deck, flashing my forged badge. "You're under arrest!"

Otto played the role of my partner this time around. His MO was to say next to nothing but maintain a steady, hyper-alert expression that said, *If you try to run, not only will I catch you—I will destroy you.*

Kurtz knew better. Clearly, he had been on the other side of a Miranda warning before. He put lifted hands, palms out, to indicate he wouldn't be reaching for a weapon (to shoot his way out) or a wallet (to buy his way out).

His young boss, however, was clearly a law enforcement virgin. Jamie Halsey's face burned bright red, as if he'd been caught in the act of something naughty, and he began to stammer a weird blend of explanation and threat.

"W-wait wait! We weren't d-doing anything! We were due to leave tonight because I have a meeting in the morning. Ask Captain Kurtz—I swear it's the truth. You can't stop us! I don't even think you have jurisdiction here. My father will make you both sorry you ever set foot on this boat!"

Kurtz shook his head and muttered, "Jamie, quit it."

I nodded at Otto, who pulled a pair of handcuffs from a case strapped to his belt and approached Kurtz. Otto cuffed Kurtz in front, an indication that we could be civilized about this whole thing.

"What's the charge, Officer? Or is that Special Agent? Or perhaps some other title you guys made up?"

Otto merely smiled.

Halsey, on the other hand, was freaking out at the sight of the cuffs in my hand. He looked like a schoolboy who'd just watched his teacher pull out a whipping cane.

"You're not putting those on me. I know my rights. I get a phone call!"

I shook my head. "Jamie, calm down. You still have the chance for this to go relatively easy."

Halsey turned to his captain. "Kurtz—do something!"

"Kid, let her put the cuffs on and get this whole thing over with."

"No—no way!"

And then he went for it. Some primal part of his brain made the calculation. Fight was impossible, so he chose flight. Perhaps he thought his youth, combined with a small element of surprise, would do the trick. With Otto busy with Kurtz, he bolted and attempted to go around me, out of arm's reach.

So I dropped down, crouching on my knees and using my fingertips for balance on the boat deck, and kicked out my left leg. His foot hooked over mine and *BAM,* down he went. He probably didn't know what had happened until he kissed wood and blood began to gush from his nose and mouth.

"Kid, I told you," Kurtz said with a sigh.

Within a second, I had a knee in the middle of his spine and was cuffing the brat's hands behind his back—an indication that we could go the uncivilized route, too. His body began to shake, and at first I thought he was trying to throw me off. But then I realized he wasn't fighting. He was crying.

"W-why are you doing this to me?" he blubbered through tears.

I removed my knee from his back but kept steady pressure on his wrists as I leaned in to whisper in his ear. "Because you took a young girl, a beautiful girl with everything ahead of her, and then you murdered her."

"I didn't do it!" Halsey said. "I'd s-swear on anything I didn't do it!"

"You murdered her and then you and your captain buddy over there buried her body in the cold, wet sand with nothing but an empty beer bottle for a headstone."

"W-what?"

"You put her family through more than a week of living hell, all because, what...she wouldn't sleep with you?"

"Jamie, for God's sake, don't listen to her!" Kurtz cried out. "She's trying to psych you out!"

"Please, *please,* I'm telling you the truth, I didn't even know she was dead! The last time I saw her she was drunk, sure, but she was alive!"

I pulled Halsey up to his knees. His face was a wasteland from all the crying and bleeding.

"Well," I told him, "we're going to give you one last chance to see her again."

CHAPTER 27

KATE (continued)

THE BUILDING LOOKED OFFICIAL enough. Gotta hand it to you, Quinn—procuring a CDEMA facility? That was an effective touch. Even stoic Captain Kurtz swallowed hard when he saw the official government seal.

By this time, I'd given Halsey a towel to mop off his face, allowing him to regain some semblance of dignity. But he was still petrified. I almost felt bad for the punk.

"Come on," I told him. "She's in here."

The moment I pulled back the tarp, Halsey's face turned white and then a strange shade of purple as he tried to hold back the tidal wave of bile rocketing up his throat. Otto, fortunately, got him over to a metal slop sink in the corner of the room before he could vomit all over the body.

By the time we stepped inside the facility, I had already received your text, Quinn, telling me that the corpse under the tarp wasn't Paige Ryerson. No matter who she was, the girl could still be used as an effective prop to shock our two suspects into admitting the truth.

Jamie Halsey was clearly rattled. But Kurtz was another

story. Ever since we'd set foot on the *Hostile Wake-Over*, the captain had been the coolest of customers. And you know the old riddle, Quinn. Who sleeps the most soundly during his first night in prison? The guilty.

Otto helped Halsey clean himself up more thoroughly—which was no easy task, considering the kid's hands were still cuffed behind his back. Then he brought him back over to the table. Halsey's face looked like he had traveled to the far side and back. What do the kids say? Worst. Night. Ever.

"Is that her?" he asked quietly.

"Yeah," Otto replied.

"I swear to God, on my parents, on my life, on *everything*...I did not kill her. Someone else did this."

I watched Kurtz carefully. He said nothing. Expressed no emotion whatsoever. He just stared at the corpse on the slab like he was looking at something a deep-sea trawler had dredged up from the ocean floor. Whatever this was, it didn't concern him in the least.

That's the kind of person who could stalk a young girl, grab her, strangle the life out of her, and bury her body.

And consider Kurtz's advantages. He was mobile, thanks to the yacht. He was afforded the same protections as Jamie Halsey. Nothing ever blew back on the kid. And Kurtz could be confident he'd enjoy the same kind of immunity. After all, he was a virtual member of the family.

I'm convinced we've found our killer.

CHAPTER 28

QUINN

"TELL ME ABOUT THE last time you saw her," Quinn asks.

Jamie Halsey is seated in a chair so that he's facing Quinn directly. Behind Quinn: the corpse of the unknown woman. This arrangement is not accidental. Quinn will be watching his suspect's eyes as much as listening to his words.

"I don't really remember. I was kind of drunk myself."

Quinn's expression doesn't change. "Try harder. This is *your* ass on the line, not mine."

"Okay, okay." He glances over at the corpse behind Quinn, who notes the movement of Halsey's eyes. "I do remember her friends laughing like lunatics—they were really drunk. And I think Paige...Ms. Ryerson...was dancing with Jake."

"Captain Kurtz," Quinn says.

"Yeah. I struck out, so maybe he thought he'd give her a try. I do remember that she was really strange. Flirty one minute, then next, cold fish. You know?"

"No, I don't."

"Come on, man, don't be that way. You know how these girls can be. They're total teases. They come down here to party and get out of control, right up until the minute they decide they want to be good girls and go home."

"Is that what made you angry? That Paige wanted to go home?"

"No, I'm just saying..."

"Is that why you trapped her on your boat? So that you could party?"

"Trapped? No, man, it wasn't like that...wait, I remember now! Those crazy loud girls—they pulled Paige away from Jake. He held on to her hands, trying to convince her to stay, but her friends wouldn't let her. They practically dragged her away."

"And that's the last time you saw her."

Halsey glances behind Quinn. "Yeah, I swear."

A short while later, Captain Jacob Kurtz is placed in the same seat while the others guard Halsey in another room. Kurtz doesn't look behind Quinn. Not even once. No matter how many times Quinn says her name.

"The last time anyone saw Paige Ryerson alive," Quinn says, "was when she was dancing with you. Why did you kill her?"

"That's not true," Kurtz says, "and you know it. Those Clee girls dragged her away. And anyway, I heard she was making out with some islander cop later that night. So why don't you go talk to him and let us be on our way?"

"Nobody saw you on that yacht after your dance with Paige. You followed her down the beach. You couldn't get over her turning you down, even though you're old enough to be her father. You followed her and saw her kissing that cop and it drove you insane...."

"Come on, man. You know that's not right."

"And it drove you insane," Quinn repeats, "that she would be with someone else instead of you. So after she broke things off with the cop you followed her. You strangled her. You buried her body. That"—Quinn pauses to jerk a thumb at the corpse behind him—"body right there. And then you just...sailed away."

"This is all crazy. If you've got proof, then show it to me. Otherwise, you need to let me go."

Quinn calls for Otto to take the suspect away. All of that suppressed emotion comes bubbling out of Kurtz now. He yells about how this farce of an interrogation will never stand up in court, how Halsey's lawyers will crucify Quinn for this, and so on and so on.

But Quinn is barely listening. After a moment, Jana enters the room, touches Quinn's shoulder. "What are you thinking, my dear?"

"I'm thinking we let them both go. They didn't do it."

CHAPTER 29

QUINN (continued)

"I'M RESISTING," THEO SAYS.

"Resisting what, exactly?" Jana asks.

"Resisting the urge to dance around and do this...."—at which point Theo starts to do an exaggerated Broadway dance number, all to the nonexistent tune of "I Told You So."

"Come on, get into character," Quinn snaps. "Here he comes."

Indeed he comes. And Paolo Salese the playboy lifeguard is furious. He scans the crowd outside the casino, searching for the face that did him wrong. And then he finds it. Theo Selznick, standing on the corner, giving him a shy little wave. Which seems to infuriate Paolo even more.

Quinn and Jana, meanwhile, stroll down the sidewalk, arms locked, taking in the laid-back decadence of a Caribbean-style resort.

Paolo crosses the street, finger pointing at Theo. "You gave me a bag full of fake rocks!"

"What are you talking about? You had your guy there. He authenticated them."

"Whatever, man. You fooled him, but you didn't fool the guys who mattered—the guys who almost killed me for trying to pawn off fake diamonds! Look, I don't know what kind of scam you're pulling, but you're going to give me my money *right now*."

"I know you're upset, but hey...so am I. You led me to the wrong dead girl."

This statement acts like a bucket of ice water on Paolo's growing rage.

"W-what? What do you mean, wrong girl?"

At this very moment, Quinn and Jana pass by, and Jana heaves a punch into Paolo's midsection that certainly would have made him double over—if Theo hadn't been there to grab his shoulder and the waist of his pants to keep him upright.

"Come on," Theo says, "let's talk this whole thing out."

Talking this whole thing out, in this instance, means hustling Paolo into the back of an idling SUV. Quinn knows this is technically kidnapping, but he doesn't care. Jana takes the wheel, and Quinn and Theo sit on either side of the lifeguard, who is struggling to catch his breath.

Quinn says, "We know the girl wasn't Paige Ryerson. Who was she?"

"I'm telling you...it's the girl...."

"No, it's not, Paolo," Theo says. "You stole Paige's ring and watch and put them on a fresh corpse. So who was she?"

"You can't do this to me...."

Quinn places two fingers on Paolo's chin and moves his head to the right so they're looking directly into each other's eyes. "You have no idea what we're capable of, Mr. Salese."

The head tilt is a distraction so that Theo can inject the lifeguard with a knockout cocktail. Paolo feels the pinch, but two seconds later, the lights go out.

"Take us to the beach, Jana," Quinn says.

By the time the lights come back on for Paolo Salese, he's lying on his back in a grave in the same bottle-littered stretch of beach where the corpse with Paige's ring and watch was buried. He's three feet down, with enough sand shoveled onto his body to immobilize him while keeping his head uncovered.

It's four o'clock in the morning, so when Paolo starts screaming, there's nobody awake to hear him.

"Shhh," Quinn says, crouching down. "Calm down. If we wanted to kill you, you wouldn't have woken up at all."

This seems to calm the lifeguard down a little, as he realizes there might be a way out of this. Theo and Jana are standing on either side of Quinn, looking down into the grave as if they're pallbearers at a secret funeral.

"But if you lie to us," Theo says, "you'll stay down there for good. You understand?"

"Yeah . . . I understand."

"Who was the girl?" Jana asks.

"I don't know," Paolo says. "I swear to God, I don't know."

"Then how did you know where her body would be?" Theo asks.

"The day before you and I met, I got this call—the guy wouldn't tell me his name. But he said that people would probably be asking me about the girl. And if that happened, I should play along, and he'd give me further instructions."

"In exchange for what?" Theo asks.

"Money. Like you, he gave me a little down payment and promised me the rest when it was all over. That's why I was trying to make a deal with you—I knew this guy was up to no good, and I didn't want any part of it. I just wanted to get out of this damn place and put all of this behind me."

"How did this man contact you?" Quinn asks.

"Through the hotel. He left me his number at the front desk and said I should call him back within an hour."

"What did he sound like?"

"Uh...rich."

Theo is not so quick to believe Paolo. "So we have no way of backing up your story. Isn't that convenient for you." Idly, he begins to kick sand into the grave, pelting Paolo's face.

Paolo starts to scream again. Quinn motions for Theo to knock it off.

"The hotel! Check the front desk phone records! I called him back using the lobby phone. Maybe you can trace him."

"Anyone smart enough to run this kind of cover-up would use a burner phone," Jana says. "Nobody calls from landlines anymore."

"Is that my problem?!" Paolo shouts. "Come on, I told you everything I know. Let me out of here."

"Let's go," Quinn says, already strolling toward their SUV. "The others are meeting us in a couple of hours." When Jana and Theo shake their heads and begin to follow, Paolo freaks out all over again, screaming with all of his lung capacity. Quinn suggests that Theo give the man a hand, and he does, reluctantly: clearing the sand away from Paolo's left arm.

"Dig yourself out."

CHAPTER 30

THE STINGRAYS

UP IN THE PENTHOUSE suite Quinn has ordered a full breakfast for the team, but no one feels like eating. Aside from Otto, of course, who never turns down a hot meal. He tucks into an egg-and-sausage scramble bowl as if a guard is about to knock on his door at any moment and lead him down to the executioner's block.

"Okay, Quinn," Theo says, "so to recap, the lifeguard didn't do it, the rich kid didn't do it, and his yacht captain didn't do it."

"That's correct," Quinn replies.

"Which leaves us with Nigel James, the islander cop. I've liked him for this crime since the moment I met him. So what are we waiting for? Let's nail him."

"Hold on," Jana says. "Just a few hours ago you were about to bury the lifeguard alive because you were convinced *he* did it."

"No, I said he *knew* about it. I didn't think he actually did it."

Kate interrupts. "Are we really discounting Jamie Halsey

and Jacob Kurtz? Quinn, you said you thought this was a conspiracy—that we most likely have two suspects working in tandem. I can think of no better pair."

"Sure," Otto says through a mouth full of scrambled egg, "but everybody agrees that Nigel James was the last person to see her alive. I'm with Theo on this. Let's put this cop in our crosshairs and see what he does."

"No," Quinn says. "We've pushed Officer James as far as we can. If we try a full-court press on him now, he'll have the entire police force looking for any flimsy excuse to boot us off the island."

"So then…we go into stealth mode and lay an extremely clever trap?" Jana asks with a hopeful smile on her face.

"No," Quinn says. "Right now, I suggest you all finish your breakfast and go for a swim. Loosen up your muscles a bit."

"Wait—what?" Kate asks.

"I'll be flying back to the US," Quinn tells them. "I've got a noon flight up to Boston."

A sour look washes over Theo's face as he throws up his hands. "Well, that's just awesome. Some killer got the best of us? Are we seriously giving up?"

"Matthew, dear," Jana says, "is there something we're missing?"

"Look, I'm not leaving until we find Paige," Kate says. "Or her body."

Otto grunts his agreement.

Quinn, perhaps sensing the minor mutiny brewing in the penthouse, shows them his palms. "I didn't say anything about any of you leaving. I suggested you take a leisurely swim, because you're going to have a long night ahead of you. By the time you return, I'll have made a phone call, and your assignments will be waiting for you."

Theo smiles and shakes his head. "Can you imagine what it was like to be this guy's roommate in college?"

CHAPTER 31

THE TWINS

EVEN THOUGH THEY HAVE papers due the next morning, Hannah and Brooke Clee head back to Turks and Caicos for the night.

Brooke laughs and says they'll have plenty of time to write them on the Gulfstream—or download them from the internet, whichever's easier. But Hannah doesn't find this amusing in the least.

"I can't believe you're joking at a time like this. Do you even realize why we're headed back down to the island?"

"Because maybe, oh, I don't know, you're hopelessly OCD?" Brooke asks. She means it to sound devastating, but there's enough uncertainty in her voice to let Hannah know her sister's not entirely sure what those three letters stand for.

"No, it's because we need to know if they really found her or not," Hannah says. "And there's only one way to do that."

Hannah, of course, was the one who arranged the impromptu trip. Ordinarily such a lavish expense would have to pass through her father's office for approval—the jet is company owned, after all.

But Hannah has had eighteen years to practice her powers of persuasion and manipulation. A sob story about a lost ring (allegedly a gift from her stepmother, Daddy's second wife) and the delicate need to search for it in person was enough for the jet crew to scramble to get the Gulfstream down to Turks and Caicos for the second time in a week. Flying the jet for an hour costs about $9,000; the round trip would set the company back about $100,000. But the staff knows that if it makes Hannah Clee happy, then it's wheels up.

"All we know is that somebody found a body," says Brooke. "If it really is Paige, wouldn't it be all over the news?"

"Exactly," Hannah replies. "We can't trust *anybody*. For all we know, those jerk FBI agents spread a fake story. We have to be sure."

"Why? We didn't do anything!"

"Well," Hannah says, "we did *something*."

Brooke sighs, then sneaks in a mumbled complaint. "We should never have invited her along for spring break."

"Oh, don't even go there, Brooke. If we hadn't invited her along, you know where you'd be right now?"

Brooke has no response to this, because deep down she knows her sister is right. Throughout their childhood Brooke was always the one to run her mouth off at the wrong time, and Hannah was the one who'd have to bail her twin out of the mess. More than once using her fists.

Hannah, feeling a little guilty, tries to reassure her sister. "Don't worry. We'll be there soon, and we'll know for sure."

Brooke frowns. "I don't know why we didn't just call the police right away and tell them what happened. They'd *have* to understand. None of it was our fault...."

Hannah takes her sister by the shoulders and refuses to let go until she finally makes eye contact.

"Listen to me. We did the right thing. Some people would like nothing more than to use this to embarrass or hurt Dad. We're not going to let them."

At the airport, the twins are met by two vehicles. One is a private limousine, white, chartered to Paul Clee & Partners. A uniformed driver pops out from behind the wheel the moment the girls clear the gate. He is efficient and the girls barely notice him. They don't ask for ID because why would they? Strangers have been taking care of them their entire lives.

The other vehicle, parked thirty feet behind the limo, is a rented SUV, also white. But this second vehicle is *not* under the employ of Paul Clee & Partners.

Then again, neither is their limo driver.

CHAPTER 32

OTTO AND JANA

OTTO HAZARD, IN HIS crisp white uniform, uses the limousine intercom to ask the girls where they'd like to go. "The hotel, to check your bags? Or perhaps a quick stop at Calico Jack's?"

Annoyed, Hannah stabs the intercom button. "Just go east on Leeward Highway. I'll let you know when to turn."

"Yes, miss, my pleasure."

The intercom connection is severed. Or at least, that's what Hannah and Brooke Clee believe. Any conversations the girls have will be heard clearly by Otto—and Jana Rose, who is following in the white SUV. A hidden digital video camera is also running, capturing everything that happens in the back of the limo and instantly uploading it to the Stingrays' private servers. For instance, there is this exchange:

"This is going to suck."

"Don't flake out on me now, Brooke."

"I'm not! I just don't want to see her again."

"Will you shut up? I don't want the driver hearing any of this."

"Hannah, that guy can barely speak English. Did you look at him? Um, *Neanderthal much?*"

Otto smiles. Over his Bluetooth earpiece, he hears Jana's laugh.

"I'm sorry, Otto, but Brooke Clee has said what we've all been thinking."

"Nah, she's just playing. I'll bet she thinks Neanderthals are foxy."

"Keep sharp. We're approaching the beach."

"Neanderthal out."

After their late-morning swim, the Stingrays had returned to the suite to discover that Quinn had left them all simple instructions. Otto and Jana's list read:

1. FOLLOW THE TWINS
2. RECORD THE TWINS
3. LISTEN TO THE TWINS

Their collective afternoon was busy with an insane amount of detail work—which happened to be the kind of work they did best. Otto, however, was eager to finish this whole thing so they could maybe kick back and relax over a proper meal.

His reverie is interrupted by the static pop of the intercom. "Turn left here, driver. Then follow my directions."

"Yes, miss, my pleasure," Otto says, adding a little more of an islander accent to his speech this time around. If nothing else, he wanted to live up to Brooke's expectations.

After a series of turns, he is told to park the limo about a block from a deserted stretch of beach.

"This isn't where we found the other body," Jana whispers.

"No, it's not," Otto replies.

Another loud static pop. "Wait here, driver. We'll be right back. You stay in the car. Do you understand?"

Like he's a moron. "Yes, miss, I understand."

But the moment the girls make it a safe distance away, Otto springs into action, gathering his mobile recording gear and swiftly tightening the distance between himself and the Clee girls. Jana joins him a few moments later with her own recording devices. There's no time for chatter now; they nod at each other, then slip into the cover of darkness and follow the twins.

Hannah and Brooke are on the beach, gingerly stepping around a patch of sand a few yards away from a crumbling lifeguard station.

"This is it," Hannah says.

"Is it?"

"You know it is. You put the bottle there."

"I was making sure."

"No, you're not. You just don't want to dig."

"Neither do you!"

"Come on. Let's get this over with."

Jana is able to capture their conversations with a long-distance microphone; Otto, meanwhile, records the visuals, focusing in with his digital camera. The Clee girls drop to their knees as if they've suddenly decided to build a sandcastle here on this dark, sinister strip of beach.

They push the sand away with their hands, slowly at first, as if sifting dirt for flecks of gold. But then they grow impatient and begin grabbing great handfuls and flinging them off to the side. The wind catches some of the sand and blows it back into their faces. They pout with annoyance.

But then one of the girls—Jana has to really listen to determine the difference in their voices—shrieks loudly.

"Oh, God," she says.

Even with those two syllables, Jana knows it's Brooke speaking.

"It's her."

CHAPTER 33

KATE AND THEO

"YOU SURE YOU DON'T want me to drive?" Theo asks.

"Dude," Kate says, "I've driven a Humvee through two hundred heavily armed Taliban guerrillas in Quam. Pretty sure I can follow a huge black limo through the streets of a resort town."

"Yeah, but he's a cop. Pretty sure he'll know if he's being tailed."

They're in a Honda Whatever, some generic import that's guaranteed not to raise eyebrows because so many tourists rent them here. They waited outside police headquarters on Old Airport Road until Nigel James finally stormed out, looking irritated. Then the cop climbed into an unmarked car and sped away. At that point, Kate took off in pursuit.

Quinn's list of instructions to Theo and Kate were as simple as Jana and Otto's:

1. FOLLOW THE COP
2. RECORD THE COP
3. DETAIN THE COP (IF NECESSARY)

Kate is following the cop like a pro. But there isn't much mystery as to where he's going. About three minutes ago, Theo intercepted a text transmission from a burner phone to James's personal cell, asking him to meet at a certain location on the southeast end of the island. At the same exact moment, Otto Hazard observed Hannah Clee holding a cell phone and thumbing an urgent message that said:

UR GONNA HELP US FIX THIS

All transmissions are documented and uploaded to the Stingrays' servers.

After a frenzied five minutes, James arrives at the given location. The white limo is kind of a dead giveaway; the cop must be fuming at the girls for being so utterly and completely indiscreet.

"Look at him," Theo says. "That man is *not* happy."

"Tell me something I don't know," Kate replies. "Come on, let's get our gear."

Nigel James smooths out his clothing, checks his personal weapon (a Glock, Kate notes), stuffs it into a jacket pocket, and then shuffles up the beach toward the twins.

As soon as he's in range, Hannah Clee points at the unmarked grave in the sand, barking orders.

"You need to get *this* out of the ground right now and dispose of it properly!"

"Take it easy, Ms. Clee," James says. "I didn't expect you back here so soon. You know, what you're doing is not very wise."

"Oh, really? You want to know what I didn't expect? A phone call telling me that somebody pulled the body of a girl out of the sand. And that it could be you-know-who."

James shakes his head. "There have been some private investigators causing trouble on the island. I told you both: you have nothing to worry about. You are under my personal protection. And by extension, that of the entire police force."

"No," Hannah says. "That's not good enough. We need this…thing up out of the ground and, like, shoved into a wood chipper or something. I don't want any trace of her left behind!"

"You have to be patient. The evidence was planted else-where, which will satisfy local investigators, and eventually everyone else."

"You don't get it. *I'm* not satisfied! It should be *me* you're worried about!"

James can't help but chuckle, which unnerves the twins. They look at each other, wondering if they've made a deal with a lunatic.

"Ms. Clee…you don't understand your position." James removes the Glock from his jacket pocket. "In about five seconds I could be a hero and the two of you could be dead, next to the corpse of your friend. Murder solved. Everyone's happy."

"What?!" Brooke exclaims, the first word she's uttered since the cop arrived. Life has always been a bunch of laughs for her—until this moment. "But we didn't kill her! It was just an accident. She was crazy drunk and running too fast and then she tripped and fell and hit her head on a rock."

James smiles. "Oh, is that the story your sister told you?"

There is a look of growing horror on Brooke's face as she begins to put it together. *Oh, no. Her sister murdered Paige.*

"Brooke, don't say another word," Hannah snaps. "I did what I had to do. To protect *you*."

"But...I d-didn't ask you to do that!" Brooke stammers, still trying to process everything. "This is bad, Hannah. Dad's going to be so angry!"

"Ladies, ladies...I don't care who did what. What happens on the island can stay on the island...if we can successfully renegotiate our deal."

"What do you mean, *renegotiate*?" Hannah says.

"The heat on this case has intensified. I'm sure you understand, it's going to take a lot more money to keep this under wraps. I know you both have stellar credit lines, so it'll only be a matter of discussing payment."

"We're not paying you *more* money," Hannah says. "That's unfair!"

James sighs, then points the Glock at Brooke with a two-hand grip, elbows bent, feet shoulder-width apart, just as he was taught in the police academy. This is called the Weaver stance, and it allows you to fire repeatedly and accurately at multiple targets without the muzzle flying all over the place.

"Guess I'm going to be a hero, then."

CHAPTER 34

THE STINGRAYS

THEY WERE ALL EXPECTING the gun to make an appearance, mostly as a way to frighten the twins.

But none of them really expected him to actually *use* it.

The four of them, however, scramble from the surveillance locations the moment James pulls the weapon from his jacket pocket. A few seconds later, his body language is practically screaming, *I'm pulling the trigger.*

Kate is the first one to make it within range. There's a loud crack and pop and then Nigel James's body jerks and twists like a marionette caught up in the wake of a jet engine. Kate holds the Taser steady until the Glock tumbles out of his hands and the cop collapses completely, by which point Otto is on top of him. Jana and Theo run onto the beach, Tasers in hand.

But then a voice surprises them: "You're all dead."

They all look over at Hannah, who has picked up the Glock in the momentary confusion. And she is pointing it at Otto.

"I remember you. You were that fake security guard back at school. *And you!*" Now she points the weapon at Jana.

"You're the fake FBI agent! You people have been after us this whole time."

"Well, technically, only since this morning," Theo offers.

"ALL OF YOU SHUT UP!" Brooke screams. She can't handle it anymore.

"I don't care who any of you are," Hannah says with a creepy calm in her voice. "But I'm not going to let you ruin our lives."

"Pretty sure you did that all by yourselves when you murdered Paige Ryerson and paid off a local cop to cover it up," Theo says.

Hannah might be trying to smile, but instead it comes across like the leer of someone who's just realized she's lost her mind.

"You probably think I'm some silly schoolgirl who can't do anything right without her daddy helping out. Well, you're wrong. We grew up by ourselves, left to fend for ourselves. I've gotten us out of trouble before, and I'll do it again."

"How?" Theo asks. "By shooting us?"

"Yes. And then you can join Paige under the beach here," Hannah says. "I've been to the shooting range plenty of times. My daddy used to take me, and he always told me I'm an excellent shot."

"I don't doubt that, sweetie," Jana says, speaking in the soothing tones of a therapist. "But killing us wouldn't help anything. We've recorded everything you've said since you stepped inside that limo."

Hannah is momentarily gobsmacked by that piece of news, because it's the worst possible thing she could hear. *The whole world is going to know what we've done!*

Brooke, however, doesn't seem to get it. In the moments since she's learned the truth, Brooke has done what she's always done: taken Hannah's side. After all, Hannah's always known what's best for them.

"Yeah, well, after we kill you," Brooke says, "we'll just find all of your phones and cameras and whatever and bury them, too."

"Honey," Jana says, "to cover this up you'd have to take down the whole internet."

Hannah, meanwhile, knows it's over. She allows the Glock to fall to her side. Weirdly, the first thing that pops into her head at this moment is the paper she'll never write, never hand in. But what do papers matter now?

The message still hasn't reached Brooke, however, because she snatches the weapon out of her sister's hand and screams as she points it at Theo.

"Look who's defending us now, Hannah! Look who's cleaning up *your* mess!"

Now, Brooke Clee hasn't spent any time at shooting ranges. But she's confident she can squeeze the trigger and spray these annoying jerks with enough bullets to make them *all just shut up....*

And maybe Brooke would have gotten in a lucky shot or two, if Kate and Otto hadn't rushed in, Tasers in hand, and lit up both of the Clee girls like Roman candles.

They both shriek before tumbling down onto the cold sand. A full minute later you could still smell the ozone in the ocean breeze.

Otto secures the Glock, unloads it. Kate checks the killers' vitals. They'll be hurting later, but they'll certainly live. Jana texts Quinn with the latest developments. Theo, however, simply stands there, enjoying the moment.

"Man, I hope we got all of that, because I'm totally binge-watching it later."

Jana says, "First we need to get the room and the equipment ready. We're not finished yet, and we don't have a lot of time."

CHAPTER 35

QUINN

THIS TIME, MATTHEW QUINN enters the offices of Paul Clee & Partners the way he is expected: through the lobby, up to reception, and with an appointment. All perfectly respectable and businesslike.

"You didn't have to make a special trip," Clee says as he shakes Quinn's hand. "I presume there's news?"

"There is, but perhaps not the kind you might be expecting," Quinn says.

Clee sets his jaw and frowns, then shows Quinn to a chair on the other side of his massive desk. Other clients might place Quinn on the office couch and take a seat nearby, as if to imply, *Hey, we're in this thing together*. But this seating arrangement says something different. *I'm the boss, you're my employee. Now impress me.*

"Go on," Clee says.

"None of the four major suspects you gave me did it. My team cleared them all."

"That's impossible."

"Salese, Halsey, Kurtz, and James—none of them killed Paige Ryerson. That I can guarantee."

"You guaranteed closure, Mr. Quinn," says Clee. "I'm paying you people a lot of money to end this nightmare. For my girls' sake, and for the poor Ryersons' sake."

"The Ryersons will have closure. Because we found the killer."

"Well, who is it?"

Quinn gestures: *May I?* Since Clee has no idea what he means, Quinn walks around the other side of the desk and helps himself to Clee's desktop computer, which has an absurdly huge display. A few clicks, and he's bypassed Clee's password and connected to the Stingrays' servers. Clee is about to protest, but then digital footage begins to play.

It's his daughter Hannah, who looks like she's hungover. The ghosts of mascara lines run down her cheeks.

"Yes, I killed her."

An unseen voice demands, "Who did you kill?"

"Paige Ryerson, our hallmate. But you have to understand...she was such a snitch! I swear, it was like she was keeping notes on Brooke. You should have heard her—that's a violation of the St. Paul's honor code, that's a violation of the honor code, honor code, honor code, blah blah blah."

Paul Clee's jaw drops. Quinn watches him carefully— especially the man's eyes. They reveal everything.

"She threatened to turn Brooke in?" asks the unseen interrogator, though Quinn, of course, knows this is Kate speaking.

"All the time! So we figured it was time for that honey and vinegar thing. You know, sweeten her up, get her to change her mind. So we invited her to the island. We showed her a really, really good time. And that little snitch had fun!"

"So why kill her?"

"Because around two in the morning I found her sitting on the beach, alone," Hannah says onscreen. "She must have sobered up a little because she started saying all of this nasty stuff about the two of us, pointing her finger in my face, saying that we were bribing her and it would never work. That's when I realized this little ungrateful bitch would never quit."

"So you killed her."

"No! I didn't mean to. I pushed her down, to show her she couldn't mess with me. But then she tried to push back, so I punched her in the face. And she hit me back and started screaming and I knew Brooke would be coming along any minute and I wanted the little bitch to stop so I grabbed a rock and I..."

Clee can't stand any more of this. He lunges for his keyboard and fumbles for the key that will turn off the feed. Quinn calmly returns to his seat on the other side of the desk. After a few moments, Hannah's voice is cut off. Both men sit in the office in silence.

"So the only people who know the truth are you and your team," Clee finally says.

"That is correct. You hired us, we report directly to you."

Clee nods. "I knew about this. Well, I didn't know for sure that it was Hannah, though I should have guessed. She was always the more...*rambunctious* of the two."

"Of course you knew," Quinn says. "You also hired men to spread misinformation and offer bogus testimonies. And then you hired us to throw suspicion away from your daughters. You heard that we were the best, and that if you could convince the best that someone else killed Paige, your daughters would be safe."

Clee puckers his lips a little as he considers this. "And you're not going to keep this quiet, are you?"

Quinn smiles, then shakes his head. "Never try to sting a Stingray."

Paul Clee shifts in his seat. "You know, Mr. Quinn, one of the advantages of having your own floor is that you can soundproof the walls to studio quality. Not a single noise will escape."

Then he opens his drawer and removes a large silver revolver as if it's nothing more than a tape dispenser or stapler. He points the gun at Quinn's chest and shows his teeth, his expression somewhere between a sneer and a predator's grin.

CHAPTER 36

QUINN (continued)

"MR. CLEE, YOU'RE NOT thinking clearly," Quinn says.

"On the contrary, I considered the possibility that your team would discover the truth. So I've planned everything to the last detail. Your body will be removed along with the rest of the office refuse. The chair you're sitting in will be replaced, as well as the carpeting beneath your feet. Within the hour, everything will look brand-new. I have a very loyal staff. We're like a family, really."

Clee leans forward over his desk with the gun, as if to shorten the distance for the bullet that's about to make its way into Quinn's chest.

Quinn, however, remains motionless. "What about my team? They're not going to let you get away with this."

"Who? Your precious Stingrays? Without a leader, they'll be easy pickings. If they're still on the island, they're as good as dead. *You're* the slippery one, Mr. Quinn. But you're not going to slip out of this."

Quinn nods, then leans forward, too, mimicking Clee's body language.

"After you kill me," Quinn says, "I'd like you to do me a favor. Check your surveillance recordings from this very soundproof floor from…oh, somewhere between four and five o'clock this morning."

"What? Why?"

Quinn shrugs.

Clee's expression morphs from one of confusion to anger—all of which culminates in a roar as he pulls the trigger. But instead of a blast, there is nothing but a loud hollow snap of the hammer connecting with the firing pin. Clee looks down at the pistol in his hand as if it's an employee who has disappointed him.

"I'm a planner, too, Mr. Clee."

"So you broke into my office…."

"…Early this morning and removed the bullets. You should thank me. This means you'll only be arrested for attempted murder rather than the real deal. Oh, along with obstruction of justice, accessory to murder, and a host of other charges I'm sure the FBI will be reading to you in just a moment."

Those words are the cue for the federal agents standing by to swarm into Clee's office and take him into custody. Their entire conversation has been recorded, too, which will make it especially challenging for Clee's wolf pack of lawyers when it comes time for the trial.

Once he's outside the building, Quinn calls Jana, who's waiting near the luggage carousel at Logan International with the others.

"Nigel James and the twins are in custody," Jana says. "Local authorities are preparing to turn them over to the FBI."

"Good. The girls will be able to see their father soon."

"Did Clee go along quietly?"

"Pretty much," Quinn says. "How's the team?"

"Otto's going on and on about lunch," she says. As per tradition, the Stingrays will gather for a celebratory feast at the successful close of the case. "What can I tell him so he'll shut up already?"

"Tell them it'll be dinner," Quinn says. "But first I'd like you to stop by the office a little early."

"How early, my dear?"

Quinn smiles. "Well...are you busy right now?"

This is another part of the tradition. But they never mention it to the other Stingrays.

ABOUT THE AUTHORS

James Patterson is the world's bestselling author and most trusted storyteller. He has created many enduring fictional characters and series, including Alex Cross, the Women's Murder Club, Michael Bennett, Maximum Ride, Middle School, and I Funny. Among his notable literary collaborations are *The President Is Missing*, with President Bill Clinton, and the Max Einstein series, produced in partnership with the Albert Einstein Estate. Patterson's writing career is characterized by a single mission: to prove that there is no such thing as a person who "doesn't like to read," only people who haven't found the right book. He's given over three million books to schoolkids and the military, donated more than seventy million dollars to support education, and endowed over five thousand college scholarships for teachers. For his prodigious imagination and championship of literacy in America, Patterson was awarded the 2019 National Humanities Medal. The National Book Foundation presented him with the Literarian Award for Outstanding Service to the American Literary Community, and he is also the recipient of an Edgar Award and nine Emmy Awards. He lives in Florida with his family.

* * *

James O. Born is an award–winning crime and science-fiction novelist as well as a career law-enforcement agent. A native Floridian, he still lives in the Sunshine State.

During his thirty-five years in the advertising business, **Tim Arnold** had a regular column in *Adweek*. Currently a blog columnist for The Huffington Post, he continues to actively consult for a wide range of clients.

Duane Swierczynski is the Edgar-nominated and Anthony Award–winning author of *Canary* and *Revolver*. He's also written for comic books, TV, and film.

JAMES
PATTERSON
RECOMMENDS

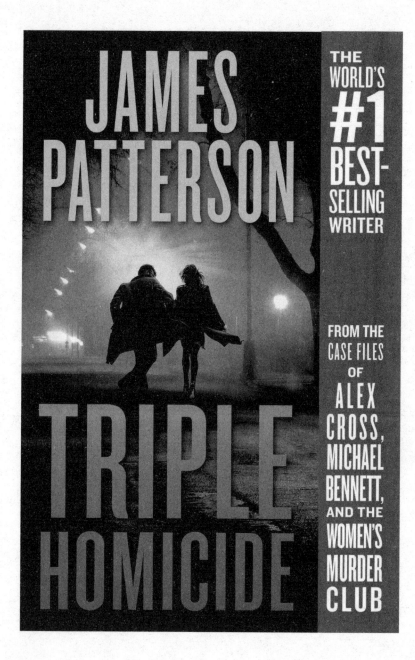

JAMES PATTERSON

TRIPLE HOMICIDE

TRIPLE HOMICIDE

I couldn't resist the opportunity to bring my greatest detectives together in three shocking thrillers. Alex Cross receives an anonymous call with a threat to set off deadly bombs in Washington, D.C., and has to discover whether it's a cruel hoax, or the real deal. But will he find the truth too late? And then, in possibly my most twisted Women's Murder Club mystery yet, Detective Lindsey Boxer investigates a dead lover and a wounded millionaire who was left for dead. Finally, I make things personal for Michael Bennett as someone attacks the Thanksgiving Day Parade directly in front of him and his family. Can he solve the mystery of the "holiday terror"?

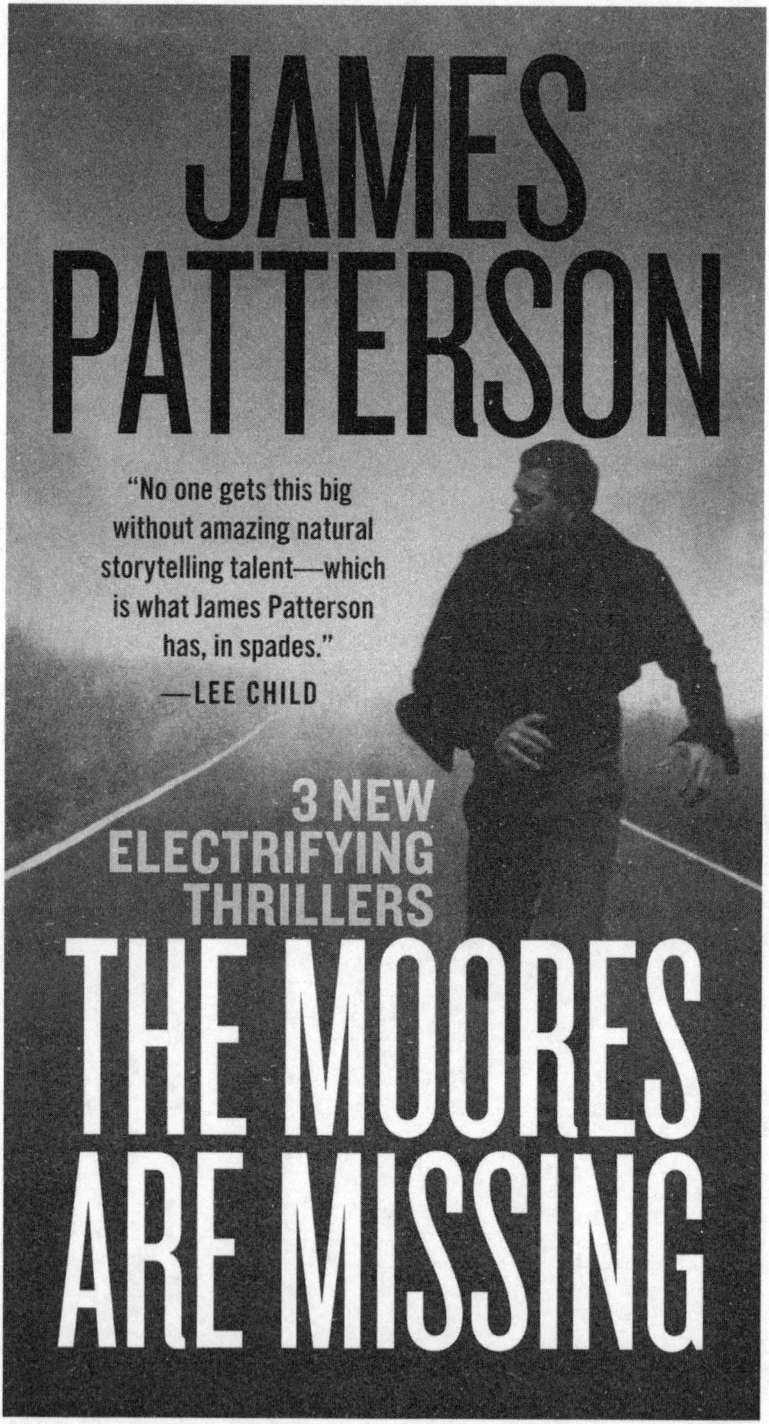
JAMES
PATTERSON
"No one gets this big without amazing natural storytelling talent—which is what James Patterson has, in spades."
—LEE CHILD
3 NEW ELECTRIFYING THRILLERS
THE MOORES ARE MISSING

THE MOORES ARE MISSING

I've brought you three electrifying thrillers all in one book with this one. First, the Moore family just ups and vanishes one day, and no one knows why. Where have they gone? And why? Then in "The Housewife," Maggie Denning jumps to investigate the murder of the woman next door, but she never imagined her own husband would be a suspect. And in "Absolute Zero," Special Forces vet Cody Thurston is framed for the murder of his friends and is on the run, but that won't stop him from completing one last mission: revenge. I'm telling you, you won't want to miss reading these shocking stories.

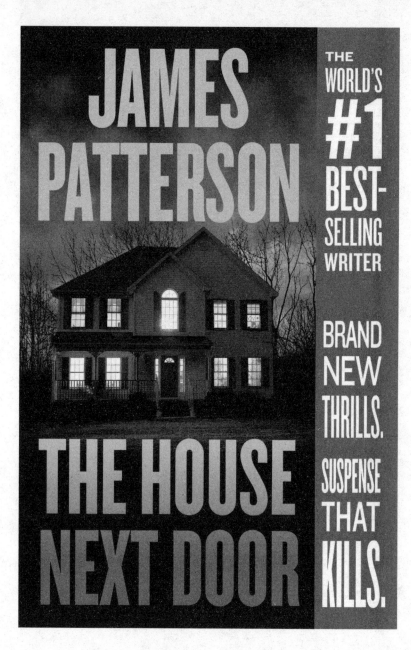

JAMES
PATTERSON

THE HOUSE
NEXT DOOR

THE HOUSE NEXT DOOR

There's something absolutely bone chilling about a danger that's right in front of you, and that concept fascinates me. Everyone always thinks there's safety in numbers, but it isn't always true, and those closest to you can sometimes be the most terrifying. In *The House Next Door*, Laura Sherman's neighbor seems like he's too good to be true; maybe he is. And then in *The Killer's Wife*, Detective McGrath is searching for six girls who have gone missing but finds himself dangerously close to his suspect's wife. Way too close. And finally, I venture out there in *We Are Not Alone*. Robert Barnett has found a message that will change the world: that there are others out there. And they're watching us.

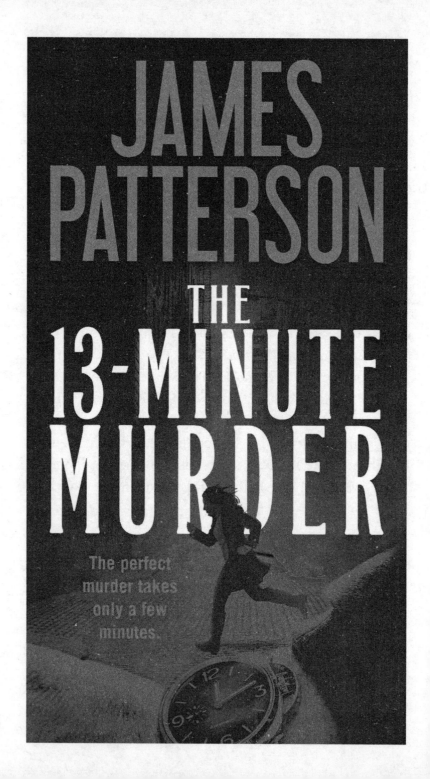

JAMES PATTERSON

THE 13-MINUTE MURDER

The perfect murder takes only a few minutes.

THE 13-MINUTE MURDER

I've really turned up the speed with three time-racing thrillers in one book! In "Dead Man Running," Psychiatrist Randall Beck is working against a ticking clock: he has an inoperable brain tumor. So he'll have to use his remaining time to save as many lives as he can. Then in "113 Minutes," Molly Rourke's son has been murdered and she's determined to expose his murderer even as the clock ticks down. Never underestimate a mother's love. And finally in "The 13-Minute Murder," Michael Ryan is offered a rich payout to assassinate a target, but it ended in a horrifying spectacle. But when his wife goes missing, the world's fastest hit man set out for one last score: revenge. Every minute counts.

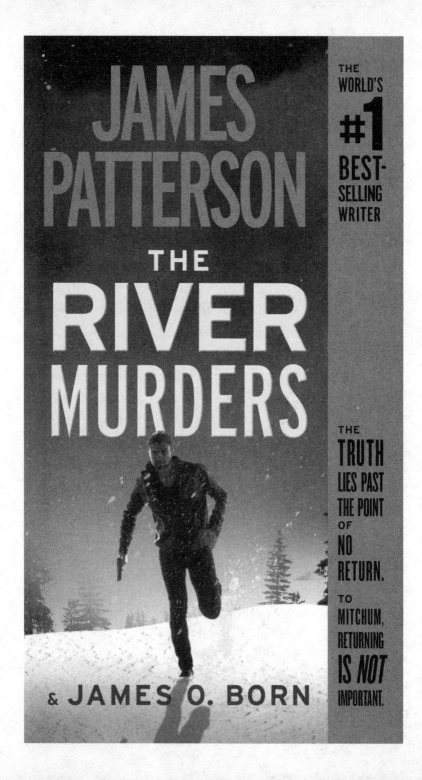

JAMES PATTERSON

THE RIVER MURDERS

& JAMES O. BORN

THE RIVER MURDERS

Mitchum is a relentless man and I've cranked up the tension with three stories just about him. In "Hidden," after being rejected by the Navy SEALs, he becomes his small town's unofficial private eye. But he never could've imagined that investigating a missing teenage cousin would lead to a government conspiracy. And then in "Malicious," when Mitchum's brother is charged with murder, he'll have to break every rule to expose the truth—even if it destroys the people he loves. And finally, in "Malevolent," Mitchum has never been more desperate as one by one, his loved ones have become victims. Now there's only one way to stop the mastermind: going on the most dangerous hunt of his life.

For a complete list of books by
JAMES PATTERSON

VISIT
JamesPatterson.com

 Follow James Patterson on Facebook
@JamesPatterson

 Follow James Patterson on Twitter
@JP_Books

 Follow James Patterson on Instagram
@jamespattersonbooks